ETCHED IN SHADOW

A CASSIE QUINN MYSTERY

L.T. RYAN

with

K.M. ROUGHT

LIQUID MIND MEDIA

THE CASSIE QUINN SERIES

Path of Bones

Whisper of Bones

Symphony of Bones

Etched in Shadow

Concealed in Shadow

Betrayed in Shadow

Born from Ashes (Coming Soon)

Love Cassie? Hatch? Noble? Maddie? Get your very own Cassie Quinn merchandise today! Click the link below to find coffee mugs, t-shirts, and even signed copies of your favorite L.T. Ryan thrillers! https://ltryan.ink/EvG_

1

Detective Adelaide Harris missed the chill of Montana's mountain air. There was something invigorating about the biting cold. Most people would bury themselves deeper into the comfort of their warm bed, but not her. She lived for the way it sharpened her senses and lit up her nerve endings.

Savannah's mornings were never cold enough. Even now, in the middle of December, the nightly temperatures rarely dipped below forty. Every morning, the soft heat of the day coaxed her back to sleep. Coffee overheated her body, so she took cold showers to remind her of those longed-for chilly mornings back home.

But today was different.

This morning, she had been awake the moment her feet hit the living room carpet. The only sound she heard was Chief Clementine's voice echoing in her head. Harris had fallen asleep on the couch again, and the peal of her phone's ringtone woke her from an uneasy rest. The sun had risen hours ago, and as she fumbled for her cell, she wondered how she could've overslept. When she finally raised the device to her ear, Clementine sounded surprised, like she had almost gotten away with not having to pass along the news.

Harris had always respected Chief Clementine's strength and dedication, her innate ability not to mince words. So when Harris heard the hesitation in the other woman's voice, something shifted inside her. Her body prepared for the worst, and when it came, she absorbed the shock to her system.

"I need you to come in." Clementine weighed her words. "Something's happened."

That's all the Chief had told her. *Something's happened.* But Harris knew what it was, even if she couldn't put it into words. The dread pooling in her stomach sent an icy chill up her spine. It worked its way into the base of her skull, causing the hair on the back of her neck to stand on end.

Still, she took the time to shower. Get dressed. Eat breakfast. She didn't dawdle, but she didn't rush. It wouldn't have changed the outcome of the situation, and she'd need her strength for the day.

Clementine had brought her into the station to break the news. Harris didn't bother asking questions or denying the validity of the Chief's claim. She had walked into Clementine's office with a stone mask on her face, and she had refused to let it slip in front of her superior officer.

Or anyone else, for that matter.

Harris had only one desire—to see the body. Clementine had protested. Harris had insisted. She would not back down, and after a full minute's deliberation, the Chief relented. Clementine drove the detective to the scene herself, which was all the better for Harris. The detective may have been able to control her face, but she couldn't control the shaking of her hands.

The twenty-minute ride to a warehouse just outside the city proper was a silent one. Harris did not feel motivated to fill the silence, and she assumed Clementine didn't either. Any words at this point would have been empty. Proof, evidence, and tangible details were the only elements that mattered.

Most of the other officers still wore their jackets despite the sun being at its zenith, but Harris had left hers in the car. The heat of the day didn't register against her skin, nor did the crunch of gravel under her boots. Even the patrol cars' flashing lights, competing with the sun's rays, were distant. All she saw was the loading dock entrance, the caution tape, and the crumpled body laying just beyond.

Clementine put out her arm to stop Harris' approach. The Chief waited until Harris looked her in the eye. "I'm giving you five minutes to do what you need to do. Scream, cry, punch a wall, whatever. After that, I need you back here with me. All pistons firing. We're going to find who did this."

Harris nodded, but when Clementine didn't drop her arm, Harris felt obligated to meet her eyes. "I got it. Five minutes."

The Chief nodded, then cleared everyone out. A few officers tried to give their condolences, but she ignored them. She didn't want the pity or the sorrow or the sympathy. She wasn't the only one suffering today, even if she was the only one who had gotten an escort from the Chief of Police. They all thought they knew what she was feeling, but they didn't have a clue.

Harris put one foot in front of the other until the toe of her boot hit the first step of the stairs leading to the dock. She took each step with deliberate care, feeling the stretch of her muscles before they contracted and lifted her upward. When she made the platform, she forced herself forward.

Someone had rolled up the bay door and draped caution tape across the entrance. Harris ducked under it, forcing her eyes to the body in the center of the room. There was no point in denying it was him. That would only postpone the inevitable, and they couldn't afford to lose that kind of time.

Detective David Klein had been shot once in the head and once in the heart. The wounds were clean. In and out. No suffering. One minute he was alive, and the next he was not. He probably hadn't even seen it coming.

It was a minor comfort, but even through the fog of her pain, Harris recognized it for what it was—a mercy. Every police officer, from the beat cops to the Chief of Police herself, had thought about what it would be like. Whether you'd suffer for days before succumbing to your wounds or feel a sharp pinch before it was lights out and you never opened your eyes again.

One arm was trapped under his twisted body. She wanted to push him onto his back, to straighten him out and maybe fold his hands across his stomach. But she resisted the urge. The crime scene had to stay intact. They couldn't afford to lose a single piece of evidence.

Harris waited for tears that never came. She wished they would, to blur the scene in front of her. Instead, she saw David's dead body in high definition. Every drop of blood, every scratch on his skin, every contorted muscle of his body was in sharp relief.

There was no doubt in her mind that she'd see him every time she closed her eyes for the rest of her life.

Footsteps echoed around the room. Harris turned to see Clementine approaching. The Chief was alone. Were the five minutes up already? She knew she wouldn't cry with the other officers so close, but Harris hadn't had time to figure out what she'd wanted to do first—scream or punch something.

"This is my fault." The words were out of Harris' mouth before she could stop them. "I did this."

"You didn't." Clementine's voice wasn't gentle. The sharp look in her eye quieted any of Harris' protests. "You didn't pull the trigger. You didn't kill him."

"I should've been here."

"If you had, then I might've had two dead detectives on my hands instead of just one."

Harris looked down at David. She heard Clementine's words, even registered they were true, but the guilt that ate away at her stomach lining didn't recede. If anything, it doubled its efforts to consume her from the inside out.

"I need to know what you know." Clementine's voice was all business, but when Harris turned back to her, the sharpness in her eyes had lifted. "All of it. Even the parts you don't want to tell me."

Harris stood, but couldn't put David at her back. She needed to know he was still there with her, at least in some capacity. "Two nights ago, we were grabbing a beer when he got a phone call from a witness who wanted to turn on Aguilar."

"Francisco Aguilar?" Clementine's eyebrows pinched together. "Why?"

"David said it was because the guy had a kid on the way. He didn't want to be part of it anymore—the drugs, the murders, none of it. He wanted out, and he wanted protection for him and his family."

"And you guys believed that?"

"David did." Harris blew out a breath, and it ruffled the hair around her face. "But I think it was more than that. The witness must've said something else because David looked scared. He told me the other guy said Aguilar had people in the department doing his dirty work for him. People you wouldn't suspect."

Clementine narrowed her eyes. "You never want to hear something like that."

"David didn't seem surprised. More resigned. He didn't want me involved, but I insisted. He'd already told me too much. He couldn't get rid of me that easily."

Clementine glanced at David's body and then back up at Harris. "So why aren't you lying next to him?"

"The witness wanted him to come alone. I wouldn't let him." She ground her teeth. "He gave me an address, told me to show up ten minutes after he did. I was to stay close but not intervene. We needed this guy to take down Aguilar and whoever he had in the department. We couldn't risk spooking him."

"I'm guessing he didn't give you this address?"

"He sent me across town. By the time I figured it out, he had already turned his cell off. I drove around for a while, but I had no idea where they were meeting. Eventually, I went home."

"There's nothing you could've done, Adelaide." Clementine put a hand on Harris' shoulder and forced the detective to meet her gaze. "I mean it. This was David's choice. Don't bear the responsibility of decisions he knew could have this outcome. He probably saved your life."

"Did he know?" Harris looked down at David, and for the first time that morning, she felt a well of emotion creep up her throat. "Did he know he was going to die?"

"Only one other person might know the answer." Clementine gave her a pointed look. "Are you going to call her, or do you want me to?"

"I'll do it." Harris wondered if Cassie already knew. Had David visited her? Had he told her exactly what happened? Would Cassie blame Harris for not being with him? "But I have to figure out what to say first."

"If you're looking for the right words for a situation like this"—Clementine returned her gaze to David–"you'll be looking for a long time."

"What about you?" Harris asked. "What are you going to say to the others?"

"Only what they need to know. If we have a rat, we need to flood the ship."

Clementine waved the other officers back inside. Harris stepped back under the caution tape, walked down the stairs, and moved off to the side of the loading docks. A small crowd had gathered on the far end, but three police officers kept them at bay. Harris drew a deep breath and blocked them all out.

As she pulled out her phone, her stomach twisted. She hadn't known Cassie for long, but they had forged their friendship in the heat of battle. She was the one person outside David's family who would understand what Harris was feeling right now, and it was her job to deliver the killing blow.

Before she could lose her nerve, Harris dialed Cassie's number.

"Hey." Cassie sniffled. "What's up?"

"Cassie." Harris' voice sounded unnatural, even to her ears. It was too full of emotion, too full of heartbreak. "Am I interrupting?"

"No." Cassie sobered instantly. "What's wrong?"

"I don't really know how to say this." She was losing it. "It doesn't feel real."

"Adelaide. What happened?"

"It's David." Harris' voice shook, despite her best efforts to stay calm for her friend. "He's dead."

2

If Cassie Quinn ever thought there was a limit to how much one person could cry, today had proven her wrong. Her throat was raw, her nose was red, her cheeks were puffy, and yet tears continued to stream down her face with great abandon.

It was a cruel trick of the universe that her life had come together for the briefest of moments before falling apart again. Cassie had repaired her relationship with her sister and her parents. She'd discovered she'd had her abilities far longer than she could've imagined. And she'd even solved the murder of her childhood best friend, finally allowing souls like little Sebastian Thomas to rest after twenty long years of turmoil.

If it were any other day, Cassie would be on cloud nine. Savannah had greeted her with open arms. The sun was warm, and the chill breeze made her want to bundle closer to the people she loved. Work was going better than ever before, and she and Jason were texting daily now. Slowly but surely, they were getting to know each other.

But today was not like any other day.

Today, Cassie watched as her best friend was laid to rest.

The funeral was beautiful, if such a word could describe the somber event. David's casket had been draped with the American flag, and his colleagues, dressed in their finest, carried him with a strength Cassie couldn't imagine mustering at a time like this.

She sat behind David's wife, Lisa, while the woman clutched her daughters' hands and cried. Half a dozen grandkids surrounded her. David's legacy watched as each person took a handful of dirt or a fistful of flowers, tossed it on top of his coffin, and said their goodbyes.

When it was Cassie's turn, she felt Lisa's eyes burning into the back of her skull. But whatever answers the other woman wanted, Cassie didn't have them. The world around her was as silent as it had ever been.

A three-volley salute honoring David's life shattered that silence. The bang of the rifles tore their way through Cassie's patchwork façade, unlocking a newfound wave of pain that existed somewhere deep inside the darkest reaches of her soul. She clung to Harris, burying her face in the detective's shoulder and sobbing until her entire body ached.

David's funeral affected every person in attendance, and when it drew to a close, Cassie witnessed some of the hardest, toughest men wiping away tears as they headed back to their cars. Some would go home and find comfort in a bottle. Others would find that same comforting bottle at Lisa's house, where she had invited David's closest friends and colleagues to eat, drink, and remember the life he had led.

Cassie rode with Harris, not trusting herself to keep a car on the road in her current state. She was grateful for the detective's presence, but it was a harsh reminder something was missing. She and Harris were no longer whole without David by their side.

The Klein residence was bursting at the seams with food, booze, and people. Clusters of men and women had formed in the front yard, and Cassie could hear crying, laughing, and the clinking of glasses. The porch sagged under the weight of a dozen men telling stories about David—some heroic, some hilarious. She and Harris had to squeeze through the front entrance, only to pop out the other side into another group of officers.

Harris put her hand on Cassie's shoulder. "Are you okay? There are some people I want to talk to, but I can stay with you if you need me to."

"I'm fine." When Harris didn't look convinced, Cassie gently shoved the woman away. "Really. Go. I need to find Lisa."

Harris nodded and left, leaving Cassie alone in a sea of people far bigger and taller than her. Immediately, a cloud of anxiety engulfed her, squeezing her lungs until she felt so lightheaded, she stumbled. Someone righted her, and she mumbled a thanks before winding her way through the crowd and ascending the stairs. Just like that, she could breathe again.

A whine slipped under the crack of a door off to her left. When she pressed her ear to the wood and heard it again, she whispered an apology to Lisa before twisting the handle and pushing her way inside.

A mass of fur launched itself off the bed in the center of the room and tackled Cassie just as she closed the door behind her. For the first time in days, she laughed as the giant German Shepherd licked every inch of her face.

"Bear." She tried to keep her voice stern, but she couldn't find it in her heart. "Bear, come on. Sit down."

Bear relented, but instead of sitting, he crawled into Cassie's lap and flipped over so she could rub his belly. His tail thumped rhythmically against the ground as his entire body wriggled with happiness.

"Oh, I know." Cassie couldn't stop giggling. "It's been days since I saw you last. Did you miss me? I missed you."

Bear answered with another whine and buried himself closer.

"David loved you so much." Cassie's giggles transformed into a sob. Bear sat up and stared directly into her eyes. "I'm sorry you didn't get to spend more time with him."

Whether Bear understood Cassie's words or just their sentiment hardly mattered. When he inched his head closer and laid it on her shoulder, Cassie wrapped her arms around him and pressed her face into his fur. Bear's fuzzy mane muffled her sobs and soaked up her tears as his stoic form held her upright.

When the door clicked open behind her, Cassie jumped. She brushed the fur from her face and looked up to find Lisa standing there, a small smile on her face.

"I thought you might be in here."

"I'm so sorry." Cassie stood and brushed off her dress. "I didn't mean to intrude. It was so packed downstairs. I just needed to get away for a minute."

Lisa shook her head and wrapped her hands around Cassie's shoulders, squeezing them until Cassie looked her in the eye. "You're family. Nothing has changed that. You're welcome here any time. Besides, Bear was looking forward to seeing you."

The dog jumped up on the bed and laid his head on his paws. The excitement in his eyes at seeing Cassie faded, soon replaced by a sadness she knew all too well.

"How's he doing?"

"He's sad. He knows David is gone." Lisa led Cassie to the bed and they sat down. Bear shifted so his head was in Cassie's lap. "He kept looking for him over the last few days. At first, he was confused, but now I think he understands. I felt bad keeping him in here, but I just wasn't sure how he would react with all those people downstairs."

Cassie placed a hand on Lisa's arm. "How are you doing?"

"I'm okay. For now, at least. It helps to have a purpose. Once the house is empty again, it'll be harder. But the girls are going to stay with me for a while. I won't be alone. It'll take some getting used to, but I'll survive."

"If you need anything from me, please let me know. You and David were my family when I didn't think I had any."

"Actually, there is something I wanted to ask you."

As Lisa looked down at her hands, Cassie's stomach filled with dread. She had known this moment would come eventually, but she had hoped to stave it off for as long as possible.

"Have you seen David?" Lisa looked back to Cassie. Her eyes were full of hope. "Have you talked to him at all?"

Cassie didn't blame Lisa for asking. If the roles were reversed, she'd want to know, too. But the desperation in the other woman's eyes made Cassie's stomach twist. Either answer would've been difficult to hear. If Cassie had seen David, that meant his soul wasn't at peace. If she hadn't seen him, that meant he was truly gone.

Tears spilled over from Lisa's eyes. Her voice was thick with emotion. "I can tell by the look on your face that you haven't."

"I'm so sorry." Cassie squeezed Lisa's hand. "I wish I had a different answer for you."

"I think this is for the best." Lisa wiped away her tears. "Really. He wouldn't have wanted to put that kind of pressure on you."

"He told me that once." Cassie couldn't help the laugh that escaped her mouth. "He said he hoped I wouldn't have to look at his ugly mug after he was gone."

Lisa joined in Cassie's laughter, and the two women hugged each other tightly. When Lisa let go, she looked a little lighter. "I can sleep better knowing he's where he belongs."

Cassie wished she could say the same. "I'll sleep better when they find out who did this."

"Have you heard anything?" Lisa's voice was even, but her eyes couldn't hide her desperation. "Do they have any leads?"

"Harris hasn't told me much. Just that they think it has something to do with some drug lord operating in Savannah. But they're still trying to piece it all together."

"Well, you know as much as I do then. That's some small comfort."

Cassie wasn't sure she agreed, but she kept it to herself. She looked down at Bear and rubbed the top of his head until the dog closed his eyes and began to snore.

"Not to spring this on you," Lisa said, "but David had hoped you'd want Bear back at one point or another."

"Oh." Cassie looked up at her. "You don't want to keep him?"

"He was never mine to keep. David's either. David told me about how you rescued him. You two have a connection."

A sense of warmth spread throughout Cassie's body. "I'm not sure how Apollo is going to feel about this, but I'll make it work."

"Oh, and there's one more thing." Lisa shifted to one side and pulled an envelope out of her dress pocket. David had scrawled Cassie's name across the front. "This is for you."

Cassie didn't lift her hand to take it. "What is it?"

"I don't know. I didn't read it." Lisa waited until Cassie took the envelope with a shaking hand. "David wrote it about a month ago. Every couple of years, we made it a point to discuss what would happen if he died. Somber, I know. And at first, I hated it. I didn't even want to think about it. But now, I'm grateful. Nothing can prepare you for this, but I can at least say I don't have any regrets. I knew how much David loved me, and he knew how much I loved him. At the end of the day, that's all that matters."

She lifted the envelope. "And this?"

"If I were to guess, I'd think that letter holds the same sentiment. He loved you like a daughter, Cassie. He'd want to make sure you knew that, even after he was gone."

Cassie nodded, but she couldn't smile. The letter was like a rock tied to her ankle, pulling her beneath the surface of her own grief. She'd open it someday, but not until she stopped hoping that whatever David had to tell her, he could do it face to face.

3

Cassie opened her fridge and surveyed the options as the cool air washed over her skin. Goosebumps formed, and she rubbed them away. Harris paced the length of Cassie's living room like she was going for a world record. "Options are limited. Water or tea? Beer or wine?"

"Something stronger?"

"Jose Cuervo?"

"I'll stick with the beer."

Cassie grabbed a bottle for Harris and a glass of wine for herself. It had been her first day back to work since she found out about David, and it had been long and miserable. Her head was pounding in rhythm with her heartbeat. If the wine didn't relieve the tension in her body, maybe it would put her to sleep.

Harris took the bottle and slammed half of it back. She wiped her mouth and sat in the recliner opposite Cassie on the couch. "Thanks."

Cassie eyed the other woman and contemplated her decision to ask Harris to watch the house for her this week while she went on a work trip. Agitation had replaced Harris' normally calm demeanor. She would sit back in the chair for a few seconds, then lean forward again. She'd shift to one side, put her ankle up on the opposite knee, then drop her foot and do the same thing with the other one. The beer was gone before Cassie had taken her second sip of wine.

Harris held the bottle up. "Mind if I grab another?"

"Go for it."

Cassie waited until she returned, but Harris didn't seem any calmer. It'd probably take something stronger than beer to do that. "How've you been?"

"You know." Harris shrugged. She didn't bother finishing the sentence, and Cassie didn't need her to. The detective pointed at Apollo and Bear, who were curled up together on the couch, inches from Cassie. "These two seem to get along."

"Yeah." Cassie couldn't help the smile that spread over her face. Only one good thing had come out of all of this, and that was having Bear by her side. "When I brought Bear home, they sniffed each other for a solid minute before he took off to explore the house. Next thing I know, they're curled up like this in the middle of my bed. Bear's still walking on eggshells. Probably afraid I'll ship him off to another house soon. But Apollo is obsessed with him."

"That's cute." Harris looked like she meant it. "I think David would be happy he's with you."

The smile slid off Cassie's face at the mention of David's name. "Yeah. I wish I didn't have to leave so soon. I'm afraid Bear will think I've abandoned him again. I really appreciate you staying here for a few days. Sending him somewhere else would make him more anxious."

"It's not a problem, I told you that." Harris tilted her bottle back and downed a third of it this time. At least she seemed to be slowing down. "But are you sure you have to leave? You can't get out of it?"

"I didn't ask." When Harris pinched her eyebrows together, Cassie rushed on. "I just took off a bunch of time visiting with my sister, and then going to Charlotte to see my parents. It didn't feel right to get out of this trip, too."

"I'm sure they'd understand. Did you tell them what happened?"

"No. Nobody knows." She refused to feel guilty about that. "I'm not ready to talk to them about it."

Harris looked away, but she stayed silent. Whatever she was feeling, she kept it locked down. "Where are you going again? New Orleans?"

Cassie bobbed her head up and down, grateful for the change in subject. "We're lending a couple pieces to the NOMA, and my boss wants me to oversee the installation and build a better relationship with the staff."

"The NOMA?"

"New Orleans Museum of Art." Cassie smirked. Harris seemed so far removed from her world at the museum. "It's one of about a dozen museums around the country to take part in a program to increase collaboration in the hope that it sparks community interest and visitation."

"You sound like you studied the brochure."

"They told me there would be a test." Their usual banter was flat. Neither of them put their heart into it. "Look, I'm sorry if it seems like I'm running out on you—"

"No, no." Harris set her bottle down, then rubbed her hands down her face and sighed into her palms. When she looked up, Cassie could see the pain and confusion in her eyes for the first time. "I'm not trying to get in between you and your job. I just—I don't really have anyone, okay? I can't talk to Lisa, I'm not about to talk to the Chief, and no one else knew David like you did."

There was a lingering question in the air that Harris seemed too afraid to posit. Cassie couldn't be mad at Harris for wanting to know, but that didn't make it any easier. "I don't have answers for you."

The pain on Harris' face aged her twenty years. She looked so tired. "It's not fair to ask you."

"You wouldn't be the first." Cassie had resigned herself to the fact a long time ago. "And you won't be the last."

"Have you seen him?" Harris had to choke out the words. "Talked to him?"

"No."

The detective stood up and peeked through Cassie's window. Bear lifted his head and watched her, then settled back down. Apollo kept snoring. When Harris faced Cassie again, the mask she'd been wearing for the last few days had returned. "I don't know what I was hoping for."

"Well, if you're anything like me, you wished the answer was 'yes,' because at least you'd have a shot at answering more questions. But you're also relieved the answer was 'no,' because maybe that means he's at peace."

"But someone murdered him." The mask flickered, but Harris forced it back into place. "How could he be at peace?"

"I don't know." Cassie remembered what she'd told Lisa about David not wanting to visit her after he died. "Maybe he doesn't want to."

"Does it always happen right away?"

"Not always." Cassie tucked her feet underneath her. Talking about this, even to Harris, still felt strange. And vulnerable. Like exposing the rawest nerve in her body to someone who had been a stranger a few months ago. "It's not like there's a rule book. Spirits come and go in whatever way they can. Sometimes it's their choice. Sometimes there are other factors at play."

"That doesn't help us solve David's case." Harris put her hands on her hips and tipped her head back. She sighed at the ceiling before looking back down at Cassie. "I didn't mean it like that. I know you can't control any of this. I'm just frustrated." She sat down and drained the rest of her beer. "Not at you. At the case. At David. At myself. At the world."

"I am, too. Trust me." Cassie took another sip of wine and felt the liquid warm her body. "But you'll figure it out. We'll figure it out. I shouldn't be in New Orleans more than a couple days. Maybe by then you'll have learned something else."

And maybe by then I'll be ready to solve my best friend's murder. But I doubt it.

"I hope we have that kind of time."

Cassie cocked her head to the side. "What do you mean? Isn't this a top priority for the department?"

"Of course." Harris shrugged. "But that doesn't mean they'll catch the right person."

"I don't follow."

"We were meeting a witness who wanted to turn on Aguilar. Then David winds up dead and the witness is missing? It was either a setup or a lucky break for Aguilar. Either way, this man is powerful. He's always been untouchable, which means even if we catch his guy, the one who killed David, it doesn't mean we'll catch *him*. Just because someone else pulled the trigger doesn't mean Aguilar isn't responsible, but it's a lot harder to prove that in a court of law."

Cassie sat with that for a minute. She knew David's job was dangerous, but as the years went by, she must've gotten accustomed to it. Of all the people they'd tracked down together, she always felt like David was in control. Or that he'd made the right decision. And she hadn't even heard of Aguilar before now. Cassie wasn't one to doubt Harris' judgment, but all this information was coming in too fast for her to process.

"Something isn't right." Harris said. She leaned forward now, her elbows on her knees, one hand wrapped around the back of her neck. She was staring a hole through the floor. "David didn't want me to be with him that night. Either he was trying to protect me, or he was trying to keep something from me."

"What would he possibly want to keep from you?"

"Your guess is as good as mine." Harris' laugh was hollow. "Probably better, actually."

"If anything comes to me, you'll be the first person I contact. I promise."

"I appreciate that." Harris stood. "I should go."

"I'll drop the keys off to you tomorrow morning."

Harris scratched the top of Apollo's head, and then ruffled Bear's fur. "I promise I'll take good care of them." Harris made her way to the door with Cassie at her heels but stopped shy of opening it. "When you get back, maybe we can team up. Find real justice for David. Make sure he's at peace."

"Yeah. Of course." Cassie smiled and watched as Harris left, pulling the door shut behind her. But as soon as the detective was out of sight, Cassie sank to the ground. Bear jumped off the couch and nuzzled her hand with his nose. "Hey, handsome man. I'm glad you're here."

Apollo meowed from the couch but didn't bother moving.

"You, too, Apollo. I don't know what I'd do without you guys."

Cassie let the tears slide down her face, and Bear cleaned them away one by one. She thought she'd feel some relief now that she'd made it through David's funeral, but the pressure still sat on her chest like a ten-ton elephant. She'd even been looking forward to this trip, to forgetting what she'd left behind in Savannah, but now it was simply an inconvenience.

Cassie didn't fault Harris for wanting her help. If the situation were reversed, Cassie would ask the same thing of the detective. It wasn't like she didn't want to solve David's murder. It would bring her as much peace as it would bring him. But the journey to justice was rarely an easy one.

And something told her she wouldn't like the answers she'd find.

4

Cassie stood in a darkened hospital room surrounded by the rhythmic beeping of machines. Though her dream had stolen her sense of smell, she could imagine the antiseptic burn that clung to the air and assaulted her nose. She was grateful for the reprieve, but confusion and heartbreak soon replaced her relief.

A clean-shaven man sat in a chair next to her. He had a buzzcut and wore wire-rimmed spectacles. Whether it was the sadness in his walnut eyes or the way his shoulders sagged under the weight of an invisible burden, Cassie thought he looked ten years older than he was. When he removed his glasses and set them on the bedside table, Cassie saw the lines on his face. They weren't from age, but from life.

As the man wrapped his fingers around the hand of the woman in the bed, Cassie's gaze traveled up her arm until it stopped at a tube inserted into one of her veins. A clear liquid Cassie couldn't identify filled the line, but something told her it wouldn't be enough to save the woman's life.

Cassie forced her eyes to keep moving up the woman's shoulder, through her mass of corkscrew curls, and to her face. Her once rich brown skin was now dull and ashen. Her lips were dry, and tears had turned to crust along her lashes. Minuscule beads of sweat gathered along her forehead. The man wiped them away with a damp cloth.

Despite knowing this was only a dream, Cassie was hesitant to disturb the moment. What if the man could sense her? What if the woman woke up? She didn't want to intrude, but an unseen thread had wrapped itself around her chest and pulled her to the woman's medical chart clipped to the end of the bed.

With deliberate movements, Cassie lifted the chart from its holder and looked down at the paper in front of her. She could see the words with crisp clarity but couldn't read them. Jumbled letters filled the page like a message written in code. None of it made sense, no matter how long she stared at it.

The man in the chair let out a strangled sob and pressed his forehead against the woman's hands. His lips moved in a silent prayer, and Cassie's heart broke for him. She didn't know what was happening to the woman, but she knew time was not on their side.

Cassie replaced the chart and returned to her spot beside the man. There was a low rumble and the room vibrated enough to rattle the machinery. The man didn't seem to notice. His prayers went uninterrupted.

Cassie looked to the ceiling, afraid it might collapse and bury the three of them in rubble, but as soon as the sensation came, it also went. The floor was stable beneath her feet, and the distant noise was now just a memory.

But not everything was as it had once been.

When Cassie's gaze returned to the scene before her, a fourth figure had emerged from the shadows. It was another woman, dressed in a white coat with a stethoscope wrapped around her neck. As the woman leaned forward, Cassie realized she didn't quite belong. She wore low-heeled pumps and a plain gray A-line dress beneath her jacket. She had done up her chestnut hair in pin curls. Everything about her looked muted and faded—including skin that once had been the color of pale sand and now was almost khaki—except her eyes, which were a piercing hazel that stunned Cassie into silence.

If her wardrobe had not given her away, then the transparent sheen of her skin would have. Cassie knew, without a doubt, this woman had died decades ago, and yet here she was, looking more alive than the woman in the bed before them.

The Ghost Doctor leaned forward to fluff the woman's pillow, and though she had no physical effect on the object, she stood back and surveyed her work as if satisfied. If the doctor registered anyone else in the room, she did a good job of ignoring them. She worked her way around the bed, straightening the blanket and tucking it under the woman's feet.

When the room shook for a second time, Cassie's gaze shot to the ceiling. The rumble was a little louder, and she could've sworn she felt something fall and hit her elbow. But it went quiet again, and the roof remained intact. When Cassie lowered her gaze, the Ghost Doctor stared directly at her.

Cassie had never seen a spirit like this one. She was almost solid, even bright compared to others she'd encountered. Even newer ghosts, ones who'd died only weeks or days beforehand, didn't look as present as the Ghost Doctor did in this very moment. She didn't flicker in and out of existence, and her hazel eyes stared unblinking, rooting Cassie to the spot.

The Ghost Doctor was the first to break eye contact, and when she did, she circled back around the bed, to the far side, and leaned over the woman. She whispered something Cassie couldn't hear and then inched forward, as if waiting for a response. When she didn't get one, the doctor checked her patient's pulse, using the delicate watch on her wrist to time it.

But as soon as the Ghost Doctor took the woman's hand in her own, alarms blared from the surrounding machines. The man jumped, first looking up at each individual screen and then back down to the woman in the bed. A stillness hung in the surrounding air.

The doctor did not seem affected by the commotion. In fact, she seemed pleased with the development, and as she took a step back, she tugged on the other woman's arm. Cassie didn't expect any effect, but when the patient sat straight up, Cassie knew something was wrong.

The woman's physical form hadn't moved from the bed, but her spirit turned and placed her feet on the ground. Cassie looked from one version of the woman to the other. They were identical, except for the way the spirit flickered in and out of existence, as though she were the embodiment of a poor connection.

Cassie only had time to gauge the confused look on the woman's face before the entire room shook for a third time. The rumble was infinitely louder, and Cassie's instincts drove her forward, reaching for the wrist of the woman in the bed. All she cared about was pulling it from the Ghost Doctor's grasp.

But when her fingers closed around the woman's hand, its warmth shocked her. And just as the room rattled one last time, Cassie locked eyes with the Ghost Doctor. Decades of pain and rage and conviction washed over Cassie, so sharp and twisted that she opened her mouth to cry out.

CASSIE'S EYES FLEW OPEN. She snapped her mouth shut, swallowing a scream that would've made everyone on the plane crane their heads in her direction. Her heart hammering, Cassie forced her lungs to pull air in and push it back out in a rhythm she could pretend was normal. It took her a moment to remember where she was and what she was doing.

She'd been forced to fly from Savannah to Charlotte before she boarded the plane to New Orleans. How ironic that she had left North Carolina last week after visiting her parents for the first time in a decade, and here she was, already on her way back. But her time at the airport had been limited—too short to pay them another visit—before she headed to her eventual destination.

Cassie breathed a little easier. The hospital room and the Ghost Doctor were already fading from memory, and her body was waking up alongside her mind.

Which also meant it didn't take her more than a second or two before she realized that while she had wrapped her fingers around the dying woman's wrist in her dream, the Cassie who lived in the real world had done the same to the woman sitting next to her on the plane.

Cassie released her grip and turned to the woman with wide eyes and an apology on her lips. She felt a flush creeping up her neck and across her cheeks. She considered opening the emergency door and throwing herself from the aircraft.

"Don't worry about it, honey." The woman's smile lit up her face. There was a golden glow beneath her umber skin that made her look ethereal. Wires of gray peppered her dark hair, and though she looked to be in her early sixties, there was something eternally youthful about her. Cassie had heard her accent before, like New York meets the South. It was uniquely New Orleans. "Bad dream?"

Cassie nodded. "You think I'd be used to them by now."

"Best not to get too friendly with nightmares." The woman offered her hand. "My name is Celeste Delacroix."

"Cassie Quinn."

Cassie took the woman's hand. It was warm and the handshake firm, but Cassie barely noticed because one minute she was staring into this beautiful stranger's face, and the next she saw Celeste standing next to her mirror image. A fire crackled between them while stars twinkled in the sky above.

And then it disappeared.

The vision hadn't ended. Celeste had taken it back.

The woman slipped her hand out of Cassie's, but she didn't look scared. In fact, she looked impressed. "Well, you're quite the surprise, aren't you?"

"I'm sorry." Cassie wasn't sure what she was apologizing for. She just knew she'd done something wrong. "I didn't mean to."

"No harm, no foul." Celeste looked like she was seeing her for the first time. "You've got a lot of power, Cassie Quinn. It's a shame you don't know how to use it."

Cassie opened her mouth and then closed it. She wanted to ask what she meant, but when she opened her mouth again, a different question came out. "Who are you?"

"There are a lot of interesting answers to that question. 'What do you do?' is a better one. I run a voodoo museum in the French Quarter."

"You're a lot more than that." Cassie was still trying to wrap her head around what had happened. "How'd you do that?"

"Practice. Discipline. Control." Celeste's eyes sparkled. "You'll get there some day."

Cassie had a thousand questions, but she had a feeling Celeste wouldn't answer them, so she started with an easy one. "You're from New Orleans?"

"Born and raised." Pride oozed from her voice. "What about you?"

"Savannah."

"Lot of restless spirits in Savannah. You've got your work cut out for you." Celeste's face tightened. "I'm getting a feeling life hasn't been kind to you. Your road might be the one less traveled, but it'll take you where you need to go."

Cassie looked away. She had pushed thoughts of David's death out of her mind for a few moments, but they were never far away. Neither was Novak nor the troubles with her family. Still, Celeste's words were kind. "Thank you."

A man's voice came over the plane's speaker. "Ladies and gentlemen, we have begun our descent into New Orleans. Please turn off all portable electronic devices..."

Celeste pulled a business card from her purse and handed it to Cassie. "If you want to see the real New Orleans, call this number. Tell her I sent you."

Cassie looked down at the card. It was black with gold lettering, and the name Sabine Delacroix flashed in the florescent overhead lighting. Was this the woman Cassie had seen in the vision before Celeste had shut her out? How much would she be like her sister?

Celeste patted Cassie's arm. "This trip will be good for you, Cassie Quinn. I can feel it."

Cassie looked out the window as the ground drew closer. She hadn't felt optimistic about the trip when she'd boarded that morning, but Celeste's confidence gave her a spark of hope. David was gone and his murder was unsolved, but life carried on. She'd have to find a path forward, one way or another.

A visit to New Orleans could be exactly what she needed.

5

Cassie had the Uber driver drop her off as close to the New Orleans Museum of Art as he could manage. The chill breeze sent a shiver down her spine as she walked the rest of the way. She pulled her jacket closer, regretting the fact that she hadn't brought a pair of gloves, especially once she pulled out her phone to call Magdalena. The device was freezing to the touch.

"How was your flight?" Nothing could dampen the cheer in Magdalena's voice, not even the wind. "Enjoying yourself so far?"

"My flight was good." Cassie almost said it was uneventful, but that would've been an outright lie. Celeste Delacroix had made sure of that. "But I haven't had too much time to myself yet. I dropped my stuff off at the hotel, and now—"

"Oh, how's the hotel? Was your room okay?"

Cassie frowned. "Bigger than I needed, but it's nice. Are you sure the museum was okay with paying for that?"

"Oh yeah, it's not a problem." Magdalena's voice betrayed the smile on her face. "George had final approval. Don't you worry about it."

"Okay." Cassie planned on taking full advantage of the room—and the jacuzzi bathtub that came with it—but for now, she wanted to get on with business. "Anyway, I'm outside the museum now. I wanted to check in on the truck and make sure it's arriving on time."

Magdalena's silence spoke volumes. "There's been an issue with the truck."

Cassie froze on the stairs leading up to the museum's entrance. She turned her back to the wind and tucked one hand into her jacket pocket. "What do you mean there's been an issue?"

"It hasn't left Savannah."

Cassie didn't know how to process the information. Her entire job down here was straightforward. Fly to New Orleans. Supervise the NOMA staff as they offloaded the truck full of eighteenth-century furniture. Offer her expertise on how to exhibit and catalog the pieces. Eat an entire pint of ice cream while watching the Food Channel in her hotel room. Return home.

"How is that possible?"

"I put the wrong date down on the paperwork." Magdalena rushed on, breathless. "I thought I scheduled it to move out at nine this morning, but it's actually tomorrow. But don't worry! I've already talked to the hotel and extended your stay another night. You won't have any issues with your room."

"That's a relief." A small one, but it released a little tension between her shoulder blades. Cassie looked at the front entrance, where a guard watched a small family file through the door. "Do the staff already know? I've practically got one foot inside the museum."

"Called them myself to apologize. Make your introductions, then take the rest of the day." Magdalena's voice brightened, but it sounded practiced. "Who knows, maybe this is a blessing in disguise. You could do worse than an extra night in New Orleans."

Cassie frowned. She didn't know what her friend was up to, but she knew better than to trust the woman didn't have backup plans for her backup plans. There was no way she got the date wrong for Cassie's trip. "Mags, what's really going on?"

"I have no idea what you mean." The smile was still in her voice. "But I've got to go. Busy day today. Eat something yummy for me. Have fun!"

The line went dead before Cassie could say another word.

Magdalena's intentions were always noble, but that didn't mean Cassie was in the mood for one of her schemes. The last few days had been hell, and Cassie wanted to do her job and eat her ice cream and forget about the real world for a few hours. But she reminded herself, Magdalena didn't know David had died, or that Cassie was barely keeping her head above water. She just thought she was doing her friend a favor.

Cassie squared her shoulders and finished her ascent of the stairs. She nodded a hello to the guard, who gestured for her to pass through the door and into one of the most breathtaking foyers she'd ever seen. Everything from the floor to the walls to the columnar supports was a brilliant white. Green garland laced through the bannisters, and a simple red rug led straight to the bottom of an elegant staircase.

For a moment, she forgot her frustration with Magdalena and simply stared in wonder.

As another family bustled through the door with two small children, Cassie beelined for the visitor's desk, where a young woman had a phone cradled to her ear. Her fingers flew over the keys as she nodded along to whatever the person on the other end of the line was telling her. A smile never left her face.

After a moment, the woman hung up and turned her attention to Cassie. Her hair, cut in a sharp bob, was jet-black against her tawny skin. Her eyes, just as dark as her hair, were wide and excited, and she wore bright pink lipstick that looked a shade too modern for the exquisite museum. "How can I help you?"

"My name is Cassie Quinn, and I'm here to—"

"Oh!" The woman's eyes grew wider, and her hair swished as she bounced in her chair. "Hello! We've been waiting for you. My name is Julie Tanaka, but you can call me Jules. Let me call my co-worker, and I'll get you set up."

Before Cassie knew it, someone had replaced Jules at the front desk, and the young woman was leading Cassie through a door to the back. Few people ever saw this side of a museum, which was a shame. It was where the real mysteries were held and where the real magic happened.

"Was your flight okay? Any trouble?"

"No, everything went smoothly."

"Good, good." Jules' twang was subtle, but it deepened when she got excited. Which seemed to be about every other sentence. "Magdalena told us you'd probably show up a day early, and I was hoping I'd be here to show you around."

"A day early?" Cassie furrowed her brow. "She said the truck was delayed."

Jules shrugged. "The truck was due to be here tomorrow, but that's okay. It gives you more time to explore the museum and meet everyone."

Cassie tried not to grimace. She didn't mind meeting new people but being the center of attention was never fun. Then she reminded herself that she had at least one thing in common with everyone who worked at the NOMA—they all loved art.

Still, too many names and faces for her to remember filled the next hour, and certainly too many fake smiles. Jules never lost an ounce of her spark, and even seemed to gain energy the more she paraded Cassie around.

"This is my office." Jules opened the door wide and let Cassie poke her head in. All the furniture was sleek and modern, either black or white. In fact, the only color came from the paintings hanging on each wall. One featured a silhouette of the Eiffel Tower set against a green, teal, and purple sunset.

"This is gorgeous." Cassie stepped closer, admiring the texture of the brushstrokes. "Who did this?"

"Oh." Jules cleared her throat, and when Cassie looked over, she was blushing. "I did."

Cassie looked around the room at the other paintings, each featuring a different landmark in silhouette against an explosion of colors. Each monument was recognizable and yet otherworldly. Red grass. A yellow ocean. Trees painted all the colors of the rainbow. "They're fantastic, Jules." She looked over at the woman and shook her head in disbelief. "Really. They're beautiful."

Jules' cheeks turned the color of her lips. "Thank you." She hid a smile as she gestured to a small foldout table at the back of the room. "I know it's not much, but that's for you, if you need it."

"I appreciate it." Cassie shook her head. "I'm sorry again about the mix up. I'm not really sure what to do while I wait."

"Have you ever been to New Orleans?"

"Once or twice. But it was a long time ago. I wouldn't know where to start."

Jules' eyes lit up, and Cassie regretted the words as soon as they left her mouth. She liked Jules' enthusiasm, but she wasn't sure she'd be able to keep up with the other woman's pace. But it was too late to take back what she'd said.

"I can show you around the museum, including where we're setting up the new exhibit."

"I'd love that." It was the truth. She'd never been to the NOMA, and even though she'd looked through the collection and as many pictures as she could, it wasn't the same as visiting in the flesh. "Thank you."

A man with black hair and sallow skin popped his head in the doorway. He had a faintly British accent. "All right, Jules? Who's your new friend?"

"It's Cassie Quinn from Savannah!" Jules didn't bother hiding her excitement. Cassie didn't think she'd be able to, even if she tried. "I'm going to show her around here in a minute. Want to join us?"

"Mack's got me working on a new contraption for the modern wing." The man looked over at Cassie and shook his head. "I'd apologize for her cheeriness, but there's no getting around it. Coffee's in the breakroom if you need it. And you will."

"Go away, Ashford." Jules rolled her eyes, but she never stopped smiling. "Let me have my fun."

"Full name, ouch. Hit a nerve then." He stepped into the room and held a hand to Cassie. "Call me Ford. Will you be coming out for drinks later?"

"Oh, um." Cassie looked to Jules, who barely suppressed a squeal, and decided she didn't have the heart to say no. "Yeah. Of course. Sounds fun."

6

CASSIE THANKED THE SERVER AS HE SET HER FOURTH OR FIFTH TEQUILA SUNRISE in front of her. She couldn't remember the name of the bar, but she knew she'd come back if given the chance. They had a good waitstaff with heavy pours, and their dinner had been hot, fast, and fresh.

Jules had insisted on ordering for Cassie, making her try a barbeque shrimp dip and Creole smoked sausage and even fried alligator. Everything had been incredible, and their table of six had emptied their plates in a matter of minutes.

Then came their entrees.

Cassie had ordered a shrimp po'boy, but Jules insisted she share her gumbo. Ford had gotten an entire seafood platter, and Cassie couldn't begin to name what the others had. It all smelled and looked delicious, and she dug in without humility or grace. She had no shame when it came to good food.

That was an hour ago. They'd started ordering drinks immediately after, enjoying the cool breeze on the outdoor patio. It was a chilly evening for Louisiana, but the bar had placed stylish propane heaters near each table. It was warm enough that Cassie had slipped off her jacket and hung it on the back of her chair.

This was the best kind of dinner, one where Jules' friends included her in the conversation but didn't grill her about what she did or where she was from or how she liked the city. If she had something to say, she said it. And if she didn't, the others made their own conversation. They were loud in a way where you wanted to be in on the jokes, and she found moments where she enjoyed their company, even if she still wanted to try out that jacuzzi tub back at her hotel.

Then there were the other moments, the ones in between the happiness where she remembered David wouldn't be texting to check in, and she couldn't pick up the phone to tell him she was at a dueling piano bar that he would've loved with every fiber of his being. The music emanating from inside was loud, and the raucous laughter accompanying the musicians' muffled jokes throughout their sets made Cassie smile. She could see David raising a beer in salute to their talent.

But he would never be able to do that again. Someone had made sure of it. The tequila turned her grief into anger, and she drained her drink in one go. No one took notice when she ordered another.

She couldn't decide if it would've been better to be by herself or surrounded by strangers she'd met a couple hours ago. At the very least, Jules and Ford's banter was entertaining. They were so obviously in love with each other, yet there was a practiced distance between them. If they got too close, their gravitational pull would keep them from ever escaping.

Cassie then thought of Jason. She wondered where he was and what he was doing. She knew he had taken a few days off to attend a funeral, but he hadn't offered specifics, and she didn't want to pry. Their text messages, while short and sporadic because of their current schedules, still filled her with a sense of hope. And longing.

Jules leaned over to her. "Twenty-six."

Cassie thought the music had warped Jules' words. "Huh?"

"Twenty-six." Jules pointed to Cassie's phone. "You've picked up your phone and immediately set it down twenty-six times in the last hour. Who are you hoping will send you a message?"

"No one." When Jules raised an eyebrow in disbelief, Cassie rolled her eyes. "This guy. He works at the museum back in Savannah. He just hasn't texted me in a while, that's all."

"That means you should text him first."

"I don't want to bother him."

"Something tells me he wants you to bother him."

"You couldn't possibly know that."

Jules winked, and her large, golden peacock earrings flashed in the fire-light. "I'm psychic."

Cassie laughed. It was a good enough reason as any to reach out to him. To at least see how he was doing. She leaned closer to Jules. "I don't know what to say."

"Ask him what he's up to." Jules nodded her head until her earrings jangled. "It's a nice open-ended question. It shows interest. But it's short and simple. You'll get the tone of the conversation from however he responds."

"You make this sound easier than it is."

Jules waved her off. "Sometimes you just have to shoot your shot."

Cassie pointedly looked at Ford, who was staring into the fire as though in a trance, then back at Jules. "When are you going to follow your own advice?"

Jules scrunched her face and cast a glance over at Ford. She didn't notice, but when she turned back to Cassie, Ford's gaze shifted and followed her every movement. "I will follow my advice on a day that's not today. But you should. I have a good feeling about this."

"Because you're psychic."

Jules' eyes twinkled. "Because I'm psychic."

Cassie sighed and picked up her phone, unlocking it and tapping on her conversation with Jason. She read through his last few responses, but none of them indicated whether he was in the mood to talk. Cassie felt the tequila taking the reins, and before she backed out, she typed up the message and hit send.

His response was immediate.

I was just about to ask you the same question.

Cassie's heart kicked into high gear. She looked at Jules, who had a smug look on her face. She tapped her head and smirked. "Psychic."

Cassie was about to ask what she should say—Jules was clearly better at this than she was, even if she couldn't follow her own advice and take the leap with Ford—when Jason sent through another text message. "It's a video."

Jules leaned so close she was cheek to cheek with Cassie. "Looks like he's out with friends, too."

Cassie hit play, and Jason's face filled her screen. His sepia skin glowed in the light of an overhead lamp, but his eyes locked her in place. She had stared into them countless times, but she'd never seen them so bright before—like topaz illuminated from behind. He was so close to the camera, she could see a caramel-colored flame circling his pupil.

"Hey." Jason's voice was deep and easy. He had to move the camera closer so she could hear him over the din of the music in the background. Even with a screen between them, Cassie felt a blush creep up her neck at his proximity. "I'm out with my cousins. We wanted a couple drinks before the funeral tomorrow. I hope you—"

Suddenly, someone wrenched the phone from his grasp. A young woman with the same smile and same eyes stared into the camera and fluffed her downy curls. She looked over at Jason, who was reaching for his phone from just off-camera. "Who are you talking to?"

"No one." Jason laughed as she held him at arm's length, with the phone just out of grasp. "Kiki, come on. Give it back."

"You're not talking to yourself. Who is it?"

"I told you, it's—"

Her eyes lit up. "Is it Cassie?" Kiki turned back to the camera, as though she were looking directly into Cassie's eyes. "Girl, he is so into you. He won't shut up—"

Someone pulled the phone from her grasp, and for a minute, Cassie could only see the floor. Then another unfamiliar face filled the screen. He was broader than Jason, with a bit more weight in his face, but he and Jason could've been brothers.

"Cassie. Ty here. Nice to meet you." Ty laughed as Jason yelled from across the table. "We're having a great time. Wish you were here. Jay does, too. Is he playing hard to get? If he is, let me know. I'll set him straight."

The phone tilted again, and Kiki came into view. "I'm going to send this before Jason del—"

The video cut off there. Cassie's face was flaming, and it felt like the entire table was looking at her. She was torn between laughing and crying and jumping for joy. The tequila running through her system made her want to launch out of her chair and dance across the table.

Another message came a second later. *I'm so sorry. My family is ridiculous.*

"Cassie." Jules' tone was serious. "Did you hear the song playing in the background?"

"No." She had been a little preoccupied with everything else. "What was it?"

"Go back and listen." Jules flapped her hands. "Hurry."

Cassie hit play again and held the phone up to her ear. She forced herself to ignore Jason's silken voice, to hear past Kiki and Ty's antics, and tune into the song in the background. She could just barely pick out the lyrics.

"'Piano Man'?" Cassie turned to Jules. "Kind of on the nose, don't you think?"

The video ended, and Jules pointed at the speaker above their heads. "Listen."

Cassie tilted her ear to the speaker. It wasn't hard to hear the music above the din of the restaurant, but it was difficult to pick out the individual words. Slowly, she recognized the melody, heard the harmonies, and finally—*finally*—realized what Jules was trying to tell her.

Unless the universe was playing a cruel joke on her, she and Jason were in the exact same bar, listening to the exact same song.

7

Jules pushed Cassie out of her seat and toward the door to the bar. With an encouraging nod, she returned to their table, leaning close to Ford, and undoubtedly sharing what had just happened.

For a split second, Cassie wondered if Jules really *was* psychic.

But as she pulled open the door, the heat of the room snapped Cassie back to reality. Clusters of people huddled around tiny tables and lined the walls. She tried to picture where he'd been sitting when his cousins tossed the phone between themselves and realized he must be at a booth in the back. She'd have to wade through a sea of people to get within reach of him. Then what? Pull him away from his family? She wasn't sure she could do that.

Then again, what were the chances they'd end up at the same bar in the same city, miles away from home?

Cassie wound her way through the crowd, trying not to jostle anyone's drinks. If slipping between dozens of drunk people gesticulating wildly was an Olympic sport, she'd have a gold medal. Somehow, she managed not to step on anyone's toes or start any fights.

As she made her way to the other end of the bar, she spotted Kiki's cloud of curls. Her heart dropped into her stomach and then shot up into her throat. It was pounding so hard she felt lightheaded. She knew it was Kiki, and yet, she wouldn't believe it until—

Two men sat side by side, their backs to Cassie. One had broad shoulders, while the other was taller and leaner. The smaller one had an arm slung over his cousin's back, and with his other hand, he lifted a drink in celebration. Cassie didn't need to see his face.

She would know him anywhere.

She tucked herself against the wall at the end of the bar, hoping she wouldn't be in the way of the servers as they left to deliver drinks. But nobody paid her any attention, and even when Kiki scanned the room from across the table, she didn't recognize Cassie. Jason had obviously told them about her, but had they seen her picture? What did they know about her?

It took Cassie a moment to figure out what to do. Approach the table and hope they'd invite her to sit down? Have a drink delivered along with a message to meet her at the bar? Cassie decided she'd have a little fun with it first, so she pulled out her phone.

I think someone's checking you out.

Jason immediately leaned forward to check his messages. Kiki snatched for his phone, but he was too fast. The response came seconds later.

Doubt it. She's probably looking at Ty.

No, she's definitely looking at you.

Oh yeah? How do you know that?

She told me. Cassie was grinning like a maniac. The two men at the pianos across the room ended one song and started another. *Do you like David Bowie?*

Jason looked over at the pianos, then back down at his phone. Kiki saw the change in his demeanor and said something, but he didn't answer. He just kept staring at his phone.

Cassie let him off the hook. *Turn around.*

Very funny.

I'm not joking.

Jason pushed his chair back and stood up. His table went quiet as he turned around and scanned the bar. Cassie stepped out from against the wall. When their eyes connected, it was like everything else faded away—the music, the people, the bar itself. Her heart stopped and didn't start again until Jason's face lit up in his trademark smile.

Before she knew it, they were standing toe to toe. She looked up into his face while he looked down at her, wonder and confusion and elation written in his eyes. Cassie couldn't help the giggle that escaped her mouth, even though it made her sound like a love-struck teenager. She refused to be embarrassed. His presence washed away any hint of darkness closing in on her earlier.

"How?" Jason brushed a piece of hair away from her face and shook his head, as if to reset his focus. "What are you doing here?"

"Work trip." She wasn't sure she could speak in complete sentences. "Only a couple days."

"Why didn't you tell me?"

"Didn't know." She cleared her throat and took a deep breath. *Come on, Quinn. Pull yourself together.* "I didn't know you would be here. A couple people at the museum invited me out. I almost didn't come."

Jason's smile widened. His voice was low and measured, but she didn't miss a single word. "I'm glad you did."

Cassie forced herself to look at his table. They were all staring at them. "I didn't mean to interrupt. I just wanted to say hi. I'll let you get back to your family."

"No, no." Panic crossed his face. "Have a drink with me? Just one. If I buy them a round, they'll leave us alone for at least fifteen minutes. Twenty if Kiki is feeling generous."

"Okay."

"Really? Are you sure?" Jason looked around. "Do you have to get back to your table?"

"I can stay for a drink." She was giddy with the idea. "Jules won't leave without me."

"Awesome." Jason was breathless. "Wait right there. I'll be back. Don't leave."

She laughed. "I won't." When he still didn't move, she placed her hand on his chest and pushed. *"I won't."*

Jason returned to his table, and everyone leaned in close to hear what he was saying. Simultaneously, six heads turned in her direction. Cassie could feel the blush on her face reaching her toes. She waved, and Kiki threw her head back and laughed. Ty whooped. One of the other cousins slapped Jason on the back. A moment later, he was by her side again.

"Kiki promised me she'd behave, but I don't trust her. She's had a lot of rum." They found a spot next to the bar. "What are you drinking?"

"Tequila sunrise."

Jason waited for the bartender to spot them, then ordered her drink and a round of shots for the table. He got a glass of water.

"Designated driver?"

Jason nodded. "We drew straws. I think Ethan rigged it."

She laughed. "I'm so sorry."

He shrugged. "It's okay. We'll probably be doing a lot of drinking over the next few days. My family isn't really into the whole mourning period thing. It's more about throwing parties and getting together. But it helps, in its own way."

"I'm Irish. I know how that goes." Cassie's smile faded. "Were you close?"

"Yeah. Most of us grew up together. A few of us have moved away, but most of the family still lives around here. We get together as much as we can." Jason took a sip of water and turned to Cassie. His eyes were darker now than they'd been in the video. Sadness had clouded their light. "Jasmine had a heart defect, so she'd been sick her whole life. Doctors told her she wouldn't live past forty, but she was doing well, all things considered. It's not like this was her first surgery. She got through it, but I guess it took its toll."

"Complications?"

Jason nodded. "That's what they told us. We thought she'd been doing fine, but a couple days later, she just crashed. Everyone was surprised. Her sister—" Jason's voice cracked. He cleared it before he moved on. "She's taking it pretty hard."

Cassie remembered the dream she had on the airplane. She didn't know the woman in the bed—hadn't been able to read her chart—but she hoped it wasn't Jason's cousin. If so, how would she tell him there was something more going on? How could she explain his cousin's death wasn't because of complications but a Ghost Doctor meddling in the affairs of the living?

She settled for the only other words she could think of in the moment. "I'm sorry."

"Thank you." He smiled, and though there was still pain behind it, it seemed genuine. "But what about you? How are you doing?"

Cassie fought the urge to say she was fine, that life was going great. He'd been honest with her about what was going on with him, so the least she could do was pay it back in kind. "I'm okay."

"That sounded almost convincing."

"Did it?" She laughed. "No, really. I'm hanging in there. The trip to see my parents has helped a lot more than I thought it would. Who knew working through our issues would be such a good thing for us? It's going to take time, on both ends, for things to feel normal again. If they were ever normal."

"No family is normal. I know that for a fact."

"True." Cassie's face fell as she thought of what had come next. "After I got home, I got a phone call from Detective Harris."

"The woman who came to talk to you at the museum?"

"Yeah." Cassie shook her head. "You have a good memory."

"I'm pretty good with names and faces. Part of the security thing. Gotta remember people."

"Well, Adelaide called to tell me some bad news." She had told her sister soon after she found out, but Cassie still wasn't used to saying it out loud. "We had a mutual friend, Detective David Klein. He was very important to me." How could she tell Jason what David had meant to her? How could she sum that up in a couple of words? It was impossible. "Like a father, really. Like family. She called to tell me he died."

Jason moved closer. He placed a hand on her arm. It was comforting, but she could feel her emotions threatening to spill over. He waited until she looked him in the eye before he spoke. "I'm so sorry, Cassie. This is probably a dumb question, but are you okay? I mean, down here, working?"

She shrugged. Her voice was thick with grief, so she took a swig of her drink. The tequila helped burn it away. "Honestly, no. I'm still processing it. We don't know exactly what happened, other than someone murdered him." When Jason's eyes grew wide, she hurried on. "His funeral was the other day. I wanted to come down here to get away from everything for a while. Maybe it wasn't the right call, but running into you makes it feel like it was."

The alcohol made Cassie's head swim, and her entire body felt warm and tingly. Jason was right there, so close, and she could feel the heat of his hand on her arm. It sent electric shocks throughout her body that were anything but painful. The sting of David's death was never out of reach but looking into Jason's eyes made her feel like everything could be okay. One day.

"If you need anything, let me know. Whether it's a distraction or a shoulder or a pint of ice cream."

Cassie laughed, even as a tear escaped from the corner of her eye. Jason was quick to wipe it away. He cupped her face and held her gaze. She couldn't look away if she tried. The tequila wasn't the only thing making her dizzy now.

"I'm really glad we ran into each other." Jason's voice was deeper than a moment ago, and Cassie could see a hint of a blush in his cheeks. "I like how the universe keeps bringing us together."

"Me too." Cassie felt a pull to lean closer. Her last encounter with Jason hadn't gone over well—she'd accidentally punched him in the face, after all—but she was a different person now. She was brave, and she was ready.

But it turned out the universe had a sense of humor. Just as they leaned closer, someone bumped into Jason, sending his glass of water across the bar. He jumped to clean it up and apologize to the woman on the other side of Cassie who now sported a soaking wet arm. The man who hit Jason didn't even look back to say he was sorry.

With the moment properly ruined, it didn't come as a surprise when Jules showed up with Cassie's jacket in hand. She looked at Jason with wide eyes and an enormous smile but said nothing.

After all, they'd have the entire ride home to discuss everything that hadn't happened.

8

Detective Harris took a deep breath and brushed the fur off her jacket before she knocked on Chief Clementine's door. She didn't mind watching Apollo and Bear, but she needed to add an extra ten minutes to her morning routine to use a lint roller before heading to the station.

This morning, she'd been less than successful at removing the evidence.

But it was too late now, and she didn't want to waste anymore of the Chief's time. She heard a muffled response to her knock, so she twisted the doorknob and walked inside, closing the door behind her with an audible *click*.

Chief Sandra Clementine was a constant picture of perfection. Her dark copper skin was flawless, and the lines on her clothes were always sharp. She had pulled half her hair back into a ponytail, but her locks still fell past her shoulders. She was a tall woman with broad shoulders and rippling muscles, and every ounce exuded power and control.

Her office always smelled like oranges, and it was the only comforting part of the room. There was a single picture of her husband on her desk, but the rest of the office was void of any personal touches. If nothing else, everyone knew the Chief kept her personal and professional lives separate.

"Have a seat, Detective."

Harris followed orders. She unbuttoned her jacket and sat down, crossing her legs to appear more comfortable than she was. She didn't know why the Chief had called her into her office, but she had a few guesses.

Clementine pushed a few pieces of paper out of the way and folded her hands on top of her desk. She waited until Harris met her gaze before she spoke. "How are you doing?"

"I'm fine."

Clementine leveled her with a stare.

Harris had to resist the urge to roll her eyes. "I've been better. I'm not really sure what you want me to say, Chief."

"The truth, to start." Clementine leaned back in her chair with a sigh. "Look, I'm not your therapist, so you don't have to tell me anything. But it's still my job to make sure my people are taken care of. I want to know what you need. What I can do for you."

Harris knew better than to tell her what she really needed. Revenge. That wouldn't sit well with the Chief of Police. So she went for another version of the truth. "I want to nail Aguilar to the wall. I want to make sure David gets justice."

"We don't know if Aguilar killed David."

"Even if he didn't pull the trigger—"

"We still don't know." Clementine shook her head. "We have to be smart about this, Adelaide. I'm on your side, but we can't be rash. I have to know you won't be rash."

Harris froze. "Do you know something I don't know?"

"You have as much information as I do. We've got everyone working on this. The second cop shot within the last two weeks. I don't know if there's a connection, but if there is, this could get out of hand. It already has. The newspapers are running stories on how there's a cop killer on the loose."

"I don't care what the newspapers say."

"You should. I do." Clementine tossed her hair over one shoulder, and Harris could feel the frustration behind the movement. "You know the media can influence our case. The more they sensationalize it, the harder it's going to be for us to solve it. I need you on my side here."

"I am on your side." She wanted nothing more than to be given the reins on this one, but Clementine hadn't handed them over yet. "Just tell me what you need me to do."

"To start, I need you to answer my question."

Something told Harris the Chief wouldn't believe her if she insisted she was fine. So, once again, she went for a version of the truth. "Like I said, I've been better. I keep expecting him to call me or text me. I look over at his desk, and it takes a minute to remember he's not just grabbing coffee in the break room."

"Every once in a while, he'd bring me a cup of coffee if I hadn't left my desk in a few hours." Clementine chuckled at the memory. "I didn't realize how much I appreciated that until I remembered it would never happen again."

"I'm angry." Harris hadn't intended to tell her that, but it was hard to hide. "Angrier than I've ever been. I'm angry at whoever did this. I'm angry at myself. I'm angry at David."

"A lot of people will tell you not to be angry. They'll say anger doesn't solve any problems. But they're wrong." Harris must've looked shocked because Clementine smiled. "Didn't think I'd say that, huh? Anger can be a powerful tool. But it can also be a dangerous one. I want to know if you can get a handle on your anger long enough to solve this case for us."

"I can." Harris sat up straighter. "I promise I can."

Clementine didn't answer right away, and when she did, she chose her words carefully. "You're a good detective, Adelaide. A great one. David liked you a lot. He saw a lot of potential in you. For the record, so do I. You're by the book, and I like that. There are too many cops out there who think they can break the rules and get away with it because they caught the bad guy. That's not how the real world works."

"I feel like I won't like what's coming next."

"*But*," Clementine said, "even good cops get wrapped up in bad shit. I'm not saying you will, but I'm warning you to keep your head clear. David needs you at your best. If Aguilar is behind this, then we need to do it right. Otherwise, we lose our shot at putting him behind bars."

Harris knew Aguilar deserved worse than sitting in a cell for the rest of his life, but she wasn't about to say that to the Chief. "I understand. I want him in jail as much as anyone."

"I know you do." Clementine opened her desk drawer and pulled out a manila folder. "This is David's case file. It has everything we know about how he died and what we found on him. I want you to talk to Lisa first. We've done some preliminary interviews, but she knows you best. Asked for you by name, actually."

Harris looked up from the file folder. "Did she say why?"

"No. That's what I want you to find out." Clementine hesitated before she spoke again. "Listen, this won't be an easy case. For anyone. Are you sure you can do this?"

Harris had never felt so sure in her life. "I want answers."

"You'll get your answers," Clementine said. "What I want to know is if you're ready for them."

Harris thought she knew if she was ready, but when she opened her mouth to respond, no words came out.

9

THE TWINGE OF A HEADACHE MADE CASSIE SQUINT AGAINST THE SETTING SUN, even though she wore sunglasses. Her pounding head had abated for a while, but her Uber driver's choice in music opened the door for its return. With every guitar riff and drumbeat, she felt like puking. It was hard to say if she'd ever drink another tequila sunrise again.

Cassie pressed her head against the cool window and shut her eyes. Last night felt like a fever dream. One minute, she was moping around a table full of strangers, and the next she was sitting at a bar with Jason, hoping the universe wasn't playing a cruel joke on her.

But as many times as she replayed it over in her mind, she couldn't deny it had been real. It was a quick conversation—and, true, they had mostly talked about the people they'd recently lost—but it had happened. And so had that almost-kiss.

Statistically speaking, she was due for a moment alone with him void of disaster—right?

The car hit a bump and jostled Cassie, causing her forehead to smack against the window. She stifled a groan and squeezed her eyes shut tighter. She'd spent the entire morning chugging water and feeling like death warmed up. After a hot shower and an equally hot breakfast, she felt almost human.

The only thing that kept her going was a text message from Jason earlier that morning, inviting her out to dinner. She had agreed on one condition—

she got to pick dessert. He'd made some smart-ass comment that, given their history, they probably shouldn't go for ice cream, but little did he know she had something much more unpredictable in mind.

But they'd only get there if she could make it through the meal.

By the time she pulled up to Armand's Bar & Grill, her headache had receded, and hunger replaced nausea. It didn't hurt that the aroma of surf and turf emanating from the restaurant made her mouth water. It wasn't a large establishment, but it packed a flavorful punch.

Jason was waiting for her at a table inside. He stood up as she entered, wearing a collared shirt and dark wash jeans. She was glad she'd dressed casually, but the way he was looking at her, you'd think she looked like Cinderella at the ball.

She didn't hate the way it made her feel.

"Hi." He couldn't keep the smile off his face. It was contagious. "How are you?"

"I'm great." When he leveled her with a look, she rolled her eyes. Which made her head twinge again. "I'm still hungover. Don't judge me."

"I would never." The waiter came to take their drink orders, and Jason could barely keep the smirk off his face. "I'll take water. Cassie, do you want a tequila sunrise?"

"Water." Cassie tried to scowl, but she couldn't hide her smile, either. "Water will be perfect."

"I'll get that right in for you."

"Oh, and could you tell Armand that Jay Broussard is here? He'll kill me if he knows I ate at his restaurant and didn't say hi."

The waiter laughed like he and Jason shared a secret and then retreated to the back. Cassie raised an eyebrow. "I feel like I should call you Jay instead of Jason."

"I like when you call me Jason." His eyes lit up as he caught the blush on her face. "Everyone I knew as a kid still calls me Jay."

As if on cue, a large Black man wearing an apron and a chef's hat pushed through the kitchen doors with a slight limp to his walk. He stopped in the middle of the room. The man was twice as wide as Jason and at least two heads taller. He would've been one of the most intimidating men Cassie had ever seen if it weren't for the smile that stretched from ear to ear, pushing his cheeks up so high you could hardly see his eyes.

"Jay Broussard as I live and breathe."

"Armand."

Cassie liked the way Armand said Jason's last name, with the slightest hint of a French accent. He sounded like the woman from the plane, and it was clearly the result of a New Orleanian upbringing. Jason stood to hug the other man, and Armand slapped him so hard on the back, Jason's knees almost buckled.

Then he spotted Cassie.

"And who is this beautiful woman you're sharing your table with, Jay? Where are your manners?"

"This is Cassie Quinn." Jason hesitated for only a fraction of a moment, but Cassie thought Armand caught it, too. "I know her from back in Savannah. At the museum."

Armand's eyes sparkled. He reached out and engulfed Cassie's hand in both of his. They were warm, and at this close range, she could smell the garlic emanating from him. It was not an unpleasant aroma. "It is wonderful to meet you, Ms. Quinn."

"Please, call me Cassie."

"Cassie." He patted her hand one last time and let go, spreading his arms wide. "I am Armand, the owner of this fine establishment. I cook every meal myself. Anything you want, it's on the house."

"Armand—"

Armand ignored Jason. "I owe this man my life. We go through this every time he comes here. I say his meal is on the house, he tells me he has to give me something, I threaten him, and he leaves my servers a hundred-dollar tip." He clapped his hands together. "For the sake of expediency, let's just get to the part where you both order anything you want off the menu."

"Pasta." Cassie hadn't even looked at her options. "Your biggest bowl of pasta. Please. I need carbs."

Jason laughed. "I'll take the second biggest bowl of pasta."

"Coming right up!" Armand slapped Jason on the back again, almost sending him face first into a goblet full of water. As the larger-than-life man walked away, Cassie could hear him muttering, "Jay Broussard, as I live and breathe," under his breath and chuckling.

The server didn't look at all fazed by Armand's entrance or his departure, though Cassie couldn't imagine ever getting used to how that man filled a room. The other guests had turned to watch their interaction, and she saw a few people leaning close to whisper to each other, probably wondering who Jason was.

"Let me know if you need anything else," the server said.

"Thank you." Cassie waited until he left to turn back to Jason. "Saved his life, huh?"

Jason shook his head. "I was a combat medic for a few years. He was wounded in the field. It was a while before we found him. He lost his leg, but it could've been worse. I was the one who pulled him out of the pit and treated him until we got back to base. The doctors at camp did the hard part, but the way Armand tells it, I brought him back from the dead."

"He seems like a good friend." She took a sip of water, knowing her curiosity was about to get the best of her. "I didn't know you were a combat medic."

Jason shrugged. It was a motion she could only describe as humility. "I've done a bit of everything. I was probably an MP for the longest, though."

"Military Police?" Cassie cocked her head to the side. "I don't think I know much about what they do."

"Depends on the branch. And the assignment. It took me to a lot of different places. Met a lot of different people." He smiled. "I just realized who you remind me of."

"Who?"

"This MP I used to know. She was probably the toughest person I've ever met. I hated training with her. She'd kick my ass without breaking a sweat."

Cassie laughed. "That sounds nothing like me."

"You're tough, too."

"Oh yeah, you definitely want me on your side in a bar fight." She flexed her arms. "The other guys wouldn't stand a chance."

Jason shook his head, but he laughed. "I think you'd be pretty scrappy in a fight. But that's not what I mean." He paused, like he was searching for the perfect words. "She always looked like she had the entire weight of the world on her shoulders. Like she dared the universe to throw her something she couldn't handle just so she could prove it wrong. You look that way sometimes."

"Is that a good thing or a bad thing?"

"Neither." He shrugged. "I like it, though."

"Well, that's good to know."

"Last time I saw her, she had these scars running up and down her arm—"

Cassie's hand automatically went to her shirt and tugged it higher on her chest. She hated how she was still self-conscious of them, hated that Jason had noticed them. It was the one physical aspect of Novak she couldn't remove from her life. She might push him out of her mind, but there were still remnants of what he'd done all over her body.

Jason reached out a hand but stopped short of touching her. "I'm sorry. I shouldn't have said that. We've never talked about it, and that should've been my sign to keep my mouth shut."

"No, no. It's fine." When he didn't look convinced, she forced a smile. "Really, it is. I just wasn't sure if you ever noticed. If it bothered you."

"I notice everything about you, Cassie. I couldn't ignore you if I tried. And if I'm being honest, I don't really want to." He let the tips of his fingers come down on her arm. "We don't have to talk about it. But for the record, there's nothing about you that would scare me away."

"Even if I were a serial killer?"

Jason looked like he was trying to stay serious, but the corners of his mouth went up. "Depending on the circumstances, I might give you a free pass."

"Good to know." Cassie's smile faded. She hadn't planned on doing this tonight, in public, but it was as good a time as any. Sometimes you had to rip off the Band-Aid in one swift motion. "I was looking for a way to tell you about that. About me. I just didn't know how."

"You don't have to if you don't want to." He rubbed the side of her hand with his thumb. "I don't know if you've noticed, but I'm a pretty patient person."

"I have noticed." She smiled, and it was genuine. "And I do want to tell you."

"Then I'm all ears."

Cassie took a deep breath and a sip of water before she started. "There was a man named Novak. About ten years ago, he attacked me in a graveyard. He stabbed me and left me for dead. Somehow, I survived. They arrested him, but last year, he escaped. He came back to finish the job. That didn't work out so well for him. He got the electric chair. He's dead now. And I'm still here."

It was strange to boil down the last ten years of her complicated life into a few succinct sentences. It felt good to get it out, but there was so much more to the story, even if you didn't consider how she sometimes got visions or saw ghosts.

She shook her head to clear away those thoughts. "You know, I've practiced that speech in my head a thousand times, give or take a million. I don't even know if I explained it well enough." Her face was feverish now. It was probably the color of her hair. "I'm sorry. That's a weird thing to spring on someone. Not exactly dinner conversation."

Jason squeezed her hand and waited for her to look him in the eyes. "Thank you for telling me. I'm sure that wasn't easy. But a couple of scars won't scare me away. I've got a few, too, you know."

The release of her anxiety was overwhelming, and Cassie could feel the tears forming in her eyes. Luckily, Armand saved her by pushing through the double doors from the kitchen with a massive plate in each hand. She used the distraction to blink back the tears, but she could still feel Jason's eyes on her.

"For you, sir, Cajun shrimp and scallops over angel hair in a creamy white sauce." He put Jason's plate down in front of him and turned to Cassie. "And for you, ma'am, a seafood medley containing shrimp, scallops, lobster, and calamari in a mushroom and garlic red sauce."

"Armand, this looks amazing." She looked up into his smiling face. "Thank you."

"It is my pleasure." He brought his hands together like a clap of thunder. "Bon appétit!"

10

Cassie kept her hands deep in her jacket pockets as they trekked down Basin Street toward their destination. The temperature had cooled considerably, and while she would've appreciated the excuse to lean into Jason's side and soak up his warmth, she relished the way the chill in the air cleared her head.

The rest of their dinner conversation had not been as heavy as it was before Armand had delivered their food, and for that she was grateful. They talked about the city and Jason's cousins. They discussed how the truck with the NOMA's new pieces got delayed yet another day. What a strange coincidence that Magdalena had suddenly stopped texting them both now that she knew they were in the same city together.

Mission accomplished, I guess, thought Cassie.

The restaurant's owner had joined them for dessert, bringing out an enormous slab of tiramisu for each of them. Cassie knew she couldn't refuse, even if she'd wanted to. And she didn't. Somehow, she found room for every last crumb while Armand regaled her with stories of his childhood adventures with Jason.

They had excused themselves after a round of handshakes, which turned into backslaps and hugs. Jason had slipped several twenties into the hand of their server on the way out the door, and Cassie caught Armand beaming after them. She wasn't sure when she'd visit New Orleans again, but she knew she'd be back to Armand's Bar & Grill the second she landed.

Now the two of them walked off their meal, groaning and complaining about their full stomachs, but knowing full well they didn't have any regrets. It felt good to stretch her legs, and it helped Cassie rid herself of the nerves that had built up over dinner.

"Since we've technically had dessert already," Jason started, "I feel like you have something else up your sleeve."

"Busted." Cassie gestured down the street. "We're supposed to meet someone around here who'll give us a special tour of the city."

"A special tour?" Jason raised an eyebrow. "A friend of yours?"

"Not exactly." She winced. "More like the sister of a random lady I met on the plane down here."

Jason looked caught between comedy and concern. "Well, this should be an interesting night." They stopped in front of a large metal gate. There was a plaque next to it that read SAINT LOUIS CEMETERY NUMBER ONE. "It's probably not the cemetery. They don't do tours at night."

"There are some exceptions." Jason and Cassie both jumped as a woman stepped out of the shadows. "But you have to know the right people. And I am the right people."

Sabine Delacroix was the spitting image of her sister in all the ways that mattered, from that same golden glow beneath her skin to the wiry gray peppered throughout her dark hair. But her eyes were a shade cooler and her smile a fraction sharper. And while Celeste had dressed in muted tones that oozed elegance and class, Sabine, it seemed, didn't mind sticking out in a crowd. She wore a full-length dress with a heavy shawl over her shoulders. The layers of purple and blue flattered her figure as they draped across her chest and pinched in at the waist.

Magdalena would've approved.

"Ms. Delacroix?" Cassie held out her hand. "I'm Cassie Quinn. This is Jason Broussard."

Sabine's smile grew wider. "Two for one, my lucky night. The Broussards have a long history in New Orleans. I'm happy to make your acquaintance." She shook Cassie's hand, and then Jason's. "Both of you."

Sabine's mind was as quiet as Celeste's had been, but without the momentary lapse that had brought about the vision of the two sisters standing in front of a raging fire. If they were twins, Sabine likely had the same ability to close herself off to Cassie. Had Celeste warned her sister? The way Sabine lingered on her face made Cassie think she had.

"It's true that most people can't enter the cemetery at night, but I don't think the spirits will mind, as long as you stay close to me."

Cassie couldn't tell if Sabine was being theatrical, but considering there was something more to the Delacroix sisters than they let on, she had an inkling the warning held some weight. Ghosts weren't usually dangerous, but there were exceptions to the rule. And Cassie was sensitive to the spirit world. How many would come up to her seeking help? She hadn't prepared for this, and she wasn't sure how she'd be able to hide it from Jason.

As if on cue, Jason leaned close as the older woman unlocked the gate. "Are you okay with this? A cemetery, I mean. It won't bother you?"

Cassie's heartbeat ratcheted up and then smoothed out to a steady rhythm. Novak's attacks were fresh in his mind. That was the only reason he was asking. She felt her features soften. "I've been in a cemetery or two since then. I should be okay."

Not that it would've mattered. Sabine Delacroix waited for no one.

Cassie and Jason barely slipped through the gate before it clanged shut behind them. Cassie's body tensed, ready for the onslaught of spirits walking aimlessly through their final resting place, reaching out to the first person to acknowledge their presence.

But it never happened.

The graveyard was quieter than expected. Cassie could feel the spirits in the surrounding shadows, but none showed their faces. They lurked at the edges of her vision, pressing forward, only to shrink back. Sabine hadn't been kidding about staying close to her side.

Sabine walked forward at a measured pace, her dress billowing out behind her, taking on the air of someone who assumed everyone else would fall in line. And they did. Both Delacroix women had an aura about them that demanded respect, and Cassie had no interest in behaving otherwise.

"Welcome to St. Louis Cemetery No. 1. This will not be your average tour of one of New Orleans' most haunted corners." Sabine stopped and twirled to face them, forcing Cassie and Jason to pull up short. She spoke to them like they were just two people in an audience of observers. And maybe they were. "Not only do we have a local in our midst, but someone who, I assume, would rather see our city for what it really is."

Jason looked to Cassie, whose cheeks colored. Cassie had no more doubts that Celeste had told Sabine about her. Cassie wasn't sure what the women knew of her abilities, but she hoped Sabine would keep that knowledge to herself.

One major reveal of her past was enough for tonight.

"New Orleans wears a false mask of color and chaos. We're known for food and festivities, and while murder is always on the menu, those who yearn to peek at our true face rarely like what they see."

Cassie waited for Sabine to continue, but the silence of the graveyard was resounding. She knew the other woman was waiting for her to ask the question on the tip of her tongue. "What do they see?"

"Magic." Sabine's eyes lit up as though a fire burned behind them. "Ghosts. Demons. A darkness that stays with them, long after they've left New Orleans behind."

Sabine turned, flourishing her dress, and moving deeper into the cemetery.

"St. Louis is New Orleans' oldest extant graveyard." The woman had discarded some of the effect in her voice, but it still sent chills down Cassie's spine. "The Spanish established it at the end of the eighteenth century, and it is still used after two hundred years. One hundred thousand souls have been laid to rest on these grounds, and some have never left."

Until this point, the pressing darkness of the graveyard had felt like a lover's touch on Cassie's cheek. Sabine's declaration lifted the veil just enough for Cassie to see the true extent of the restless spirits around her. Most of them didn't take notice of the trio in their midst, but a few stared at Cassie, as though trying to burn a hole right through her chest.

Sabine continued forward, while Cassie and Jason followed in her wake. The eerie silence stretched to every corner of the graveyard, despite the world raging outside the fence. It was like the cemetery acted as a portal through time. Broken cobblestones and chipped grave markers looked whole in the dark of the night. Here, the spirits reigned supreme, and they could warp your sense of time.

"There are dozens of famous men and women buried in this historic spot, though none of them attract as much attention as the Voodoo Queen herself, Marie Laveau. Born at the turn of the century in 1801, she had a Haitian mother and a white father. She was a hairdresser to the wealthy, but she gained fame for her herbal remedies. She saved many lives."

"People believe she can help them from beyond the grave," Jason added. "That's why they still leave her trinkets, isn't it?"

"Correct." Sabine smiled and took a step closer to him. "How is your grandmother? Is she still well?"

Jason blinked. "She's good, yeah. Healthy."

"Please tell her my sister and I say hello. We'd love to have a cup of tea with her next week. She has my number."

"Okay." Jason glanced at Cassie and then turned back to Sabine. "I'll let her know."

Sabine wound her way through tight alleyways, turning at this gravestone and that crypt as easily as if she were following street signs. "They call this place the City of the Dead, but it's more alive than you might think. It is a portal to another realm, and that veil is never thinner than it is right—" she took two steps, stopped, and turned around, holding her arms wide, "—here."

A chill passed over Cassie, as though hands made of ice trailed their frozen fingertips down her spine. She kept her eyes on Sabine, but she could see the spirits closing in around her. Men and women of the past had seen the future come and go without them. This knowledge tortured them into a restless sleep. They sensed Cassie could help and inched closer, reaching out as if to touch her shoulder or stroke her face. Whatever Sabine had been doing to keep them back was fading.

"Who are you?" Cassie asked. Had this all been a ruse? She hadn't realized how crowded the cemetery was until this point. Sabine had taken her to the deepest part of the ocean and snatched away her lifeboat. Now she was drowning. "What do you want?"

Out of the corner of her eye, Cassie saw Jason stiffen at the tone of her voice. He took a step closer, looking between the two women. If he had any idea what transpired between the two of them, there was no indication on his face.

"You're afraid, Cassie Quinn. You don't know what you can really do." Sabine kept her unblinking eyes trained on Cassie's face. "Today, I will help you. And someday, you may pay me in kind."

This is how deals with the devil are made, Cassie thought. But she couldn't resist the promise of answers in Sabine's voice. "How?"

"I've met many people like you. Some of them are afraid of what they can do. They push it down into the deepest part of themselves until they think it's gone. And then something happens, it comes rushing back, like a nightmare long forgotten. Does that sound familiar?"

Cassie nodded. Swallowed. Found her voice again. "I almost died. I thought that was the reason I could see them."

"But it wasn't, was it?"

She shook her head. "I've had it all my life. I just didn't remember."

"You've spent the better part of your life holding yourself back. You've pushed your abilities down until they all but disappeared. A brush with death cracked the façade you had created. Now, it's time to shatter it."

Cassie could barely breathe. "I'm afraid."

"I won't tell you not to be. You know better than most that we should be wary of what stalks us in the dark." For the first time since they met, Sabine looked older than her years. "But you can't fight what you can't see, Cassie. You have to look. Even when you're afraid. *Especially* when you're afraid."

Cassie tore her gaze away from Sabine's eyes. She barely knew this woman, but there was a truth in her words that rang bright. Whoever Sabine Delacroix was, she knew more about Cassie than Cassie knew about herself.

When she turned to look at the surrounding spirits, it was like she was seeing them for the first time. Their outlines, once blurred, were now crisp. They were in high definition. She could feel what they wanted. Like a thousand voices talking at once. Her knees buckled, but Jason's muscular arms were there in an instant.

"Don't push them away, Cassie." Sabine took a step closer, and Cassie felt her legs straighten. "Acknowledge them and move on. They don't have any power over you. You're so much stronger than they are."

Cassie couldn't speak. She wouldn't know what to say if she tried. The spirits drew closer. Jason looked between the two women with a slack jaw, but Cassie barely noticed him. Barely felt his hands on her shoulders. Through the haze of the graveyard's ghostly inhabitants, Cassie caught sight of someone who didn't belong.

On the other side of the invisible veil that kept her world separate from the next, a man stood etched in shadow. He was nothing more than a tall figure with broad shoulders, and yet he felt familiar. She could see the slant of his nose and the curve of his lips, but the truth of him was just out of reach.

Before she could ask him who he was or why he wasn't like the others, Sabine took a step back. The moment, which had occurred between one breath and the next, was over. The man had disappeared, and Cassie stood there, feeling lost at sea once more.

Sabine took her hand. It was warm and soft. "Our inner demons feed off our fear. They lose their hold over us when we choose to stand and fight. You can either run from all of this"—she gestured around the graveyard with her free hand—"or you can embrace it. The first option hasn't worked out so well for you. Maybe it's time to try the second."

Cassie nodded her head, but she didn't know what to say. Jason's voice broke the silence. "Anyone want to fill me in on what just happened?"

"Cassie got a new perspective on life." There was a smile in Sabine's voice. "Now it's up to her to decide how she wants to move forward."

"There was a man hidden in shadow." Cassie swallowed. She didn't want to say his name out loud. It would only make it more difficult later when she proved her theory untrue. "It could've been—I thought I might know him. Why did he look like that?"

Sabine shrugged. "I don't see them like you do. But if he was shadowed, there's a reason. Either he's holding himself back from crossing through the veil, or someone else is."

Jason looked more apprehensive than scared, but Cassie hated it all the same. Still, his voice was gentle. "Are you okay?"

She nodded. She didn't feel all that different. But she couldn't stop thinking about what Sabine had told her. For years, Cassie had witnessed the dead through a crackling television set distorted by static. And for a few moments, she'd seen that other world with perfect clarity. There was so much noise and pain and desolation that it had nearly brought her to her knees. But she had felt something beyond the fear.

Hope.

Sabine frowned. "Your grandmother never taught you how to spot a psychic? I'm disappointed."

Jason clenched his jaw. Propriety kept him from talking back to Sabine. He turned to Cassie instead. His eyes didn't betray his thoughts. "Is that true?"

What was the point in denying it? "Yes."

Jason bobbed his head up and down for a few seconds and stuck his hands deep into his jacket pockets. When he met her gaze again, his eyes were somber. For a fraction of a second, Cassie worried he'd walk away. Instead, he squared his shoulders.

"Then there's someone I'd like you to meet."

11

Jason pulled into the driveway of a pale-yellow house and parked behind at least half a dozen other cars. Each one was as different as the next, from a brand-new Ford pickup truck to a shiny BMW to a rusted-out burgundy Honda Civic.

The house was much bigger than the bungalow Cassie called home, and every inch of it looked like sheer perfection, from the rainbow assortment of wind chimes along the porch and the elaborately decorated front door to pitch-black shutters and an iron balcony around the second story. The street-lamps cast a cozy glow over the house's façade.

Jason twisted in his seat to look at her. "There are a lot of people inside, but you already met half of them at the bar last night."

"When you said you wanted me to meet someone, I didn't think you meant your entire family."

"Trust me, this isn't the entire family." Jason caught her look and smiled. "We don't have to go in if you don't want to, but I promise they're going to love you. And I think you should meet my grandmother."

Cassie's stomach twisted. "Any particular reason?"

She was stalling, and Jason knew it. "It'll be easier for her to explain."

Cassie blew out a breath and steeled herself. "Okay."

Jason pushed his door open but looked back at her before he got out. "If anyone should be nervous here, it's me. Kiki warned me she'd tell you all the worst stories."

"Oh, yeah, because I'm sure you were such a bad kid."

His eyes twinkled. "I got into some shenanigans here and there."

Cassie let her response die on her lips. They were already inside the front gate, up the steps, and through the door, and her nerves hit her all at once. She let Jason lead the way through the living room to the kitchen while she smoothed down her shirt and tried to take slow, even breaths.

Three women occupied the room. Two of them sat at the table drinking tea. They looked like sisters, with shoulder-length hair that fell in waves around their faces. One of them wore rings on every finger. The third woman wore a head wrap and looked older than the other two. She was taking cookies out of the oven. The smell was divine.

Jason walked up to the woman sitting closest to the doorway and kissed her on the cheek. "Mama." He turned to the one with all the rings and kissed her, too. "Auntie Kay."

"Jay, what are you doin' back so soon?" The older woman hadn't turned around yet. Her voice was deep and rich. Her words came slowly, like she had all the time in the world to sit and talk with you. "I thought you were out with that young lady from the museum. Figured you wouldn't be back 'til mornin'."

"That's actually why I'm here." Jason gestured for Cassie to step out of the shadow of the doorway and into the light of the kitchen. Auntie Kay was the first to notice her. She set her teacup down and pinched her eyebrows together. "Granny, this is Cassie Quinn."

Jason's mother and grandmother turned at the same time. The smiles fell from their faces the second they laid eyes on her. There was a beat of silence, and Cassie considered bolting for the door. Her heart would've been pounding like a jackhammer if it hadn't given up and stopped altogether.

"Oh, honey." Granny crossed the room and took Cassie's hands in her own. "You poor thing."

It was Cassie's worst nightmare. She could save face and lock her emotions up when she had to, but the moment someone saw through her, the tears started flowing. Jason's grandmother had looked deep into her soul and saw more than Cassie wanted to admit.

Auntie Kay grabbed a box of tissues and handed it to Cassie, who took one and dabbed her eyes. "I'm sorry. I don't know why I'm crying."

"It's okay, you let it out." Granny steered Cassie to the last open seat and sat her down. Before she knew it, there was a cup of tea and a plate of cookies in front of her. "You take your time, honey."

The three women in the room turned to Jason and leveled him with an identical glare. The force of it made him take a step back. He held up his hands. "What'd I do?"

"You tell me," Granny scowled.

"Tell you what?"

Cassie bit into a chocolate chip cookie and instantly felt more at ease. She washed it down with a sip of tea and then turned to Jason's mom. "Please don't be mad at him. He's had kind of a strange night."

"Strange how?" she asked.

Cassie looked to Jason, who rubbed a hand across the back of his neck. "Well, it started with a trip to the graveyard with this strange woman," he said, like that should be explanation enough. With three faces still blinking up at him, he sighed. "I think Cassie might be kind of like you."

The woman with all the rings on her fingers laid a gentle hand on Cassie's arm. "My name is Kianna, but you can call me Auntie Kay." When she gestured to her sister, the jewels sparkled in the light. "This is Tanesha, but—"

"—you can call me Mama T."

Auntie Kay gestured to their mother. "And that's Granny Mabel."

"It's nice to meet you all." Cassie meant it, even if she still felt like crawling into a hole and never coming out. "Thank you for the cookies."

"You're welcome, honey." Granny Mabel put a gentle hand on her shoulder. "You're strong. You can handle whatever you're going through. You remember that."

"Granny, do you know someone named Sabine Delacroix?"

Three heads turned to face Jason. Mama T was the first one to speak. "She was the woman in the graveyard?"

Now it was Jason's turn to look like he was the one ready to bolt for the door. "Yes."

"Tell us everything."

As Granny Mabel made another pot of tea, Jason and Cassie took turns telling the three women what had happened that night. Jason told them about the graveyard tour, and Cassie finished the story—only hesitating for a moment before telling them everything. Including the part about the shadowy figure on the other side of the veil.

"Sabine wants you to call her to have tea this week," Jason added.

Granny Mabel scoffed under her breath, but she pulled out a piece of paper and scribbled a note. When Cassie peered over her teacup to look at the message, all it said was *Call S.D. ASAP.* It was underlined three times.

Mama T left the room and returned a moment later with two more chairs. Jason sat close to Cassie, while Granny Mabel sank into her seat across from them. All three women exchanged a look that made Cassie think they'd just made a collective decision.

Jason must've caught it, too. "What's going on?"

"The women in our family are special." Granny Mabel patted Jason's cheek by way of apology. "We have a strong intuition."

"You're psychic, too?" Cassie asked.

"Not quite." Granny searched for the words. "We don't see visions or commune with the dead."

"Rather, we get powerful feelings," Auntie Kay added. "For lack of a better explanation."

Granny nodded. "If you're the sharp part of the knife, then we're the blunt end of the hammer. We usually hit our target after a couple of tries."

"How did you know—" Cassie could barely get the words out. She was only just getting used to saying it out loud to the people she trusted, never mind people she'd only met ten minutes prior. "I mean, how could you know I see—that I can—"

"That you're gifted?" Granny Mabel frowned. "There's a quality that hangs around people who can see what you can see. A heaviness to them. Even in a house full of people mourning, your sadness cuts through like a blade."

"I'm so sorry." A tear dripped down Cassie's cheek, but she didn't bother wiping it away. "I don't know how to stop it. If I could—"

"Your empathy gives you strength." Granny leaned forward, and her eyes locked onto Cassie's. "Don't be ashamed of it. You're powerful. More powerful, perhaps, than even the Delacroix sisters."

"Sabine said you should've taught me to see them. Psychics, I mean." Jason looked at his mom. "Why didn't you?"

She shrugged. "You can't close your eyes once they're open to something like that. It's as much a gift as it is a burden."

Cassie knew that burden all too well. Helping people—solving their murders—was a gift she was proud to have, but it wasn't easy. And it didn't mean she never had a sleepless night or a close encounter with someone who'd rather see her six feet under. "How did Sabine control the spirits in the graveyard like that?"

"The Delacroix sisters have their ways." Mama T's mouth was tight as she spoke. "They've made bargains. They know what herbs to infuse into a tea that pushes the limits of what they can do."

"I take it you don't approve?"

"We see the world differently."

Cassie heard the finality in Mama T's voice and didn't have any interest in overstaying her welcome. But she had one last question she needed the answer to. "The man covered in shadows. Who was he? Why did he look like that?"

Everyone looked to Granny Mabel, who sighed and set down her teacup. She added another spoonful of sugar, ignoring the way Auntie Kay pinched her eyebrows in response. "Sabine helped you see through the veil to the other side. We don't know what lives there. The Shadow Man could've been who you think, your friend David, or it could've been someone else entirely. Something else. What she did was unnatural. If the Shadow Man needed your help, he would've come through the veil. Unless something was stopping him."

"What would have the power to do that?"

"I don't know." Granny shook her head and took another sip of tea. "It's beyond me."

Cassie felt disappointment and relief in equal measures. "I appreciate your help. I'm still getting used to saying all this out loud. It feels nice to know I'm not alone in it."

"Does your family know?"

"They do." Cassie smiled at the memory. "They took it well, all things considered. I'm not sure it's something my parents and I will talk openly about, but my sister and I are closer now than we've ever been. She's in my corner."

"Good. Good." Granny turned to Jason and pursed her lips. "You're further ahead than most, but there's still a lot you don't understand about what Cassie can do."

Jason met Cassie's eyes. "I'd like to find out."

"I hope you mean that." Granny's voice was firm, but not cold. Still, Jason shrunk a little in his chair. "Cassie will see things you never will. Know things you couldn't possibly know. It takes a strong person to stand to the side and let someone else shine, knowing they'll never see that spotlight. Are you ready for that?"

There was a beat of silence before Mama T cleared her throat. "Mama, they're not getting married."

"Heartbreak is inevitable." Granny's words had a ring of finality to them. "It's easier to patch a hole in the wall than it is to rebuild the entire house from the ground up."

Cassie knew Granny Mabel was looking out for Jason, but she hated the fact that she could be the person to put the hole in the wall. The one capable of knocking the entire house down. Her abilities made her own life difficult enough to lead, but dragging someone else into the mix seemed cruel.

"I'll keep that in mind." Jason stood up and kissed Granny on the cheek. "Where is everyone?"

"Husbands are in the living room thinking we can't smell the cigars they're trying to hide from us." She stood with a small groan and grabbed another plate of cookies. "The cousins are upstairs. Take these up with you?"

Jason led the way out of the room, but before Cassie could follow, Granny put a hand on her arm. "You're good, Cassie Quinn. And smart. Jason is lucky to have you. But that doesn't mean it will be easy. I hope you can forgive me for wanting to protect him."

"There's nothing to forgive." Cassie meant it. "Everything you said is true."

Granny nodded and let go of her arm. "And if Sabine Delacroix calls you out of the blue, think long and hard before you answer the phone."

Cassie wasn't sure what to say, so she nodded and followed Jason into the hallway.

12

Jason led Cassie up a narrow set of stairs before he stopped and turned to her. The floor creaked underfoot when he shifted his weight. His face was half concealed in shadow, but she caught the apology in his eyes. "Sorry about that."

"About what?"

He gestured vaguely. "Them. Granny Mabel. She can be kind of intense sometimes."

"I like her."

"Yeah?"

"Yeah."

There was a beat of silence. Jason took a step closer. All that separated them was the plate of cookies. Despite already having her fill, the smell made Cassie's mouth water.

"I really don't understand what's happening." He laughed. "But I've seen enough growing up to know I shouldn't question it. Whatever is going on, I want to help. I don't know what I can bring to the table." He laughed again. "But I'd like to try."

"I appreciate that." Cassie shook her head. "If I'm being honest, I don't get it most of the time either. But I like not being alone."

"Good." Jason hooked a thumb over his shoulder. "Because there's a room full of people who don't understand the concept of alone time."

Cassie groaned but didn't protest as Jason took her hand and led her to a door at the end of the hall. She could hear music pumping on the other side, quiet enough to talk over but loud enough that she couldn't make out the conversation. A peal of laughter broke through, and Jason's lips twitched up in response. He shouldered his way into the room.

"Jay! You're back!"

"Finally. Took you long enough, man."

"Are those Granny's cookies?"

"Did you bring anymore beer?"

"God, you guys are the worst. Let the man breathe."

"He can breathe after he hands over the cookies."

A large man pushed himself off the couch and took the plate from Jason. He spotted Cassie hiding in the doorway, and his eyebrows shot up. She recognized him from the other night. He was the one who had stolen Jason's phone from Kiki. It was Ty.

"Hey, Jay's brought a friend."

Cassie stepped forward as eight faces turned in her direction. Despite the size of the room, Granny Mabel had filled it wall to wall with furniture. Two mismatched couches and a pair of chairs were situated around a coffee table laden with food and drink. An entertainment center sat off to one side and a pair of bookshelves lined the opposite wall. Someone was playing music through a portable speaker. She didn't recognize the song, but she liked the beat.

Jason cleared his throat. "This is Cassie. We work together at the museum."

The entire room erupted into hellos and cheers and obnoxious wolf whistles, the latter of which mostly came from Ty. Kiki jumped up from the couch, her downy curls now in two puffs, one on each side of her head, and crossed the room to give Cassie a hug and steer her to the last remaining seat.

The next hour was a whirlwind of names and faces and raucous laughter. Jason was in his element. Cassie had never seen this side of him. He was quiet at the museum, more interested in observing than interacting with people. But here, surrounded by family, he was someone new. She liked the way his eyes crinkled when he laughed.

Kiki properly introduced herself this time, though she clearly had no regrets about the first impression she'd made on Cassie when she sent her that video at the bar. She kept the louder boys in line with her sharp tongue, but her voice turned soft with the younger cousins, checking in on them to make sure they had enough to eat or to see if they needed a ride home or to ask about their day.

Kiki's presence was magnetic, drawing you closer with every laugh, every joke, every story. Each person in that room had their own quirks, their own personality, but Kiki was the rope that bound them together. She was special.

In fact, all the women in the room were. Granny Mabel had said they had a strong intuition—something they didn't share with the men in the family. And every once in a while, she'd catch one of them staring like they could see right through her.

Though she would've been happier to sit back and bask in everyone else's enjoyment, Cassie allowed Kiki to drag her from person to person, making introductions and sharing stories. She was quick on her feet, which made even more sense when Cassie found out she had a successful career as a lawyer.

Jason's gaze followed Cassie around the room as she made small talk and laughed at everyone's jokes. He sat between Ty and Ty's brother Evan, who had a thick beard and a bright smile. Ty was in construction, which explained his bulging muscles, while Evan was a personal trainer, which explained why he was even bigger than Ty. The two had a friendly rivalry, which Cassie assumed extended to the gym. When she quietly joked that Evan seemed to be winning that race, Ty scowled, and Evan howled with laughter.

And on it went. The other couch held three more people. Jamie couldn't have been older than twenty-two. He was going to school to be an accountant. His little brother, Daryl, sitting on the other end of the sofa with a book in his hand, was two years younger and going to school for computer science. The woman in between them looked hilariously out of place in her sleek dress and giant hoop earrings. Janelle, Kiki explained, was going to school for fashion design. She even had a small following on Instagram who looked to her for advice on clothes, jewelry, and hair styles. Janelle politely said hello, only gazing up from her phone long enough to make eye contact.

Kiki turned to the last two people in the room. One was a short, stocky woman sitting in an armchair. She had a shaved head, dyed fuchsia, and wore baggy pants and a tight top. Her arms were covered in tattoos. She shook Cassie's hand as Kiki introduced her as Dionne, her younger sister. She was a professional artist with several paintings hanging in a local gallery. Sitting next to Dionne on the arm of the chair was a woman with tawny skin wearing a dusty rose-colored hijab and tailored pantsuit. She had one arm draped around Dionne's shoulders as she introduced herself as Imani, a personal chef. She didn't seem at all intimidated by the vibe of the room, which led Cassie to assume the two had been dating for quite some time.

As the first hour stretched into the second, Dionne invited Cassie to visit her gallery before she and Imani drifted out of the room. Soon after, Jamie and Daryl packed up to go back to their dorms. Janelle followed moments later, promising to meet Kiki for lunch the next day. Ty gave Cassie a bear hug on the way out, and Evan, not to be outmatched, lifted her up and spun her around before gently setting her back down on the floor. He punched Jason in the shoulder before grabbing a cookie and sauntering out of the room.

Cassie slumped onto the couch, turning to Jason. "How do you do that all the time? I'm exhausted."

"I've built up a tolerance." He sat down next to her, shoving several potato chips into his mouth. "You'll get used to it."

Cassie tried not to grin at the idea that she might see Jason's family again, but it was no use.

Kiki must've caught it. She was sitting across from Cassie in one of the chairs. "For the record, everyone liked you, too."

"That's nice to hear."

"It sounds like you don't believe it."

Cassie looked to where Janelle had been sitting. "I just hope no one thought I was intruding on family time."

Kiki followed her gaze. "Janelle?" She smiled and shook her head. "Janelle is super quiet. You wouldn't think that by looking at her. She looks like a supermodel. God, I can't believe she's going to be twenty-five soon."

Jason groaned. "When did we get so old?"

"I don't know." Kiki's smile faded. "It was Janelle's sister who died. Jasmine. She was a year older. Their mom, our aunt, died when they were little. Now it's just Janelle and Uncle Roger."

"I'm so sorry." The silence of the room was suffocating. "Were they close?"

"So close." The smile returned to Kiki's face. "I've never even seen them get into an argument. Not a real one, anyway. They were best friends."

"How is she holding up?"

"I don't know. She's not talking a lot, but she's around. I take that as a good sign. If it were Dionne—" Kiki broke off. Shook her head. Smiled without smiling. "I'd bury myself alongside her."

The three of them let that hang in the air for a moment. Cassie couldn't stop herself from asking. She remembered what Jason had said at the bar. "She had a heart defect?"

Kiki nodded. "She had routine surgery about a week ago. At least they told us it was routine. She made it through okay. But apparently there were complications after the fact."

"But you don't think that's what actually happened?"

"I don't know what happened." Kiki leaned back in her chair with a huff. "One minute, she was fine. Like, *completely* fine. The next? She crashed. They can't tell us anything other than her heart gave out."

"She had a lot of surgeries." Jason's voice was gentle. "I wouldn't be shocked if that were the case."

Cassie remembered the woman from her dream. The one who had been resting—maybe not peacefully—before the ghost of the doctor had pulled her from her own body. She had no idea what hospital the woman had been in. It could've been back in Savannah. Or it could've been here in New Orleans. Or anywhere in between.

"Cassie?" Kiki's gaze flicked to Jason, and Cassie realized that while Kiki had figured out she was psychic, she couldn't possibly know if that was information Cassie'd shared with Jason. "You looked a little lost there for a second."

"Can I see a picture of Jasmine?"

Kiki pulled out her phone, tapped on the screen a few times, then held it out. "This is her Instagram."

Cassie took the device. Jasmine had a natural glow about her. In nearly every photo, her head tipped back in laughter. There were dozens of pictures with her sister. Even pictures of her in the hospital. She didn't try to hide it. She wasn't ashamed.

Kiki moved to sit by Cassie on the couch. "She was like that in person, too." Kiki pointed to a picture of herself standing between Jasmine and Dionne. "Jazz was always laughing. She had the most reasons to be mad at the world, but she always had her next joke lined up. She kept the rest of us humble."

"She sounds amazing." Cassie handed the phone back. "I had a dream on the plane ride down here. A woman in the hospital. She was asleep, but she looked sick." Cassie paused. It still sounded strange to say it out loud. "Then the ghost of a doctor pulled her spirit right out of her body. She died, just like that. It wasn't Jasmine, but I'd imagine it could look the same. One minute, she was fine. The next minute, she was dead."

The room was silent. Cassie risked glancing over at Jason. He had his eyebrows pinched together in concentration. "What does it mean?" he asked.

"I'm not sure." Cassie didn't want to make any major leaps, but she usually had dreams for a reason. "It could mean I'm supposed to help this woman move on. Give her family some answers. Or it could mean I need to figure out if a ghost is killing people."

Kiki didn't look fazed by the conversation. "I know it's a lot to ask—"

Jason stiffened next to Cassie. "No."

"—but will you help us?"

"Kiki." Jason's voice was sharp. Disappointed. "Cassie has enough on her plate. That's a lot to ask someone."

Kiki met his gaze. Cassie was once again reminded of how formidable she'd be in court. "You could help, too, you know. It's not like you don't have experience with this stuff."

Cassie looked between the two of them. "What experience?"

Kiki folded her arms as if to say *go on, tell her.*

Jason pinched the bridge of his nose. "I used to be an investigator. When I was an MP. I'm good at talking to people. Getting them to open up." There was pain in his voice. He didn't look proud. "I know my way around a crime scene."

"But this is your cousin. It's different. Harder."

"It wouldn't be the first time." Jason's words were clipped. "Not a cousin. Someone else. Someone I was close to."

A friend? Cassie wondered. *A girlfriend? A partner?*

"What if it's not a conspiracy, and Jasmine's heart really did just give out? And what if it's not, and someone murdered her?" Cassie thought of David. Of what waited for her when she got back home. "What if you learn her death wasn't an accident, but you can never bring that person to justice?"

Kiki's eyes brimmed with tears, but she didn't let them fall. "I need to know the truth. One way or another. Jay, you know I wouldn't ask. I wouldn't put you in that position. But this is *Jazz.*"

"I know." Jason's eyes were watery, too. He set his jaw. "I can go to the hospital tomorrow. Ask around. I'm sure somebody knows something they didn't tell us."

"Stacey still works there," Kiki offered. "She was on call when it happened."

Jason bobbed his head. Turned to Cassie. "Her brother and I went to college together."

"I want to help." When Jason opened his mouth to argue, Cassie held up a hand. "Please, let me help. This is what I'm good at. This is what I do."

Jason closed his mouth. He looked exhausted but relieved. He nodded once. It was sharp and quick, but it was all the permission she needed.

Cassie let the full weight of it hit her. She'd gone on two dates with him. The first one, she'd accidentally punched him in the face. The second, she'd agreed to help him investigate the murder of his cousin. If they had any relationship at all in the future, at least it wouldn't be a boring one.

13

Cassie waved to the security guard as she entered the museum, stuffing her phone into her purse and taking a sip of her coffee. It was still too hot to drink, but she ignored the burning on her tongue and tipped the cup back for a second time. She needed the caffeine more than she needed her taste buds.

Last night had been a whirlwind of emotions, and as soon as Jason had dropped her back off at the hotel, she'd face-planted into her bed. She didn't feel like she got a full eight hours, but according to her alarm clock, she had. The night had been full of dreams—part memories, part premonitions—jumbled into one confusing mass that Cassie was still trying to untangle.

She remembered seeing the Ghost Doctor again, but this time Jason was in the hospital bed, fighting for his life. Then the scene shifted, and Cassie stood in the middle of the cemetery while Sabine and Granny Mabel watched on, silent. Kiki stood before her, but it was really Jasmine. She complimented Cassie's hair, then faded away. No different from any of the other spirits that circled them. Cassie tried to find her again, but she tripped and fell into a grave. When she looked up, David stood above her, poised with a shovel in his hands.

As soon as the first heap of dirt hit her face, Cassie had jolted up in bed.

Now, staring at the front entrance, she took another long pull from her coffee cup and wished it would work faster. Jules had called her just after eight to let her know they had unloaded the van full of antique furniture.

They'd cleaned the exhibit area days prior, so Cassie only needed to supervise the placement of the pieces and ensure the informational placards were correct.

When she finished, Cassie would meet Jason at the hospital where Jasmine had died. They'd track down the nurse he knew, see what she could tell them, and go from there. Cassie was still glad to help, but Jason's apprehension had rubbed off on her. There was a reason he'd given up investigating crimes as an MP, and an even bigger reason he hadn't told her. And she'd be lying if she said she wasn't dying to know.

Jules waved Cassie over to the information desk. Her bob swung with excitement, and her wide eyes looked like they were ready to burst from her head. Cassie had only met the woman two days ago, and she already felt like an old friend. A bright spot of normality in a world full of strange shadows.

"How did last night go?" Jules bounced up and down in her chair. "How was the date?"

"The date was good." It wasn't a lie, but Cassie found she had to force some cheer into her voice. "It was good."

Jules frowned. "What happened?"

"Nothing." Cassie set her coffee down on the counter and ran a hand through her hair. "Nothing bad, I mean. I had a great time. Things are just complicated right now. For both of us."

"Complicated doesn't mean impossible." Jules shrugged, and her frown dissipated. "I saw the way he looked at you at the bar. Trust me, he wants this."

Cassie couldn't find the words to explain how that was the least of her worries at the moment. She was more concerned with what Jason thought of her abilities, and whether he'd ever get used to what she could see. Then there was the fact that, in a matter of hours, they'd be investigating the death of his cousin. Would he appreciate how she helped him find answers—if they even found answers—or would he resent her for it?

Too late to turn back now. But she couldn't say that either, so she smiled instead. "Thanks. That's nice to hear." Ford emerged from the back and waltzed up to Jules. He tipped his head back in acknowledgment of Cassie. She returned the favor. "Good morning."

"Morning." Ford plucked the stapler off Jules' desk. "Need this." He opened her drawer and pulled out a pair of scissors. "And this." He grabbed two pens and a paperclip. "This, too."

"Help yourself." Jules' voice was sarcastic, but she had trouble hiding her smile. "Anything else? My coffee mug? My desk chair? The computer?"

Ford looked at the chair as if weighing his options, but Cassie had a feeling he was using it as an excuse to look her up and down. Jules blushed under his scrutiny. "It's safe for now."

"What in God's name are you doing?"

Ford spun on his heel. He said nothing until he was halfway across the room. "Crime."

Cassie lifted an eyebrow when Jules turned back around. "Crime?"

Jules shook her head. "He's always saying that. Probably fixing"—she fluttered her hand in the air—"something."

Cassie noticed Jules' blush hadn't receded. "And you're the only person in the entire building with office supplies?"

Jules rolled her eyes. "He likes to pick on me."

Cassie grinned. "I wonder why."

"Ford's impossible."

"He likes you."

Jules scrunched her face. "What kind of drugs are in your coffee?"

"Just good old-fashioned caffeine." Cassie took another sip. It had finally cooled to a reasonable temperature. She could almost taste the caramel now. "Seriously, though. Take it from a completely neutral source. He's into you."

"Ford's a flirt with everyone. Have you seen him? I'm not his type. And he's not mine."

"I beg to differ." Cassie shrugged. "But if you insist."

Jules huffed, but Cassie could tell she heard what Cassie said. "Anyway, you have a visitor."

"A visitor?" Cassie looked around, but the entire entranceway was empty. "Who? Why?"

"Don't know why. He said he's from Savannah. He's waiting in my office. I told him I'd send you back when you got here."

"You could've led with that." Cassie kept her voice even, but her stomach churned.

"I had to get the good gossip first."

"Fair enough." Cassie pushed away from the counter. "Thanks, Jules."

"Are you okay?" Her voice was already fading as Cassie wound her way to the back.

"I'm good."

But she wasn't. A visitor from Savannah? Cassie's first thought was Jason, but he wouldn't have met her inside the museum. They already had plans for later, and he would've texted if something had come up. She checked her phone just in case, but there were no messages waiting for her.

Against her will, Cassie's brain conjured another image. David. She shook it away. She knew he was gone. She'd been to his funeral. But if this had been any other time, it would not surprise her to see his frame filling the doorway. Delusions of some cosmic correction filled her with hope, even as she turned into the office to see a stranger sitting in Jules' chair.

He was the exact opposite of David. Tall. Lean. Comfortable in a suit. He had gelled and coiffed his hair. His tanned skin was two shades too dark to be real, and it made the blue of his eyes stand out even more. The smile on his face was genuine, yet it made her think of a shark. If she wasn't careful, he might open his mouth and swallow her whole.

"Ms. Quinn." It wasn't a question. He knew who she was. "My name is Dan Palmer."

When he held out his hand, she shook it. "I'm sorry, do we know each other?"

"We've never met." His smile didn't waver, like it was glued to his face. "But I've heard a great deal of wonderful things about you. Please, sit."

Cassie stayed standing. How presumptuous of him to ask her to sit in what currently doubled as her own office. She didn't want to be rude, but something about Dan Palmer kept her on guard. "How can I help you?"

If the fact that Cassie hadn't complied with his request bothered him, he didn't show it. He sat behind Jules' desk, his leather briefcase before him. "My colleague has been raving about you since you two met. She suggested I reach out to enlist your services on a project I'm struggling with. It would be well worth your time. The compensation would be generous."

"Who's your colleague?"

"Anastasia Bolton."

A ripple of fear made its way through Cassie's body. "You work for Apex?"

"Yes." Impossibly, his smile grew wider. "I'm so glad you remembered. I wasn't sure if you would. Anastasia told me how chaotic things were in Charlotte. Though, she tends to leave an impression."

Cassie couldn't argue with that. Anastasia Bolton had been Senator Grayson's publicist, and while she'd only come face to face with her once, Cassie remembered the cool confidence that oozed out of every pore in her body. Detective Davenport had murdered Senator Grayson's son, but FBI agents Viotto and Mannis thought Apex had been pulling strings the entire time.

Mannis had warned both Cassie and Viotto before they parted ways—if Apex comes knocking, make sure you don't answer the door.

But it was a little late for that.

"What is it you want me to do?" Curiosity got the better of her. "I'm just an art preparator."

"I wouldn't say you're *just* anything." Palmer gestured around the office. "The museum sent you down here to oversee an installation, didn't they? Don't sell yourself short."

Cassie felt like a scolded child. "What I meant to say," she continued through gritted teeth, "is that I can't help you. I'm already gainfully employed. I don't think I have time for any extracurricular activities."

Somehow, Palmer kept smiling even while the corners of his mouth turned down in a scowl. "Perhaps I'm overstepping here, but you seemed to have time for extracurricular activities in Charlotte. You did, after all, successfully expose a corrupt senator in addition to solving his son's murder and bringing down a dirty cop in the process. You have quite a talent for solving mysteries, Ms. Quinn."

"Is that what you want from me? To solve a mystery?"

"Of sorts." Palmer opened his briefcase and brought out a checkbook. He scribbled his signature, tore the single piece of paper from the margin, then held it out to Cassie. "This is for you."

She took the check. A hundred grand. It nearly slipped from her fingers. "Nothing in life is free." She looked up. If she hadn't distrusted him before, she did now. "What's this for?"

"Think of it as an advance." He pulled a stack of papers out of his briefcase. "I'll need you to sign a contract. You can deposit the check. Once it goes through, and you're satisfied with the transaction, we can discuss details. You'll get another check when you accept your first job."

"You still haven't told me what you want."

Palmer closed his briefcase. Set the papers to the side. Folded his hands before him. "Apex is a large machine, Ms. Quinn, with a lot of moving parts. Sometimes those parts get misplaced. We'd like you to help us find them."

She didn't bother keeping the disgust from her voice. "You're talking about people."

"Yes."

"What makes you think I can find them?"

"Your track record." Palmer leaned forward. She could see his pupils dilate with excitement. "Senator Grayson in Charlotte. Noah McLaughlin before that. Dr. Langford and William Baker before *that*." He shivered gleefully. "That one was particularly gruesome. You've impressed me."

She set her disgust to the side for a moment. "How do you know all this?"

"We keep tabs on people with incredible potential. People we think could make a difference in the world."

"I do make a difference." Her own conviction surprised her. "I don't need you for that."

"Of course not." Palmer's smile shrank to a humbler size. "I wasn't implying you did. I only meant that, with our help, you could do even more."

Cassie looked down at the check. She lived in relative comfort, but she'd be lying if she didn't admit the house could use a few more repairs. It'd need a new roof in the next couple years, and that wasn't cheap. This was apparently just the beginning. With enough money, she could make sure her parents had an easy retirement. She could help Laura pay off her student loans. It's not like California was a cheap place to live, either.

"No."

The word was out of her mouth before she realized it had escaped. It was the only acceptable answer, but it still surprised her how easily it had formed on her tongue. This money was life-changing, yet she felt no remorse in ripping the check in half and handing it back to Palmer.

"Money is not an issue." He poised his pen over his checkbook. "We can double that amount. Triple it, even, after your first job."

"No."

"What will it take, Ms. Quinn?" There was no hint of a threat in Palmer's voice, and yet the atmosphere of the room shifted. "Name your price."

"I'm not interested."

"May I ask why?"

A polite question. She had a rude answer. But she knew she couldn't tell Palmer the truth. Apex had already proven to be resourceful. The company clearly had endless amounts of money. And plenty of human resources. They'd put Grayson on track to become president. They'd encouraged a veteran detective to risk throwing his career away for the chance to join their organization, and when he'd failed, they'd thrown him under the bus without blinking an eye.

"I don't need a reason." Cassie stepped to the side, gesturing to the door. "I'm working. This was an inappropriate time and place for your solicitation."

Palmer finally lost his smile. Even pretended to look humbled. "You're right. I apologize." He placed the torn check inside his briefcase. Then the contract. He snapped the buckles closed. Stood. Walked to the door and stopped. Produced his card. "Please think about my offer. Apex believes we can do a lot of good together. Help a lot of people. I know that's important to you. I hoped the money would be an incentive. Now I see I've offended you."

"No, you haven't." She wasn't sure why she was trying to make him feel better. "It's fine."

"Thank you." He placed the card in her hand. "Please call me if you change your mind. You're an incredible person, Ms. Quinn. With extraordinary talents. The world could use more people like you."

Cassie watched as Palmer left the room and made his way to the exit. She felt bad about the way she'd handled their encounter before she reminded herself who he represented. If she believed Mannis—and she did—then everything they did was part of the act. She hadn't offended Palmer; she'd frustrated him. He wasn't apologizing; he was manipulating her into feeling guilty. Worse yet, he wasn't leaving her to decide on her own; he was waiting for another opportunity to present itself.

Cassie ripped up Palmer's card into twenty tiny pieces. Then she split them between Jules' garbage and the one in the breakroom before she poured herself another cup of coffee. The last thing she needed was for Jules or someone else to find Palmer's contact information. Plus, she didn't want the temptation of his number being within reach if she ever fell into financial trouble. Besides, she had a feeling Apex would find an excuse to swoop in when she was more vulnerable. That seemed to be their M.O.

Viotto's face floated to the surface of her mind. She missed him. What was he doing, how was he faring on his next case? She tried to convince herself she was just as curious about Mannis, but her brain wouldn't accept the lie. Now would be a perfect excuse to call Viotto, to tell him and his partner about her run-in with an Apex employee. But Chris hadn't reached out to her since their time in Charlotte, and Mannis' paranoia kept her from texting him an update. It was clear Apex had dug into her past. Who was to say they weren't monitoring her communications?

That would be illegal, she reminded herself, though a voice in her head told her that hiring a detective to kill a senator's son was *also* very illegal. She shook the thought free.

She'd told Apex no. It had been her final answer. They could come knocking again, but her response would be the same. There was no point in worrying about it now. And no point in making Agent Viotto worry about it, too.

Until Apex made another move, she'd keep her encounter with Palmer to herself.

14

CASSIE STOOD OUTSIDE THE UNIVERSITY MEDICAL CENTER OF NEW ORLEANS and let the sheer size of the building wash over her. It wasn't an attractive complex, but she'd rather see funding go to its function than its form. Still, it didn't ease the anxiety in her body. Even from outside the doors, she could feel the hospital's energy lying in wait for her.

"Hey." Jason's sudden appearance made her jump. "Sorry." Then, upon closer inspection of her face, "You okay?"

"Yeah. Busy morning." She elected to keep information about Apex out of the conversation for now, but her answer wasn't a lie. Moving the pieces from Savannah took several hours, as did her sharp critique of their placement and the design of the informational cards.

Jules had off-handedly mentioned the museum had an eighteenth-century writing desk and cobalt blue sofa in storage, and Cassie had sent half the staff looking for it. When they hadn't returned after an hour, she'd joined the search. In the end, Ford had made the discovery, and Cassie had spotted a portrait of a woman in white from the same period as the couch. The two would complement each other perfectly, and by the time they made room for the additions, everyone was sweaty but smiling.

With that, her time in New Orleans was over, though Magdalena had booked her an extra couple of days in the city. Technically, it was for any follow-up questions ahead of the exhibition's opening, but once they printed the banner for the exhibit, they wouldn't need her again. She was free to do whatever she wanted. In other words, she was free to question hospital workers with Jason by her side.

"How are you?" She looked over at him and noticed the red in his eyes. "Other than tired."

"I made the mistake of telling Ty and Evan I'd work out with them this morning. I don't miss getting up before the sun." He rubbed his stomach. "But I miss my mom's cooking. Breakfast was huge. I ate way too much."

"Why'd you move to Savannah?" It wasn't the first time she'd thought of the question, but it was the first time where she felt it appropriate to ask. "You're close with your family. You obviously love the city. Why Georgia?"

"I needed a change of pace." Jason's voice was more guarded than it was a second ago. "A place where I didn't know anyone. I thought it'd help me figure out what I'd want to do with my life."

"Did it?"

"In some ways." The way he looked at her made Cassie's stomach twist. "In others it's been rough. I miss them. But it makes coming to visit even better."

Cassie thought of her parents. And her sister. "Yeah, I get that."

"You ready to go in?" He pointed to a bench off to the side. "Or we could sit a minute."

In moments like this, Cassie was grateful Jason had some idea of what was going through her head. He may not understand it all, but he knew enough to recognize how hospitals could affect her. It had been bad before Sabine had gotten into her head, but now Cassie wasn't sure what would happen when she walked through those doors. She already felt like there was a spotlight shining on her.

If she concentrated, she could hold the restless spirits of the hospital at bay long enough to get in, question the nurse, and get out. But Sabine had told her she could control their access to her. That she could decide how close they got. Unfortunately, she had no idea how to do it.

"I'm okay," she heard herself saying. "I can handle it."

Jason gave her a few seconds to take it back, and when she didn't, he led the way through the sliding doors. The smell of the antiseptic hit her, even in the lobby, and her head swam for a millisecond before her senses became accustomed to the odor.

The familiar feeling of invisible fingers trailing across her skin caused goosebumps to erupt along the back of her neck and down her arms. Cassie took a deep breath, but she didn't push the tendrils away. Instead, she acknowledged them. In her mind, she said hello to all the different beings floating in and out of existence around her. Made eye contact with the ones that stayed, the ones that begged for her help. All they wanted was to understand what was going on with them. They just needed answers.

I see you, she thought. *But I'm here to help someone else today.*

Cassie wasn't sure how long she stood there in the lobby. Long enough for her to see dozens of spirits and twice as many living beings walk by. Some people turned and stared, wondering why she was blocking traffic. But the majority just walked around her.

The anxiety fell from her shoulders. The icy fingers receded. The ghosts turned and shambled on. A few looked back over their shoulders, but they had heard her. They knew their time wasn't now, and most didn't have the strength to fight her. For the first time in a long time, she was in the driver's seat. She could decide where she wanted her life to go.

"You're smiling." Jason's voice was warm. "I take it everything is okay?"

"As good as it's going to get." It was better to be practical than optimistic. "I've got a handle on it for now, but I'm not sure how long it'll last."

"Then let's make it count."

Jason pointed to a sign that read CAFETERIA in blocky letters. They followed the arrow into a large room bustling with activity. Visitors could grab sandwiches and salads on one side and sit at small, round tables on the other. A couple of nurses sat with co-workers or friends, sharing a cup of coffee and a snack.

Someone waved to Jason as soon as they crossed the threshold. He returned the gesture and made a beeline for her table. The only thing Cassie knew was that her name was Stacey, and her brother used to go to school with Jason. The woman jumped up when they got within range, dropped her sandwich onto her tray, and wrapped her arms around Jason.

"It's been so long." She pulled back. Everything about her was pale, from her ivory skin to her white-blonde hair. Even her eyes, which were ice blue. She wore periwinkle scrubs, which only made her look more delicate. "Ricky says hi."

"How's he doing?"

"Good. He and his girlfriend just broke up, so he's crashing at my place for a while. He'll be fine, though." Her eyes shifted to Cassie. "Hi. My name's Stacey."

"Cassie." She shook the other woman's hand. "Thanks for meeting with us."

"No problem." She plopped herself back into her chair and took another bite of her sandwich. "Don't mind me while I stuff my face. I've only got about ten minutes before I have to get back."

They sat across from her. Jason let Stacey take another bite before he began the interrogation. "I know you already talked to Kiki and Janelle, but I was wondering what you could tell me about what happened that day? With Jasmine?"

Stacey put her sandwich down and wiped her mouth. She had trouble meeting Jason's eyes. "I'm so sorry, by the way. About Jasmine. I still can't believe she's gone. I know we weren't friends or anything, but it still feels weird."

"I know." Jason leaned forward and waited for her to look at him. "No one blames you, Stacey. Seriously. I know you were there. I know you tried to help. From what the doctor told us, there was nothing they could do."

Tears pooled at the bottom of her eyes. "Doesn't stop you from thinking you could've done more, though. But it was over so fast."

"Is that normal?" Cassie asked. "For a patient to just crash like that?"

"Sometimes." Stacey looked down at her sandwich, but she pushed it away. "It depends. The strange part with Jasmine was that she made it through surgery okay. She was strong. Dr. Madasani said it was one of the easier surgeries he'd done, despite all the work she'd endured. We set her up in a room, she was solid for a day, and then her heart failed."

"Is there any reason that would happen so long after surgery?"

"A million." Stacey shrugged. "But like I said, all signs pointed to her making a good recovery. To see her health plummet like that was strange."

"Could there be any other reasons that would happen?" Cassie couldn't help but think of the Ghost Doctor from her dream. "Any outside factors that could affect her like that?"

"Administration of the wrong medication. Administration of the right medication in the wrong amount."

"Is there any chance that could've been a factor?"

Stacey hesitated. "It's always a factor."

The table was silent for a moment. Jason leaned forward again. "Do you know something?"

"No." Her voice was firm, her body stiff. Then she let go of the tension. "I'm not sure."

"We just want answers. We won't name names. I promise."

The conviction in Jason's voice must've been enough for Stacey to believe him because she lowered her voice and whispered, "Did you hear about Mark Galanis? He died about a month ago."

Jason shook his head. "What happened?"

"We don't know." Stacey checked her watch. "He just stopped breathing."

"Do you have any theories?" Cassie didn't want to press the woman, but they weren't getting anywhere, and their window was closing. "Any reason people would be fine one minute and not the next?"

"Unfortunately, it happens all the time. It can be natural. If you're asking me if I've seen something, the answer is no." She looked disappointed. "But there are a lot of drugs in a hospital like this. They're not always as well-regulated as you'd think. Too much of a good thing can be just as dangerous."

"If someone got the wrong medication, or too high a dosage of the right medication, would the doctors know?"

"If the family requests an autopsy, sure." She shrugged. "But it can be costly. And if the patient had an underlying condition, it might just tell you what you already know."

"Can you think of any connection between Mark Galanis and Jasmine?"

"They knew each other. At least in passing."

"And they both knew me," Jason said.

Stacey checked her watch again. "Look, I have to get back. I'm sorry I couldn't be more help." She stood, her gaze flicking to Cassie and then back to Jason. "Vanessa's looking for you, by the way. She heard about Jasmine. Heard you were in town. I think she'd like to talk to you."

"Oh." Jason's face was passive as he took in the information. It was a controlled sort of disinterest. "Okay, thanks for letting me know."

"It was nice meeting you, Cassie." She hugged Jason again. "And nice to see you again. If I think of anything else, I'll let you know."

"Thanks."

Jason didn't wait for Stacey to pick up her tray before he turned on his heel and left the cafeteria. Cassie followed in his wake, wondering who Vanessa was and why every muscle in Jason's body had stiffened at the mention of her name.

15

BEAR GREETED HARRIS WITH A WAGGING TAIL AS SOON AS SHE PUSHED THROUGH the door. Apollo waited to rub against her legs until she kicked the door closed behind her and kneeled to scratch Bear behind the ears.

"Are you more excited to see me or to have lunch?" Harris asked. Apollo answered with a meow, and the detective was certain what it meant. She confirmed her hunch when she got to her feet and he ran over to his bowl, staring at her with unblinking eyes.

Harris went through the motions of her new routine. Feed the cat. Feed the dog. Make herself lunch. Eat and pore over David's case file, even though she had the entire thing memorized. There were no additional details to glean from the handful of pages inside the folder, and yet she couldn't stop looking for them.

After everyone had finished eating, Apollo curled up in a patch of sunlight while Bear took a nap at Harris' feet. She spread papers across the coffee table and sat back as though she needed to see them from a fresh perspective.

But it was no use. The information was the same. Someone had shot David once in the head and once in the heart. The bullet was a .308 Winchester, the type of round a police sharpshooter would use. Harris couldn't decide if it was irony or a sick joke. Maybe it was neither and they needed to look internally. But that didn't mesh well with her working theory that Aguilar was the one responsible.

Harris felt anger rising as she thought about the man who could've killed her friend, her partner. It ran red hot through her veins. Burned like acid. But instead of hurting her, it made her stronger. More resilient. More determined than ever to bring him down.

Apollo perked up, sun glinting off his fur and making him glow. He stood and stretched, then trotted to the other room. Harris watched him go, his form light and lithe. She'd only been at Cassie's for a couple of days, but she already hated the idea of leaving these two behind when their owner returned home.

Harris pulled a different folder closer. This was a new one. It belonged to Officer Steve Warren, the cop killed one week prior to David. The department hadn't mourned him any more or less than David, but his death had seemed normal, if not natural. Dying in the line of duty was a reality they all faced.

As tragic as it had been, Officer Warren's death was straightforward. Routine traffic stop. Someone had reported a suspicious vehicle. A 2010 Chevy Aveo. White. Rusted doors and a missing bumper. Suspect was a white male, dark hair, in his mid- to late-twenties. Witness said he appeared to be drinking and driving.

Warren was the first person to call it in. He did everything right. Pulled the vehicle over. Radioed his position. Ran the plates. Everything came back clean. The car hadn't even been swerving, he'd said, but he was going to talk with the driver. Then he approached the vehicle.

Body cams were a neutral party. They didn't have opinions. They recorded facts. Sometimes those facts revealed how some cops shouldn't have a badge and a gun. And sometimes those facts revealed that some cops never stood a chance.

It was quick, at least. The suspect already had the window down and his gun pulled before Warren approached the vehicle. One shot to the face and Officer Warren was dead. He had no time to react. He didn't suffer. Didn't even know what happened to him. If a silver lining was conceivable in a situation like this, that was it.

But Harris only saw the rain clouds.

They had yet to locate the man who'd killed Warren. They'd found the car and his apartment, both abandoned. He'd either escaped the city or was lying low for the time being. He didn't have a criminal record, but everyone had to start somewhere. And he apparently had started with murder.

There was no connection between Warren and David. They knew each other, of course, but had never worked together. Weren't friends. Harris would've known if they played poker together on the weekends. Or went golfing. Or whatever middle-aged men did in their downtime.

There was no connection between Aguilar and the suspect, or between Aguilar and Warren. Statistically, there was a higher chance that the two murders were unrelated. Coincidence. But that seemed too convenient to Harris. Two wasn't a pattern, but it wasn't an anomaly, either.

When Harris had interviewed David's wife, Lisa hadn't been able to tell her anything she didn't already know. David had seemed stressed the last couple of months, but given his profession, that wasn't strange. They'd recently had a talk about what she would do if he died in the line of duty, but again, that wasn't out of the ordinary for them. She mentioned David had left a letter for Cassie, but seeing as Cassie hadn't mentioned it, Harris could only assume it was personal and had nothing to do with the case.

Mostly, Lisa had wanted to tell Harris how much David had respected her as an officer and a friend. Harris accepted the compliment, but even thinking back on the moment, she was embarrassed by the way she'd acted. She'd practically run out of the house before the tears could fall.

Apollo jumped up on the arm rest of the couch and meowed, jolting Harris out of her thoughts. She ran a hand over his back, but he slinked away and returned to the floor. He meowed again, loud enough to wake Bear from his nap. The dog tilted his head to the side as though he'd be able to understand Apollo if he could just concentrate hard enough.

Apollo meowed again. It was sharp and insistent. There was a whine to his voice that made Harris put down the piece of paper in her hands and lean forward. She reached out to him, but Apollo backed away.

This time, a faint click answered his call. Bear whipped his head around. Harris stood. The dog mirrored her. Apollo skittered behind the couch. Everyone took a collective breath and held it, listening. Waiting.

It could've been the house settling. Or miscellaneous item shifting. Or the back door opening.

The seconds ticked by. Harris' lungs were burning, but she didn't dare breathe lest she miss some other sign of an impending attack. When she couldn't take it anymore, she let the air in her lungs escape. And a floorboard creaked.

It didn't sound out of the ordinary. Cassie's house was old. It popped and groaned sometimes. Goosebumps erupted across Harris' skin as she remembered Cassie's stories of visiting specters. Was her house haunted? Was Harris about to get her first glimpse at a ghost?

She unholstered her weapon. The movement made Bear's fur stand on end. A growl emanated from his throat. His hackles raised reminded Harris he was a formidable animal. Not that it would do much good if it were a ghost. She'd probably end up paying for a new wall in an attempt to see if bullets would slow it down.

Bear took a step forward, the growl still in his voice. She wanted to avoid making a phone call to tell Cassie her dog had died on her watch. Harris looked down at Bear. "Sit." He only hesitated for a moment before he complied. "Stay."

The dog whined, but Harris ignored him. She crept forward, her gun pointed to the ground. She hadn't heard another noise since the second creak. Maybe the house had settled, content with its new position. Or maybe someone had realized they couldn't walk through the house without alerting its inhabitants to their presence.

There was a back door to a small fenced-in yard. She had made sure she locked it after taking the dog out that morning, but she hadn't checked it since then. Harris usually let Bear out right before she returned to work from her lunch break. She still had ten minutes left.

Harris turned the corner into the kitchen. She raised her gun to a forty-five-degree angle. It would take a split second to lift it to center mass and squeeze off two rounds. But that was only if her life was in immediate danger. She didn't want to risk blowing the head off someone who'd made a poor decision to rob a house. A thief was not always a murderer.

A quick glance over her shoulder confirmed Bear was sitting where she'd left him. Apollo was still hiding behind the couch. She couldn't blame him. He'd done his job and alerted them to someone—or something—at the back of the house. Now was not the time to be a hero.

Harris stepped forward, and a floorboard creaked underfoot. It was as loud as a gunshot, and she winced as if someone had fired a weapon. The other sounds had been farther away when she heard them, which meant if someone was in the house, they hadn't made it this far. But it also meant they now knew she was coming for them.

Rather than delay the inevitable, Harris took three quick steps forward. She cleared one bedroom and moved on. The next step was to choose between the second bedroom and the bathroom. She picked one. Decided to take her chance. Bedroom first. Then bathroom.

She entered Cassie's room and swung her gun from right to left. Checked behind the door. Nothing. Pulled open the closet and took a sharp step back. Nothing. She risked making herself a target by lying prone on the floor to check under the bed. Nothing there either.

When she stood, a shadow shifted in the doorway. For a second, she thought she was staring into the pale eyes of a ghost. Then reality hit her. It was a man, solid and real, wearing a ski mask and a dark track suit. And he was holding a knife. One moment, he held it above his head, and the next, he let it fly straight at her.

Harris dodged the knife, which bounced off the wall and hit the floor next to her foot. By the time she righted herself and aimed her gun at the intruder, he had already vaulted over the bed. As he cleared the space between them, he raised a knee and crashed into her, sending her flying into the wall. She felt it give beneath her weight. Her vision went fuzzy at the impact.

The man was on her before her eyes could refocus. He bent her hand back until she dropped the gun, then he wrapped both hands around her neck. She didn't try to peel them away. She delivered two swift blows to his right side, then brought her knee up to his groin. He grunted and his grip loosened enough for her to drive her fists through his arms and break out of the hold.

She gasped air into her lungs, but the reprieve only lasted a second before the man tackled her to the ground. The carpet fibers scratched her face as she turned to look for her gun. It was out of reach, halfway under the dresser. The blade of the knife, however, was inches from her eye.

The man saw it a split second before she did. He wrapped his fingers around its handle and struck fast. She moved her head to the side right before the knife tore through the carpet and hit the hardwood floor below. The man pulled it out and brought the blade down again, but Harris was ready. She grabbed his wrist and stopped the downward momentum, the tip of the knife inches from her face.

She tried bucking him off her, but he weighed at least a hundred pounds more than her. If she could get her knee through his legs and against his chest, she'd have a better shot at getting away. But she wasn't sure if she could do it before the strength in her arms gave out.

Harris sucked in as much air as her lungs could take. "Bear," she yelled. The strength of her voice made the man flinch. "Come."

Nails skidding across hardwood floors. An inhuman growl growing louder with each passing second. A blur of brown and black fur leaping across the room. Teeth sinking into flesh. A howl of pain and a string of curse words.

It gave Harris enough time to wiggle out from underneath the intruder and reach for her gun. When she spun around, she took aim and fired a shot, hitting his shoulder. The crack of gunfire made Bear let go, and the man took his chance to kick the dog as hard as he could in the side. Bear yelped and skidded across the room. Harris took aim again, but her next shot only found drywall. The man was already sprinting toward the back door.

Bear got to his feet at the same time as Harris, and the two followed the man through the house. He banged the door shut behind him just as Bear leaped at his heels. The dog crashed against it, and Harris had to push him out of the way to open it again. By the time they made it into the backyard, the intruder had jumped the fence and escaped.

Bear barked until she dragged him back inside by the collar, locking the door behind them. Then she checked every room and every point of entry until she was sure no one else was in the house. She used the last remaining drops of her adrenaline to check on Bear. His ribs were tender, but he didn't bite her when she ran her hand along his sides. She grabbed a napkin and wiped blood from his mouth, folding it over and tucking it into her pocket.

Only when she was sure the intruder wouldn't return did she allow herself to sink down into the middle of the kitchen floor in relief. She holstered her gun and laid back, arms splayed to her side. Bear sat guard at her feet, his ears swiveling like satellites and his eyes fixated on the back door. Eventually, Apollo emerged and crawled onto her chest, purring and nuzzling her chin with his nose.

16

Cassie hung up the phone with Harris, dizzy with relief. She could hear her blood pounding in her ears, and the hospital lobby swam in front of her eyes as she blinked away the tears that had formed. *Everyone's okay. Everyone's okay. Everyone's okay.* She kept up the mantra until she found a chair to sink into.

"Cassie?" Jason's voice felt like it was at the other end of a train tunnel. Her heart was the whistle that warned of imminent danger. "Cassie, are you okay?"

"Everyone's okay." She looked up at him. Her eyes felt like they could pop out of her head at any minute. "Everyone's okay."

"Who's okay?" Jason sat down next to her. Took her hand. Squeezed. "What's going on?"

"Someone attacked Adelaide." When Jason's eyebrows pinched together, she forced herself back to the present. "Detective Harris. She's watching Bear and Apollo while I'm down here. Someone broke into my house. Tried to kill her."

"What?" Jason's whole bodied stiffened. The grip on her hand became painful. "Why? Were they after you?"

That hadn't occurred to her. "I don't know. She thinks it's because she's looking into David's death."

"But she's okay?"

Cassie nodded. Swallowed. Slipped her hand out of Jason's grip and shook it out, hoping the feeling would return sooner rather than later. "She shot him. Bear took a chunk out of him and got kicked in the ribs. She's gonna take him to the vet to be safe, but she doesn't think he's seriously injured. The guy got away, but Harris doesn't think he'll try again."

"She has no way of knowing that." Jason shook his head. He looked angry. "She shouldn't be staying at your place. What if they come back in a couple days, once she's gone and you're there, defenseless?"

"I'm not defenseless." Cassie stood. She wanted comfort from him, not a lecture. "I'm pretty good at surviving."

Jason's face went slack. He stood, too. "Cassie, I'm so sorry—"

"It's fine."

"No, it's not." He took her hand. This time, the touch was gentle. She allowed him to hang onto her. "You're smart and strong and capable. I didn't mean to imply you weren't."

"But?"

"But sometimes someone else is smarter and stronger and more capable." He shook his head. "I'm glad the detective is okay. I know you can handle yourself. And it sounds like Bear is an excellent guard dog. But that doesn't mean I'm not going to worry about you. Even some of the best fighters, the best soldiers"—he hesitated for a fraction of a second—"or the best cops die."

"I know." Cassie tried to ignore the wound David's death had left behind, but it was still painfully raw. "She was lucky."

"I assume she's going to look into whoever this guy was?"

"She's got some of his blood. They're going to check hospitals for anyone who fits the description. He was wearing a ski mask, but a bullet wound and a dog bite will stand out."

"And she'll keep you updated?"

Cassie nodded. "She promised she'll play it safe, but I don't know if I believe her. She's taking all of this pretty hard."

"And what about you?"

"What about me?"

"Your best friend died." Jason's voice was low and soothing, but it still made Cassie bristle. "Another friend was just attacked. Your dog was injured. And you're down here, away from it all, helping me look into my cousin's death."

"So?"

"So"—Jason ducked his head to look straight into her eyes—"that's a lot to handle. A lot to process. You're surrounded by death every day. It's bound to get to you sometimes. And that's okay. But you should talk about it."

"I have a therapist for that."

"Do you talk to her about your abilities?"

Cassie smiled, but there was no humor in it. "No. If I did, she'd probably lock me up."

"Fair enough." He sighed and stroked her hand. He kept his eyes on her while he weighed his words. "The last thing I want to do is presume you're not okay when you are. But worse than that, I don't want you to feel like you have to pretend you're fine. For my sake or anyone else's." He took a step forward. "You're not alone in this anymore, Cassie. You have your parents now. Your sister. Detective Harris." He smiled. "Me."

Cassie fought back the emotion rising in her throat. She'd felt alone for so long. It should've been a relief to know she didn't have to deal with any of this by herself ever again. Instead, she felt lonelier than ever. Her friends and family could try to comprehend what she saw and heard and felt, but they would never know. They'd never truly understand.

But she couldn't tell Jason that. So she smiled and said, "Thank you."

Jason's eyes remained troubled. She looked away so he wouldn't figure out how she was feeling. Movement over his shoulder caught her attention. When her gaze shifted, it landed on a woman standing in the doorway to the Heart and Vascular ward. She wore a simple dress with low-heeled pumps. Her hair was in pin curls. She looked faded and gray, like most of the other spirits who stalked the hospital's passageways, but her eyes, a piercing hazel that stared right through Cassie, seemed alive.

Jason didn't miss Cassie's gasp. "What do you see?"

"The woman from my dreams."

"The Ghost Doctor?"

Cassie didn't answer. The woman had turned in the other direction, and Cassie didn't hesitate to follow her. She didn't want to draw attention to herself, especially after pushing through the door to the ward. Someone would eventually ask her where she was going, and without an appointment, they would be sure to turn her right back around.

"Cassie?" Jason was right behind her. "What's going on?"

She ignored him. She locked her eyes on the other woman, who had already drifted to the end of the hall. Cassie caught sight of the edge of her skirt just as she turned the corner. She couldn't run, but she walked at a brisk enough pace that a few heads turned in her direction. If she could just see where the Ghost Doctor was going—

"Ma'am?"

Cassie didn't slow down. She heard Jason talking to the nurse behind her. It would buy her another minute or two, but not much more. As she turned the corner, she spotted the Ghost Doctor at the end of the next hall. There were doors on either side, some open and some closed. Nurses carrying charts made their rounds. Doctors spoke with families in hushed tones. Cassie knew she didn't belong here.

The Ghost Doctor was within reach. If Cassie stretched out her arm, it would only take a few more steps to reach her. And then what? She couldn't lock her hand around the woman's wrist. It would pass right through, even though Cassie had never seen a ghost so present.

But she had to try.

As Cassie whipped around the corner, she hit something solid. Could spirits become corporeal? They could move objects in short bursts, though it took a lot of energy. Maybe that explained why the Ghost Doctor had been stealing souls. Did it somehow give her the ability to walk on this plane of existence like she was a real person?

But as a clipboard clattered to the ground and papers shot out in every direction, Cassie realized that while she had run into another woman, and a doctor at that, it wasn't the one she'd been pursuing.

"I am so sorry." Cassie could feel the blush on her face and neck. "Are you okay?"

"I'm fine." The woman looked down at the papers in frustration. "I knew I should've numbered them."

Cassie bent down to help her pick them up. "That was completely my fault. I didn't see you."

The woman shook her head. "I wasn't looking where I was going either."

Cassie gathered half the pieces of paper and shoved them into the woman's hands. She stood and looked beyond her, down another hallway. It was full of hospital workers but devoid of ghosts. And with half a dozen people turned in her direction, Cassie knew she wouldn't be able to come up with a good enough excuse to keep looking for her.

"I'm sorry again." Cassie turned and nearly ran into Jason, too. "Time to go."

"Did you talk to her?" Jason hissed. "The Ghost Doctor?"

"No." Cassie sped by the nurse that had called out to her earlier, avoiding any eye contact. "But it wasn't a total loss."

Jason pushed through the door and back out into the hospital's main lobby. They didn't talk again until they were next to his car. "How come?"

"Because now I know she's here, in New Orleans." Cassie looked up at the hospital's façade, which reflected the bright December sun back into her eyes, causing her to squint. "The dream wasn't random. She's connected to Jasmine."

17

JASON PULLED THE CAR AGAINST THE CURB OUTSIDE A MODEST HOUSE WITH BLUE shutters and a two-car garage. A man was bent over a brand-new cherry red BMW that looked out of place against the driveway's cracked pavement. He seemed to be about Cassie's age, and despite the cool breeze, he wore a t-shirt and a pair of gym shorts. His muscles bulged beneath the fabric, and a light summer tan clung to his skin.

Jason put the car in park. "That's Jeff."

Jeff, Cassie had learned on the car ride over, was Mark Galanis' older brother. Jason had been friends with them as kids, and even throughout college. Then life got in the way. Careers and girlfriends and trips around the world. They drifted apart, and Jason hadn't seen either of them since he'd moved to Savannah.

And now one of them was dead.

Jeff fit the description Cassie had created in her mind while she listened to Jason's stories. The older Galanis had played football, run track, and hosted most of their college parties. He could never decide what to do with his life, but eventually his father forced him to get a degree in business. Jason had no idea what he was doing now, but considering they'd pulled up to his parents' house, Cassie wasn't sure he'd ever found his footing. Then again, his car said otherwise.

Cassie waited until Jason got out and made his way around the front of the car before she followed suit. She didn't feel at all prepared to talk to Jason's friend—they hadn't come up with a game plan or anything—and she still had plenty of questions, both about the Ghost Doctor and the woman Stacey had mentioned. Vanessa.

Cassie shook herself out of her thoughts and slammed the door shut behind her. Jeff looked up, then did a double take. His grin widened, and he tossed his sponge back into the bucket.

"Broussard, is that you?" Jeff jogged to the end of the driveway to meet them. "Damn, it's been a minute."

"Hey, man." They shook hands, which turned into a one-armed hug. When they broke apart, Jason introduced Cassie. "We were in the neighborhood."

"That's awesome. Last I heard you were in Atlanta?"

"Savannah, actually." Jason looked at ease, but Cassie could see the wheels turning. They were here for some answers, and he'd get them, one way or another. "What have you been up to?"

"Not much." Jeff looked back at the house and his face fell slightly. "Living with my parents. It's just temporary, but it makes me feel like I'm in high school again."

"I'm staying with Granny Mabel and my mom while I'm in town. I know exactly what you mean." There was a beat of silence. Cassie caught the moment Jason chose to strike. "Hey, I heard about Mark. I'm so sorry, man."

"Thank you." Jeff looked like he meant it. His face, which had been all smiles and jokes, grew tight. "Yeah, took us all by surprise, you know? Man, he would've been so happy to see you. It's been, what, ten years at least, right?"

"Yeah, about that long." More calculations. "What happened?" Jason held up his hands. "You don't have to tell me. I was just talking to Stacey, and she mentioned it. But she didn't tell me anything else."

"Stacey was great. She's been checking in on my mom every week to see if there's anything she can do. I think Mom just likes having another girl to talk to." Jeff shifted from one foot to another. "But yeah, we don't really know. He got into a bad car accident. He was riding his bike and this guy in a truck didn't see him, apparently." The tone of Jeff's voice told Cassie he thought that was bullshit. "He went to the emergency room. They patched him up, but he'd shattered his leg. They told us he'd walk again, but it wouldn't be the same. He might have to use a cane for the rest of his life."

"Oh, shit." Jason's entire body language conveyed his sympathy. He put a hand on Jeff's shoulder and squeezed. "I'm so sorry, man."

Jeff forced a smile. "So, how do you two know each other?"

Jason let his arm fall. "We work together in Savannah."

"Total coincidence we ran into each other here," Cassie supplied.

"Have you met the fam yet?" Jeff's smile widened into a real one. "They're great."

"I've met some of them." Cassie looked at Jason. "We hung out with a bunch of his cousins."

"How's everyone doing?" Jeff waggled his eyebrows. "Does Kiki ever ask about me?"

"Not even once." Jason's voice was playful, but Cassie sensed this was a joke that had gone stale years ago. He allowed another beat of silence during which he sobered. "Jasmine died."

"What?" Jeff looked between the two of them as if waiting for them to say they were joking. "How? When?"

"About a week ago. She had another surgery. Everything seemed fine, and then she crashed."

Jeff's eyebrows pinched together. "I'm so sorry, man."

"It's actually why we're here." Jason had stopped trying to be subtle. "We saw Stacey because something didn't sit right with the whole situation. She didn't know much, but she mentioned Mark. I was just wondering if something similar happened?"

Jeff backed up a couple of paces and walked back over to the bucket of soapy water. He pulled out the sponge and got back to work before he responded. His words came slowly, as though he were calculating every sound that came out of his mouth.

"Mark was pretty beat up after the crash. He had to have a couple surgeries, but they all went well. It was his leg that gave him the biggest problem. They were able to save it, but they said walking would be difficult for a while." Jeff finished scrubbing the passenger-side door and moved on to the hood. "He was on a lot of different medications. One day, he just stopped breathing. They think he reacted poorly to one of the prescriptions."

Jason and Cassie exchanged a look. They were two for two with complications causing a death. But was that a legitimate excuse, or was the Ghost Doctor causing people to die prematurely? Doctors wouldn't be able to find the real reason if it were a ghost, so the only explanation would be that they missed something during recovery.

"That's what they said about Jasmine." Jason took a step closer. "That there were complications. Do you believe them?"

Jeff stiffened. He didn't make eye contact. "Why wouldn't I believe them?"

"You said everything was going fine with Mark. That he was recovering, and then he stopped breathing. The same thing happened with Jasmine. She made it through her surgery, she was fine for about a day, and then her heart gave out."

"Jasmine had a lot of medical issues. It makes sense."

Jason worked his jaw but kept his voice even. "What about Mark? Did he have a lot of medical issues?"

"He'd just been in a major crash, man." Jeff looked up. There was pain in his eyes. And anger. "Why are you asking me this?"

"Because I think something else is going on here." Jason lowered his voice even though no one else was around. "Do you think the hospital is covering something up?"

Jeff turned to him with fists clenched. The sponge dripped suds all over his shoes. "Jesus Christ, man." He threw the sponge back into the bucket and picked up the hose. But he didn't turn it on. His knuckles were white against the green. "How could you even say that?" He finally looked Jason in the eye. "Mark is dead. Nothing is going to change that. Nothing will make it better. Just drop it."

Jason opened his mouth to say something, but whether it was to apologize or defend himself, Cassie wasn't sure. The door to the house opened and an older woman poked her head out. She smiled from ear to ear. "Jay Broussard, is that you?"

Jason waved, but he couldn't bring a smile to his face. "Hello, Mrs. Galanis."

"He was just leaving, Ma." Jeff leveled Jason with a glare. "Don't you dare say anything about this to my mother. She wouldn't be able to handle it."

"I'm sorry. I didn't mean—"

"See you around."

Jeff turned on the hose and began rinsing off the car. Jason and Cassie had to choose between backing off or getting soaked. Jason stood his ground for half a second, then relented. They walked back to the car with their heads hanging low.

Jason waited until he pulled away from the curb. "Jeff's family wouldn't be able to afford a car like that after racking up Mark's hospital bills."

"Then where did Jeff get it?"

"My guess is some sort of settlement." Jason stared straight ahead. "If it was a malpractice lawsuit, they could've settled. Forced Jeff to sign an NDA. Even if he wanted to talk about it, he couldn't."

"Didn't seem like he wanted to, though."

Jason shrugged, but there was a weight to his shoulders now. "Some people don't find comfort in the truth."

"So, what now?"

Jason rolled to a stop at the end of the street and waited while cars zipped by in front of them. "Well," he started. She could hear the hesitance in his voice. "I guess it's time to tell you why I moved to Savannah."

18

It turned out that the reason Jason had left New Orleans was because his fiancée had broken things off with him. Cassie listened to the story in silence, taking in every word, while she was hyperaware of not reacting in a way that betrayed her feelings.

In theory, she didn't have a problem with Vanessa. Nor was she jealous. Jason told her they had been drifting apart for a while, neither one happy with their direction in life. Vanessa had been brave enough to say something first. Jason hadn't disagreed, but that didn't mean it hadn't stung.

That was ten years ago. They hadn't stayed in touch. Jason had moved soon after, wanting to start over. His family had told him not to run away from his problems, but Jason didn't see it like that. He'd needed a clean slate somewhere else, somewhere no one knew him. That way, he could forge his own identity away from everyone else's expectations.

Cassie didn't think that sounded so bad.

Everyone expects a teenager to go through different phases as they figure out who they want to be. Not enough people talk about the fact that even twenty- and thirty-year-olds struggle with their identity. Hell, she was climbing toward forty, and she was still trying to figure out her life.

If Cassie knew for a fact that moving to a random city where she didn't know a single soul would give her the time and space to figure all of this out, she'd do it in a heartbeat.

And she'd told Jason as much.

When they pulled into a parking spot in front of a diner an hour later, Cassie was nervous, but not apprehensive. Jason had texted Kiki for Stacey's number, and then gotten Vanessa's number from Stacey. After a brief call full of nervous laughter, Vanessa had suggested they grab a bite to eat.

Both Cassie and Jason hadn't gotten out of the car yet, and she was the first one to break the silence. "How are you feeling about seeing her again?"

More nervous laughter. "It's strange, for sure. Like, will I even recognize her? Will she still be the same person from ten years ago? I'm not. Maybe she won't recognize me." He turned to Cassie. "Thank you for being here. I know this is weird, and I'm sorry—"

Cassie held up a hand. "It's weird, but we're all adults." She smiled. "Besides, this is about Jasmine. And Vanessa clearly wants to help. We can deal with a little discomfort."

Jason nodded and pushed open his door. Cassie's stomach churned, but she did the same. The cool air dried some of the nervous sweat that had beaded along her hairline. Her head cleared, and her resolve strengthened.

The bell to the diner rang as they pulled the door open. It was a small establishment with about a dozen retro Formica tables scattered across the floor. All the chairs were a bright, cherry red, and the staff wore uniforms to match.

An older woman with short, curly hair and ruddy cheeks called out to them from behind the counter. "Sit wherever you like, hon. I'll be with you in a minute."

Jason scanned the room. Cassie noticed the instant he spotted Vanessa. His entire body went rigid, and he lifted a hand in greeting. Cassie followed his gaze and watched as a woman stood and waited for them to join her.

Vanessa was one of the most beautiful women Cassie had ever seen. Her skin was a flawless deep brown, and her eyes were a hypnotizing shade of hazel. She had wrapped her long caramel-colored braids on top of her head, which made her look taller than she already was. Cassie couldn't help but notice her toned arms, which looked like they belonged to someone who swam or played tennis regularly.

Vanessa couldn't wait until they made it to the table. A smile erupted across her face, and she took three enormous steps forward to meet them halfway. There was no hesitation as she wrapped her arms around Jason. "Oh my God, you look exactly the same."

"So do you." Jason laughed, sounding less nervous. "Thank you for meeting us."

"No problem." Vanessa let go of Jason and pulled Cassie into a tight hug. "My name is Vanessa. It's nice to meet you!"

"Cassie." She was so surprised, her name came out as a gasp. "It's nice to meet you, too."

"Sorry." Vanessa let go and fiddled with the cross hanging on a chain around her neck. "I'm just excited and nervous. And I had a lot of coffee today." She settled into her chair and widened her eyes. "*A lot* of coffee."

As Cassie sat across from her, she noticed the badge Vanessa had left lying on the table. "You work at the hospital?"

Vanessa bobbed her head. "I'm a nurse."

"I knew you'd do it someday." Jason's voice held a hint of pride.

Vanessa rolled her eyes, but she was smiling. "Jay was the only one who believed in me. Even when I didn't. My family thought I was wasting too much money going to school. But it was the only thing that made me feel like I was contributing to the world."

"I know how that feels."

"Yeah?" Vanessa beamed. "What do you do?"

"Oh." Cassie blushed. "I work at the museum with Jason."

"In Savannah," Jason offered. "I'm a security guard, and Cassie helps put exhibits together and handles a lot of the art pieces."

"That's awesome. Is that how you two met?"

Cassie nodded, but the waitress who had greeted them earlier saved her from having to explain further. "What can I get y'all?"

The three of them scrambled for their menus. Jason and Vanessa ended up ordering burgers, while Cassie stuck with the diner's world-famous Reuben.

"A pickle and fries good for all y'all?" A chorus of yeses sounded, and the waitress tucked her notepad into her apron pocket. "All right, I'll be back with those in a jiff."

Jason waited until the woman was out of earshot before he pointed to Vanessa's left hand. "I guess congratulations are in order?"

"Oh." Vanessa looked down at a ring Cassie hadn't even noticed. "Thank you. Yeah. We're getting married next month, actually."

"I'm happy for you." Jason sounded like he meant it, but Cassie saw sadness in his eyes, too.

Vanessa stared at him for a moment and then shook her head. "Look, I know this is awkward." She glanced at Cassie and gave her a sympathetic smile. "We haven't talked in a decade. I can't speak for you, but I know I've changed a lot over the years. There are things I regret saying. There are things I regret *not* saying. At the end of the day, I know I made the right choice for me. I hope you feel the same way. And if you don't"—she chewed the inside of her cheek before committing to her words—"I'd like to know that, too. If there's anything I can do to help—"

"I feel the same way."

Cassie felt like a voyeur. She wished with every fiber of her being she'd chosen to sit on the outside of their booth. Maybe then she could've excused herself and given them a moment.

"Cassie." Vanessa was looking at her now. "I'm so sorry. I didn't mean to make you uncomfortable. I just needed to say something, or I'd regret it."

"No, I totally understand." And she did. But when Jason turned to her with an unreadable expression, she still wished she could be anywhere but here. "I can leave, if—"

"No." Jason slipped his hand under the table and wound his fingers through hers. "I want you to stay."

"Okay." She squeezed his hand. "Then I'll stay."

Vanessa smiled, a hint of hidden knowledge in her eyes. "You guys are cute together."

Cassie didn't know what to say. She and Jason had been enjoying their time together, but they hadn't discussed what life would be like once they returned to Savannah. Being co-workers always complicated things.

And if you throw ghosts and murder investigations on top of that, it was bound to get out of hand.

But Vanessa didn't give either of them time to fumble through an explanation of whatever it was going on between them. Her face sobered, and her eyebrows pinched together. "How's Janelle holding up?"

"As good as can be expected." Jason shook his head. "You know how quiet she is. It's impossible to read her. Even harder now than it was before."

"I'm sure Kiki is keeping an eye on her."

"Like a hawk." He chuckled. "I think they've gone out for lunch every day this week."

"Good. She needs to know people are looking out for her. And Kiki needs someone to take care of."

Jason raised an eyebrow. "Maybe you should've gotten that psychology degree instead."

Vanessa took a sip of water, but the glass couldn't hide her smile. "Maybe if the nursing thing doesn't work out."

"Stacey said you wanted to talk to me and I don't think it had anything to do with our breakup."

"Unfortunately, no. That would've been easier, believe it or not."

"Do you know something?" Jason leaned forward. "About Jasmine?"

"No. Or, well, I don't know." Vanessa splayed her hands across the table like she was bracing herself for what came next. She glanced around the diner before continuing. "I think something's going on at the hospital. I'm not sure if Jasmine got caught in the crossfire."

"What do you mean something's going on?" Cassie asked. Her mind flashed to the Ghost Doctor and the dream she had. "Like what?"

"I think the hospital is lying about the way people have died." She lowered her voice even more. "I think they're trying to avoid more malpractice lawsuits."

"Can you prove it?"

"If I could, I would've gone to someone in HR." Her smile was tight now. "Or the press."

Jason leaned back with a huff. "So, what's the next step?"

Before Vanessa could respond, the waitress arrived, expertly carrying all three plates at once. "Our world-famous Reuben." She set the plate down in front of Cassie. "Bacon cheeseburger and fries for the gentleman." She set the last plate down in front of Vanessa. "And the classic burger for the lady. Can I get y'all anything else?"

"I think we're all set." Jason hit the woman with a wide smile. "Thank you."

"You're welcome, hon. Holler if you need anything."

Cassie waited until she left. "We need proof. We need to see if Jasmine's death wasn't what they said it was. And if we can find that out, we'll need to see if she's connected to what happened to Mark Galanis. And that other woman." Cassie hoped Vanessa didn't ask who. "Or anyone else. Then we'll need to find a connection."

Vanessa looked down at her burger, but it appeared as though the last thing she wanted to do was pick it up and take a bite. "I've got an idea." She peered through the top of her lashes at Jason. There was fear and desperation in her eyes. "I could pull some records. Maybe we'd find a connection that way."

Jason was already shaking his head by the time she finished her sentence. "You could get fired."

"Jasmine is dead." Vanessa whispered the sentence like the air had been stolen from her lungs. "And Mark? Too many people we know. Too many people gone too soon."

"We don't know that for sure."

"Which is why we need to find out." Her eyes hardened. "I know the risks. And I'm willing to take them." She sighed. Her body slumped. "But I've already looked at everything, and I have no idea what I'm doing. I was never good at connecting the dots like you were. I know you'll see something I missed."

Jason looked at Cassie, and she shrugged. It wasn't up to her. And it wasn't up to Jason, either. Vanessa had made her choice. She could live with the consequences. And if they found their next lead, the risk would pay off.

"Okay." Jason picked up a fry and shoved it into his mouth. "Lunch first. Then we break the law."

19

After lunch, Vanessa had led them to a private room in the back of the E.R. and left them while she gathered the information they needed. Jason and Cassie had waited in near silence, scared to make a sound lest they draw attention to themselves. Cassie read through the posters on the wall to waste time. For the most part, everything was ordinary as long as you ignored the ghosts drifting in and out every few minutes.

At least Jason had no idea what was going on. Ignorance really was bliss.

There was a tiny knock on the door. Cassie and Jason exchanged looks before the door swung open, and Vanessa slipped through. She closed it with a *click* behind her and pressed the lock on the handle. They weren't about to take any chances.

"We have fifteen minutes until I'm needed elsewhere," Vanessa explained. "If someone catches us, I can lie and say you two wanted to speak to me privately about an issue, but they'll be expecting documentation of your visit afterward, and I'd rather avoid any kind of paper trail if we can."

"The sooner we're out of here, the better." Jason pointed to the file in her hands. "Ready?"

"No." But she placed the folder on the bed between them anyway. "But it's too late now."

All three of them pulled up a chair as Vanessa flipped open the folder. The first piece of paper held a list of names. There had to be at least fifty of them.

"These are some of the patients who died of complications within the last six months."

Jason ran a finger down the page. "Have you noticed any connections?"

"Connections, no. But there were some interesting cases." She flipped the page over to reveal individual patient information. If someone caught Vanessa sharing this with them, they'd undoubtedly fire her. "Here are some people I remember coming through the emergency room. People who seemed to stabilize and then crash. Obviously, that can happen from time to time, but this was more frequent than it should've been. And I wasn't the only one who noticed."

"Other people were talking about it, too?"

She nodded. "A couple. A few of my friends. Martin, one of the nurses, overheard a doctor yelling about it in the breakroom. Then Stacey mentioned something, and I realized it wasn't just here. It was happening all over the hospital."

"Which means there's less likely to be a connection between the patients," Cassie offered.

"Right." Vanessa gestured to the notes. "Different doctors. Different nurses. Different wings of the hospital. Their conditions were different. The ways they died were different."

Jason picked up the first two pages and scanned them side by side. "Even if something is going on here, and the hospital is trying to cover it up, a few of these patients have to be the real deal. The question is how we separate the real ones from the suspicious ones."

"Have any of the patients jumped out at you?" Cassie asked. "Even if you couldn't find a connection, have any of them seemed stranger than the others?"

"Strange how?"

Cassie caught Jason's look of warning out of the corner of her eye, but she ignored him. They needed answers. "Abnormal in any way. Maybe a doctor went against procedure and the risk didn't pay off. Or a patient was halfway out the door when they collapsed. Or the family made a scene because they didn't think the staff was doing their job. Something that tells us the person died when she shouldn't have under normal circumstances."

"Lots of families make scenes." Vanessa sounded tired. "You can't blame them, but it doesn't make our jobs any easier."

"So, that wouldn't be out of the ordinary." Cassie kept her voice gentle, but she could feel the desperation building. "Anything else?"

Vanessa flipped through the paperwork. She pulled out a few charts. "Here's Jasmine and Mark." She handed them to Jason, who took them like they were made of glass. "And a third patient that I remembered coming through here."

Cassie took that one. "What was so memorable?"

"He'd been stabbed. The blade had perforated his lung and his liver. He was left to bleed out on the sidewalk, but someone found him and brought him in." Vanessa shook her head at the memory. "We almost lost him on the table, but they stemmed the bleeding and patched him up."

"Let me guess," Cassie interrupted, "he died of complications a few days later."

"Exactly." Vanessa sat up a little straighter. "But the strange part was that he still had stitches in from his last fight. I went looking through his charts, but we hadn't operated on him the first time. He'd been to the Tulane Medical Center. I called and talked to a nurse over there." She rolled her eyes. "Not an enlightening conversation."

Cassie lifted an eyebrow in question.

"Every time we go to a function or a convention or a seminar, he hits on me. His name is Alan Wolcott."

Jason looked up. "He hits on you even though he knows you're engaged?"

Vanessa and Cassie exchanged a knowing look.

"He doesn't care," Vanessa said. "I told him it makes me uncomfortable, and he made such a scene about how I need to loosen up and stop being so self-obsessed." She rolled her eyes again. "As if he's not the one making passes at me every chance he gets."

"Sounds like a charmer." Cassie said. "Did you get any information out of him?"

"Actually, yes. The one upside, I guess," she speculated. "He remembered the guy coming in. Said he was in some gang or something, so it wasn't a surprise that someone stabbed him again." She shook her head. "I'm sure his commentary never gets old. Anyway, he also told me they almost lost him in recovery. His organs started to shut down, but they saved his life. Only for him to wind up here and go through the same thing."

"Could this be happening at two different hospitals? If so, we have a much bigger issue on our hands." Cassie looked over at Jason, who had been quiet for too long. "Find anything?"

"No." He placed Jasmine and Mark's notes back in the folder. "It's nothing we didn't already know."

The squeal of a sneaker came from the other side of the door, followed by an eruption of laughter. Someone was right outside. All three of them froze, eyes wide, and waited for the door handle to jiggle. Seconds ticked by. Then a full minute. The laughter faded. They breathed a collective sigh of relief.

Vanessa checked her watch. "Our time's up. If I'm gone any longer, someone's gonna ask questions."

Jason stood. "Thank you for your help."

Cassie seconded him. "It means a lot. I know you took a risk putting this together."

"I want to help." Her hazel eyes glossed over with tears. "If something's going on, and I don't do something about it, I wouldn't be able to live with myself. I wish I could've given you more."

Jason flipped the folder shut and held it out for Vanessa. "You gave us another lead. That's more than we could've hoped for."

Vanessa pushed the folder away. "Those are for you. Just make sure no one else sees them. Or they'll do more than fire me."

Cassie took the folder from Jason and slipped it into her purse. "We promise. And we'll keep you updated if we figure anything else out."

"Thanks." Vanessa's gaze landed on Jason. "It was nice seeing you again. You look good." She laughed awkwardly. "Happy, I mean. I think Savannah's treating you well."

"Thank you." He looked at Cassie and smiled. "I think it was the right decision."

20

Vanessa had had the forethought to bring along a clipboard with a random array of papers. She held it to her chest as she left the room, stepping aside to let Cassie and Jason out. No one paid them any mind, even though Cassie felt like a neon sign pointed to the papers folded into her purse.

Vanessa spared them a small smile and then parted ways. The plan was to separate as soon as possible, with Vanessa heading back to the nurse's station to resume her shift, and Cassie and Jason making a beeline for the exit. If they looked like they knew where they were going, no one would stop them. The ward was too busy to worry about a couple of people leaving on their own accord.

But the universe had a different idea.

Cassie felt a pull on her senses, like an invisible line attached to the back of her head. Someone tugged on the other end. She twisted, just in time to catch the skirt of someone's dress disappear around the corner.

"She's here."

"Who?" Jason had his eyes on the exit. "We should go."

Cassie looked up at him. She'd already made her decision. "I'll meet you there."

"What?" He looked at her now. "No. Why?"

"The Ghost Doctor. She's here." Cassie turned to stare at the spot she'd last seen her. "I need to know more about her. I have to figure out how she's involved."

"If they find out we're not supposed to be here, it could get back to Vanessa." He lowered his voice. "And then they'll know about what she gave us."

"They have no reason to think we don't know where we're going." She started down the hall. "And the more we stand here arguing, the more suspicious we'll look. You go, I'll meet you."

Jason sighed behind her, but it wasn't until his shoulder bumped hers that she realized he'd followed her. "I want to know what's going on, too," he explained. "Even if I can't see what you can see."

Cassie nodded but didn't respond. They had turned the corner, but the Ghost Doctor was nowhere in sight. Had she lost her so soon? Cassie had a feeling the doctor was coaxing her forward. She wanted to be followed. Cassie just had to be patient.

They stopped to glance inside each room that lined the hallway. Vanessa had taken them to a room in minor care, which meant most of the patients here just needed a couple of stitches or some meds to get them back on their feet. They had drawn most of the curtains for privacy, but it didn't matter. Cassie knew the Ghost Doctor wasn't here. She could feel the invisible line tugging her forward.

"There's bound to be security around here somewhere," Jason whispered. "What's your plan if we get stopped?"

"I don't have a plan."

Jason winced. "At least you're honest."

Cassie hoped she'd find what she needed before anyone noticed them roaming the halls aimlessly. She kept a quick pace, with Jason on her heels, to make it look like she knew where she was going. It would work for a short time, but she felt the clock ticking.

Ahead, a pair of double doors led to the short-stay wing. People who'd had surgery or needed to stay for overnight observation would be through there. Cassie skidded to a stop and pressed her face against the glass. At the end of the hall, the Ghost Doctor waited for her. As soon as their eyes locked, the doctor turned and walked straight through a wall.

Cassie had already pushed through the doors and was halfway down the hall before Jason caught up to her. "I don't think we're supposed to be back here."

"It'll just take a minute," she said, though she had no way of knowing that. "She went into one of these rooms."

Cassie peered into each one as she passed, just to be sure, but the invisible line tugged her forward until she was standing outside the last door on the right. It was open, with the curtain pulled back as if someone had left the room for just a moment.

The brightness of the room illuminated the man on the bed. His skin was yellow and bruised, and he looked deflated, like a balloon with all the air let out. His skin sagged off his bones, which only added to the effect. Cassie couldn't tell what was wrong with him at a glance.

As harrowing as he was to look at, the man on the bed did not hold Cassie's attention. The Ghost Doctor drew her gaze as she hovered over the man, like she was inspecting every freckle and mole on his body. She laid her spectral hand on his head and looked up at the ceiling, as if calculating his exact temperature. She shook her head. Prognosis not good.

Cassie had been so focused on tracking down the Ghost Doctor that she hadn't thought of what to do once she found her. Should she stand back and observe? She'd already seen what the doctor could do from her dream, but more data could paint a better picture. If she wanted to save this patient, however, she had to act. But how could you fight a ghost? Even if she chased the doctor off now, Cassie couldn't watch over this stranger for the next ten minutes, let alone the several days it would take for him to recover. Besides, there was a whole hospital of victims to choose from. The Ghost Doctor had free rein and the ability to appear wherever she wanted.

There was no way Cassie could stop her forever.

But she didn't need to.

Two things happened at the exact same moment. Just as Cassie decided she'd do what she could to save the man before her, the Ghost Doctor plunged her hand into the middle of his chest cavity. Cassie gasped and faltered, caught between shock and terror. Jason asked her what was wrong, but all her senses were attuned to what was happening in front of her. He was as much a part of the background as the buzzing of the electricity overhead.

At Cassie's exclamation, the Ghost Doctor turned to her, hazel eyes bright and wide, with her hand still in the man's chest. Cassie was once again struck by how alive she looked. There was a consciousness behind her gaze that Cassie had never seen before. This woman, despite likely dying sometime in the '40s, had held onto herself for eighty years.

That meant she was a lot more powerful—and a lot more dangerous—than anything Cassie had seen before.

The Ghost Doctor held Cassie's gaze for a second longer before scowling. She turned to the man before her and took a step back, only she didn't let go of whatever it was she'd grabbed onto inside his chest. A paler, glowing version of the patient sat up in bed, more animated than his physical form. The doctor pulled her hand back, and alarms from the machine around his bed began blaring a warning for all to hear.

Cassie took a step into the room, but Jason latched onto her elbow and wrenched her back. She fought against him, but his grip was iron-tight. Meanwhile, the Ghost Doctor wrapped her own hand around the brand-new spirit and pulled him from the bed. He stumbled, but found his footing. All the while, he stared back at his body while the Ghost Doctor led him across the room.

"We have to leave."

"What?" Cassie's ears were full of pumping blood and blaring alarms. "We have to help."

"That's not our job." Jason forced Cassie to look at him, turning her away from the room. "They're going to wonder what we're doing here. They might think we did something. We have to leave."

The first nurse came sprinting around the corner and charged into the room. The movement snapped Cassie out of her stupor. She and Jason backed up until they hit the wall opposite the room. No one was paying them any mind, but that wouldn't last forever.

Cassie chanced one more glance inside the room but couldn't see the Ghost Doctor or her latest victim. Her head swam with a million explanations for what had just happened, but no matter how hard she thought about it, she kept coming back to the same one:

Their prime suspect in multiple murder cases might just be a ghost only Cassie could see.

21

Cassie wasn't sure where Jason was taking them, and she didn't care. She pressed her forehead to the window, relishing in the way it sent goosebumps across her skin. They'd had no trouble leaving the E.R. despite the commotion, but the run-in with the ghost had left her drained.

"Just to make sure I understand this," Jason said, "you think a ghost is killing people at the hospital."

She'd already explained what happened to the man in the bed, and Jason had taken it as seriously as she'd told it. He was doing well for someone who'd been unceremoniously dropped into her world the night before. But that didn't mean it was easy for him to take. Or easy for her to explain.

"I don't know what I think."

That was the truth, at least. She knew what she saw, but she wasn't sure what it meant. It was the second time she'd witnessed the Ghost Doctor kill someone, but in all the time Cassie had experienced ghosts, she'd never seen one do anything like that before.

Then again, she'd never seen one quite like this before, either. Every ghost was unique. The serial killer Robert Shapiro had manifested by taking on the visage of an angry red spirit. He'd manipulated Cassie's emotions, but she felt a different type of power emanating from the Ghost Doctor.

"She reached a hand into his chest and pulled his spirit out." Cassie rolled her head to the side to look at Jason. "And then he died. Kind of hard to argue with that."

Jason's hands tightened on the steering wheel. They were barreling down a major highway. He switched lanes before he answered. "Maybe she wasn't a ghost," he offered. He glanced at Cassie, who had raised an eyebrow in question. "You said she looks different from all the others. Maybe she's an angel."

"Like the Angel of Death?"

"Maybe not *the* Angel of Death." Jason cleared his throat. "You know, just *an* angel of death. Lowercase letters."

Cassie chuckled, but the humor didn't last. "I've never seen an angel before. Not saying they don't exist, but this would be a first." She returned her forehead to the window and goosebumps resurfaced on her skin. "I can't explain it, but I know she's a ghost. I just don't know why she's different. Or who she is. Or what she wants."

"That's a lot of unknowns."

Cassie made a noncommittal noise.

The conversation died as Jason made another series of turns. Cassie paid no attention to the signs they passed. It was only when they pulled into a parking lot that she bothered lifting her head from the window.

"Where are we?"

"Kiki's work." Jason looked at his watch. "She should be getting back from lunch with Janelle soon. Maybe we can catch her before she heads inside."

They only had to wait a couple of minutes before Kiki pulled into her designated parking spot. Cassie remembered the shiny BMW from the night they'd visited Granny Mabel's house. She had thought it was black, but the afternoon light revealed it was midnight blue.

"What are you two doing here?" Kiki slammed her door shut and waited for them to finish their walk across the parking lot. She looked at her watch. "I only have about five minutes."

Kiki looked both different and exactly the same as she always did. She wore a taupe suit with a pale pink shirt underneath. She'd pulled her hair back into a sleek bun, and her makeup was less dramatic than it had been last night. This was Lawyer Kiki, and if Cassie was being honest with herself, Lawyer Kiki was a little intimidating.

"That's all we need." Jason turned to Cassie, who was already pulling the folder out of her purse. He spread its contents across the trunk of Kiki's car. "We've got some leads, but I'd like your opinion."

Kiki bent over the papers, inspecting them one at a time. There must've been something there she recognized because she straightened and leveled Jason with a look. "Where did you get these?"

"Vanessa."

Kiki sucked in a breath, then put her hands on her hips. "What did you do? Did you make her do this?"

"What?" Jason blanched. "No, of course not. She was already looking into this before we even saw her. We went to go visit Stacey, and she told me Vanessa was looking for me." Jason glanced at Cassie. "I wasn't going to at first. We stopped by Jeff's house. Did you know Mark died?"

"Oh my God, no I didn't." Kiki put a hand to her mouth. "What happened?"

"He was in a car accident." Jason blew out a breath, leaned against the fender, and folded his arms across his chest. "He made it through surgery okay. They said he'd walk again, but it might be with a cane. Next thing you know, he stops breathing."

Kiki stood a little straighter. "That sounds hauntingly familiar."

"My thoughts exactly. I went to talk to Jeff." Jason shook his head. "As soon as I asked him if he thought the hospital was covering something up, he froze me out."

"Which means he knows something."

Jason bobbed his head. "Rather than overstay my welcome, I got Vanessa's number from Stacey and we met for lunch." He gestured to Cassie. "All three of us."

Kiki turned a sympathetic gaze on Cassie, but she waved it off. "I know I've only known her for, like, an hour, but I kind of like her."

"Vanessa's a good person." Kiki's smile was soft. "Always has been."

"Did you know she's engaged now?" When Kiki shook her head, Jason chuckled. "It's weird, but I'm kind of relieved. She seems happy."

"You seem happy." Kiki looked at Cassie, who blushed.

Jason beamed, but he sobered as soon as he looked back down at the paperwork before him. "I'd be happier if I could figure out what's going on here."

Kiki checked her watch again. "You've got two minutes. Walk me through it."

And so they did. Jason led the charge, with Cassie filling in extra details along the way. Kiki gave them a new perspective on the patients they'd already discussed, but every time they'd find a connection, something else broke the streak.

Neither Jason nor Cassie brought up what happened after they met with Vanessa at the hospital. It was a silent agreement between the two of them that it would be better not to discuss it until they had more tangible evidence. There was no point in telling Kiki a ghost had killed her baby cousin unless they could prove it without the shadow of a doubt.

Kiki looked at her watch again and hoisted her purse higher on her shoulder. "I'm late."

"At least tell us what you think," Jason pleaded.

"About what?"

He gestured to the folder. "What do you mean? About all this."

"It's a good start." Kiki's voice was gentle, but she sounded as confused as Jason. "But this doesn't tell us anything."

"It tells us we're on the right track." Jason sounded desperate now. "It tells us something is going on at the hospital."

"You have a pattern," Kiki said. "But that's not proof. We're going to need a lot more than this if we want to take on the entire hospital."

"I know." Jason shook his head, as though he were shaking loose the last vestiges of desperate hope he'd been clinging to. "I expected you to see something we didn't."

"I'm sorry. Trust me, I want this to be real as much as you do." For the first time since Cassie had met her, Kiki looked worn. "Then we'd at least have an answer."

"Go to work." Jason squared his shoulders, though the determination in his eyes looked forced. "We'll keep looking."

Kiki smiled and hugged them both. "Keep me updated, okay? I want to know everything." Her voice faded as she walked farther from them. "And don't get into any trouble. I'm not bailing you out again!"

Cassie turned to Jason and gaped. "Again?"

"Long story." He was smiling, too. "And with luck, you'll never hear it."

Cassie gathered the papers from the back of Kiki's car before they blew away. When she'd secured them back in her purse, she looked up at Jason. "What now?"

He rubbed a hand across the back of his neck. "As much as I don't want to meet the guy, I think we should track down that nurse Vanessa was telling us about."

"The one who's been hitting on her?"

"That's the guy." Jason started back toward their car. "Someone clearly wanted that one guy dead if they followed him from one hospital to the next. If we can find the connection between that patient and the others, we might crack this wide open."

Cassie nodded but stayed silent as she got into the car. Part of her wanted them to find what they needed at the other hospital, and the other part felt certain they'd left behind their biggest clue when they walked away from the Ghost Doctor and allowed her to continue stealing souls unchecked.

22

Jason drummed his fingers on the steering wheel. "I don't like this plan."

Cassie shrugged. "Doesn't mean it's a bad one."

"I don't like the idea of you going in there alone." Jason shook his head. "This guy is a creep."

"I won't be alone. He won't do anything."

"I don't like the idea of him ogling you."

Cassie placed a gentle hand on Jason's shoulder. "I hate to break it to you, but your presence will not stop men from ogling."

Jason didn't laugh. "Call me if you need backup."

"I will." Cassie had the urge to lean in and kiss his cheek. She resisted. "Be back in a few."

Cassie stepped into the breeze and let it refresh her senses. It was late afternoon now, and the sun had done its job of warming the city to a moderate temperature. She still needed her jacket, but she let it hang open as she walked up to the Tulane Medical Center's entrance. The hospital buzzed with activity, which suited her needs perfectly. If she could get in, talk to this nurse, and get out without anyone asking questions, she'd call it a win.

It took Cassie a few seconds to realize her apprehension over going inside a hospital had faded. It may have only been by a few percentage points, but it was a noticeable enough difference to make her smile. The icy fingers of the building's ghostly inhabitants still reached for her, but she acknowledged them all and kept moving forward. It was the best she could do, and only a few lingered longer than they were welcome.

Cassie walked up to the main desk in the waiting room. This was the only part of the plan she wasn't sure about. If her lie didn't work, she'd have to get Vanessa involved, and Jason and Cassie had both agreed to limit their contact with her as much as possible until this was over. As much as they wanted answers, they weren't willing to risk her job more than they already had.

Cassie put on her best customer service voice. "Hello, my name is Vanessa. I'm a nurse over at UMC. I'm looking for Alan Wolcott?"

The woman behind the desk looked exhausted, bored, and at the end of her rope. "I can tell him you're here, but I can't guarantee he'll have time to see you."

"That's fine." Cassie reined in her excitement. Step one complete. "I'll sit over there until he comes down. No rush."

The woman didn't respond. She picked up the phone, dialed a number, and relayed the message. When she hung up again, she turned in her chair, got up, and walked away. But Cassie didn't care. The hardest part was over.

She hoped, anyway.

Cassie found a chair in the corner of the waiting room where she could see both doors that led through to the hospital. She didn't know what Alan looked like, but she hoped it would be obvious he was looking for Vanessa. After that, she'd have to rely on her charm to get him to stay. Something told her it wouldn't be too hard.

The waiting room was busy. People walked in and out every few minutes. Some went through the doors into the back of the hospital, while others waited until a nurse called them. A man came in with his finger in a lunch pail full of ice, and they immediately escorted him away.

But Cassie was more interested in what everyone else couldn't see. Spirits paced the length of the waiting room, as though they'd been cursed to do so for all eternity. And maybe they had. As much as she saw and knew about the world beyond this one, there were still so many unanswered questions.

Some of the ghosts looked whole, a sign that an invisible disease or an internal wound had killed them. Those were the easiest to watch. The ones with missing limbs or gory holes in their heads were much more difficult to stomach. Those were the living nightmares that made her job difficult.

But Cassie made herself look at them each in turn. If she couldn't help them, the least she could do was recognize their existence. They were already invisible and forgotten. Maybe her acknowledgement could offer some small comfort.

She had another purpose in studying them: Discovering if any were as strong or as present as the Ghost Doctor. Cassie looked for the older spirits, the ones who had walked the earth for decades. She spotted a man dressed as though he'd lived long enough to see the turn of the century. What he was doing here, she didn't know, but he looked even more faded and feeble than the others.

That confirmed the Ghost Doctor was different. Special. But it didn't tell Cassie anything she hadn't already guessed. What she really needed to know was whether the Ghost Doctor could kill a person. And if she could, then Cassie needed to learn how to stop her.

Before her thoughts could run further down that path, the doors to her left opened, and a man walked through. He wasn't like the other nurses, standing in the doorway with a chart in their hands, calling names, and waiting for someone to hobble forward.

No, this man walked into the middle of the room with a grin on his face, turning in circles as though looking for someone. Cassie waited just long enough to make him wonder if someone had played a prank on him before approaching.

If she was being honest with herself, he was a handsome man. His scrubs were tight in all the right places, and his biceps bulged under the material. He looked Italian, with dark features and a natural bronze tone to his skin. At the very least, he looked like he'd be fun at a party, though that wouldn't grant him any favors with her.

"Alan Wolcott?" Cassie walked up to him when his back was turned. She waited until he faced her. "Alan?"

"You're not Vanessa." The disappointment only lasted a second. "But I'd still like to know your name."

"Cassie." She held out a hand. Alan shook it gently, hanging on for two seconds too long. "I'm a friend of Vanessa's."

"Any friend of Vanessa's is a friend of mine." His voice deepened. "What can I do for you?"

This was why Cassie had wanted to come in alone. She'd be able to get a lot more out of Alan if he thought she was here alone and interested in him.

Jason's presence would've thrown the whole thing off. They couldn't afford to miss out on this opportunity.

"Do you have a minute?" She gestured to her vacant seat. "I know you're probably busy."

"I can make time."

Alan placed his hand on the small of Cassie's back as he led her over to the chairs. She had to resist the urge to wiggle out of his reach. Even through her jacket, his touch made her skin crawl.

"Thank you so much." She made her voice breathy and plastered a smile on her face. She was grateful when they finally sat, so he'd stop touching her. "I really appreciate it. Vanessa told me you wouldn't mind talking to me about one of your patients."

Alan had the wherewithal to check that no one was listening. He at least pretended to care about breaking the rules. "I could get in trouble for that."

She batted her eyelashes. "I'll make it worth your trouble."

"Sold." Alan smirked, and Cassie had to resist rolling her eyes. It was all too easy. "What do you want to know?"

"She called to ask you about a patient who died at the other hospital. She said he'd come through here first and almost died, too."

"Yeah, I remember him." Alan squinted. "Can't think of his name, though."

"Don Chichetti." She'd studied his chart.

"Right, right." Alan shook his head. "He was in some sort of motorcycle gang. It wasn't the first time he'd been through here. I'd say 'and it wouldn't be his last,' but I guess it kind of was."

She didn't laugh at his joke. "You said he almost died after surgery? What happened?"

"Don't know. His body started failing. They fed him an IV. Pumped him full of meds. He stabilized." Alan shrugged. "He walked out of here a couple days later. Only to wind up in the hospital again. Stupid bastard."

"And you don't know why he crashed like that?"

"Not a clue." Alan narrowed his eyes. "What's this all about?"

Cassie flashed him a smile and leaned forward. The easiest way through this conversation was to stroke his ego. "He was my friend's brother. She wants to know what happened to him. Vanessa told me you were the only one who could help."

"She said that?"

"Yep." Cassie didn't linger in the moment. "Something's fishy about the way he died. We think maybe someone was trying to hurt him."

"Someone did hurt him." Alan didn't bother hiding the condescension in his voice. "That's why he was here."

"What I meant," Cassie said, forcing her voice to remain flirtatious, "was that someone tried to hurt him while he was here. And while he was at UMC. And they succeeded the second time."

"They fired a girl after they fixed him up, but I don't think she has anything to do with this."

Cassie sat a little straighter in her chair. "They fired someone? Who? Why?"

"This hot volunteer chick. She was in the room when he crashed." He shook his head. "They couldn't prove anything, not really, but they let her go because they said she may have accidentally increased his dosage. But I don't buy it."

"Why not?"

"She didn't fit in around here. She had tattoos and piercings. Some of the older patients complained it was inappropriate. I didn't care. It was hot." He sneered in a way that told her she didn't want to know what he was thinking. "She didn't mind showing me all of her tattoos."

"You think they were just looking for an excuse to fire her."

"Pretty much."

Cassie smiled. "So, you hooked up with her?"

He wasn't good at playing coy. "Maybe."

"Your place or hers?"

Alan laughed. He looked intrigued. "Hers. Why?"

"You know where she lives. Can I get her address?"

He thought about it for a moment. "I'll give you her address if you give me your number."

Cassie didn't even hesitate. "Deal."

23

HARRIS SHIFTED IN THE FRONT SEAT OF HER CAR, SHAKING OUT A CRAMP THAT had formed in her calf. It'd been half an hour since she'd seen Francisco Aguilar enter the Brazilian steakhouse, and she was moments from making her move.

The attack at Cassie's house felt like it had happened days ago rather than a few brief hours. The vet had cleared Bear, saying he had some bruising, but would be fine with rest and extra love and attention. As much as it pained her to leave him alone at the house after such a traumatic event, Harris had work to do.

She'd returned to the office long enough to inform Clementine what had happened and to turn over the bloody napkin, hoping to find out who had attacked her. Not that she needed to know. The man who'd broken into Cassie's house didn't matter. Only Aguilar did.

After all, he was the one behind all of this. She was sure of it.

But there was protocol. And procedure. And bureaucratic bullshit. She'd fired her weapon, so there'd be an inquiry and more paperwork than Harris had patience for. Clementine told her to sit and wait for the results. She did. It didn't take long. Harris had almost become the third dead cop in as many weeks. Everyone wanted answers.

When the hit came back, Harris was the first to get the call. Stanley "Shark" Gibson. He had a few priors, but mostly breaking and entering. He'd never gone to jail for murder. Didn't mean he'd never committed it, though. If he had no qualms attacking an officer in broad daylight—even if it had been in the privacy of someone's home—then this wasn't his first rodeo.

Harris found all the information she could on the man. It wasn't hard. Not only was he in the system, but his social media presence was far from quiet. He enjoyed checking in at restaurants and Instagramming his food. He was either a complete idiot or had no regard for his own well-being. Then again, those usually went hand in hand.

Against her better judgement, she'd followed his last known location to the Brazilian steakhouse. Clementine would be pissed, but Harris would deal with that later. Consequences be damned. Harris rarely went off book. They'd have to give her a pass on this one.

When Aguilar arrived, her heart kicked into overdrive. It hadn't surprised her, but she didn't expect coming face to face with him so soon. As far as kingpins went, Aguilar wasn't shy. You'd find him all around the city, eating out, going to festivals, catching a movie. He was a big-time hotshot in Savannah, though most people assumed he was just a rich business owner. Those who knew what he was really into tended to keep their mouth shut.

The buzz of her phone made Harris jump. She stopped rubbing her calf and flipped over the device to see who was calling. Clementine. She was either calling to ask where she was or to chew her out because she already knew. Harris sent it to voicemail, knowing she'd regret that later.

Harris had tracked Gibson down on her own, but she was only ahead of the game by a few minutes. Soon enough, Savannah PD would show up to arrest him, and Harris couldn't take that chance. She wanted to do this on her own.

What was that she'd said about idiocy and no regard for one's own well-being?

The detective pushed the thought out of her head while she shouldered open her door. She had her phone, her badge, her gun, and a hope that they would be enough. She banked on the fact that being in the restaurant would help avoid any kind of scene. Most criminals didn't want to draw too much attention to themselves, and Aguilar didn't seem to be an exception. He emerged when it was convenient for him and stayed out of the limelight when it wasn't.

That's how he'd stayed out of jail for so long.

As Harris crossed the road, she compiled a list of scenarios in her head. It's not like she didn't know she was being stupid by going after Gibson alone. But the reward outweighed the risk. She'd get the guy and be able to look Aguilar in the eyes at the same time.

What would she say? She was still working on that part. She had a feeling it'd come to her when the time was right.

Harris resisted the urge to draw her pistol before she walked through the door. It'd put her at a disadvantage if they were lying in wait for her, but unholstering her weapon around innocent civilians could escalate the situation in a way she couldn't handle on her own. Risking her own life was one thing; risking someone else's was another.

Outside the door to the steakhouse, Harris took one sharp breath and blew it out, releasing a portion of her amped-up nerves into the air. It grounded her momentarily, and that was all the reprieve she allowed herself before pulling the handle and walking inside.

The restaurant was dimly lit, despite the blazing sun outside the windows. The staff had drawn the shades, but the art deco lamps emitted a hint of light. It took a moment for her eyes to adjust, and her fingers twitched to her gun out of reflex.

When the room came into view, Harris relaxed. The restaurant was half full, with members of the staff darting from one table to the next, trying to keep up with everyone's requests. There was a dim murmur of conversation, and an occasional laugh would break through.

A blond woman in her early twenties with pink cheeks and dark eyes walked up to her. "Detective Harris?"

Whatever had uncoiled inside of her had grown taut again. "Yes?"

"I can take you to your table."

Without waiting for an answer, the waitress sped off toward a table in the back. Harris followed her, dodging servers and patrons, and attempting not to knock anything over as she tried to keep up. The room was packed to the limit with tables, which Harris took to mean that it maxed out in the evenings and on weekends. She had no interest in ever dining around that many people.

Once they reached the back of the restaurant, the woman slid a curtain to the side to reveal a private room. Inside were half a dozen men, including Francisco Aguilar. He was already standing with his arms splayed to the side.

"Detective Harris. I thought you'd never come inside."

The table chuckled as the waitress retreated, leaving Harris to deal with the men on her own. On the one hand, the half-full restaurant eased her mind. On the other, she didn't like the idea of cutting herself off from her escape route by entering the room.

She scanned the faces around the table. She didn't recognize anyone except for Aguilar, which meant Gibson wasn't here. Was Aguilar covering for him, distracting Harris while he escaped out the back? Harris leaned back to scan the restaurant again. She didn't see the man anywhere.

Harris returned her gaze to Aguilar. He'd dressed in a burgundy suit with a navy shirt underneath. She could just make out a white paisley pattern from her vantage point. It looked good on him. Then again, no one had ever tried to argue he was anything other than handsome. With his tailored suits, his bronze skin, and his perfect stubble, Francisco Aguilar turned heads wherever he went.

The worst part was, he knew it. Aguilar's arrogance had gained him everything he'd ever wanted in life, from his home-grown shipping business to the loyalty of his men to the affection of his women. While Harris had never met him face to face before, she had met men like him. Their confidence was intoxicating. You gave them what they wanted because they expected it from you. Disappointing them never even crossed your mind.

"Please, sit." Aguilar motioned to one of his men, who stood and held the chair out for her.

"No thanks."

"I insist."

"That's too damn bad."

The mood in the room shifted. Harris could feel it in the way the hairs on her arms stood on end. No one made any quick movements, but each of the men at the table imperceptibly tilted their heads as if to ask Aguilar if he wanted one of them to take care of her.

Aguilar smiled, and though it seemed genuine, she could feel the power behind it. Was he annoyed by her defiance, or impressed? Was he willing to risk getting his hands dirty to make a point, or would he let it go?

Harris banked on the fact that Aguilar was smart, and it paid off. He sat down and folded his hands in front of him. "Suit yourself."

"Where is he?"

"Who?"

Harris rolled her eyes. Folded her arms. "I've decided you're not an idiot, Mr. Aguilar. I hope you can do me the same courtesy."

His smile broadened. "Fair enough, Detective Harris. For clarification's sake, I assume you're looking for Mr. Gibson?"

"Correct."

"He'll join us in a moment." Aguilar nodded to the man on his left, who stood and left the room. "Are you sure you don't want to sit?"

"I'm sure."

For the first time, Aguilar looked less than bemused by her attitude. "I was sorry to hear about Detective Klein. I sent flowers to his wife on the day of the funeral. He wasn't young, of course, but it's still a tragic loss for the community."

Harris ground her teeth together. "Cut the bullshit."

"I promise you I'm not bullshitting." The man on his right smirked, and even Aguilar's mouth twitched up at the corners. "I'm going to miss David. What happened to him was unfortunate for all of us."

Before Harris could form a retort, the man who'd left earlier returned with another man in tow. This newcomer was taller and leaner, but that's not what caught Harris' attention. A bandage wound its way around his forearm, and blood seeped through his shirt from a shoulder wound.

If Harris had any doubt Gibson was the guy who'd attacked her, it was gone now.

"Stanley Gibson." She pulled her handcuffs out. "You're under arrest for aggravated assault of an officer of the law."

Gibson didn't run. He didn't resist. In fact, he turned around and put his arms behind his back. Harris only hesitated for a moment before wrapping the metal cuffs around his wrists. She ratcheted them closed tight enough to make the man grunt, but he didn't say a word of protest.

Now that Harris had Gibson in custody, she felt like there was a shield between her and Aguilar. She turned to face the man. "Why are you doing this?"

"Mr. Gibson and I talked." Aguilar's voice was somber, but it sounded practiced. "He had a change of heart. He regrets his actions. He wants to turn his life around."

"Is that so?"

Gibson finally decided to speak for himself. "It is."

"See? He's already on the road to reformation."

"What's your play here?" Harris asked. "Just between the two of us."

"You promise? Just between the two of us?"

"I promise."

Aguilar steepled his fingers. He thought for a moment. Really pondered the question. When he had formulated his thoughts, he sat back in his chair. Completely relaxed. "I want to prove to you I'm not a bad guy. I know my reputation, and I'm here to tell you you're wrong about me."

Harris had plenty to say to that, but she bit her tongue.

"I'd like to work with you, Detective Harris," Aguilar said.

"The feeling's not mutual."

"Come on." He spread his arms wide again. "If it was good enough for David, it would be good enough for you. He held you in high esteem, you know. He told me that. On more than one occasion."

"You're lying." Harris gripped Gibson's arm until the man cried out.

"I'm not. But I see you're not ready to have that conversation." He frowned, like a father disappointed in his daughter. "Perhaps the time will come soon enough. Until then, I'll see you around, Detective Harris."

Harris stayed rooted to the spot. She knew Aguilar was taunting her, but she didn't know with what. She'd never believe David would willingly work with the man, but she couldn't write off the possibility that he'd been trying to get close to Aguilar.

As Harris hauled Gibson out of the restaurant, one thing became abundantly clear.

David had been hiding much more from her than she ever could've thought possible.

24

"YOU GAVE HIM YOUR NUMBER?"

Cassie couldn't hide the smile on her face. She had left the hospital imme-diately after getting the address of the volunteer worker from Alan Wolcott. As soon as she entered the car, she relayed the entire conversation to Jason, from start to finish.

"Of course not." Cassie laughed at the look of relief on his face. "That guy was a creep."

"Then who's number did you give?"

"I almost considered giving him yours." Cassie teased as Jason blanched. "But that guy one hundred percent would've sent an unsolicited dick pic, and no one deserves that. I took his phone and put in all zeroes. He won't know until later when he tries to text me."

"Nice." Jason leaned forward and looked up at the building in front of them. It had been about a fifteen-minute drive from the hospital to the woman's apartment complex. He checked his watch. "It's almost dinnertime. There's no guarantee she'll be home. How do you think she'll react when we question her about getting fired?"

"Not sure." Cassie got out of the car and waited for Jason to catch up to her before she continued. "It's not like we know much about her. Her name is Charli—as in Charlie without the *e*—and she's covered in tattoos and piercings. She's super hot according to my new friend Alan, but she's got a problem with authority. Which he also found super hot."

Jason rolled his eyes. "I'm liking this guy more and more."

"If she can help us figure out what happened with Don Chichetti while he was at Tulane, maybe we'll be able to figure out what happened to him at UMC. And if he's connected to Jasmine, Mark, the woman from my dream, and all the others."

Jason motioned for Cassie to step into the elevator before he followed. He pressed the button for the seventh floor and didn't speak until the doors closed with a *whoosh*. "We don't have much to go on. We're miles away from Jasmine. How could she be connected?"

Cassie shrugged. She didn't know either. But she did know they had a responsibility to follow any leads, and the line connecting Jasmine to the volunteer was a straight one, even if they didn't see its true meaning yet. Unfortunately, something inside her said the answers they were looking for were back at the hospital with the Ghost Doctor.

The elevator *dinged* and opened. Once they oriented themselves, Cassie led the charge down the hallway to apartment 718. She and Jason hadn't practiced what they would say, but then again, they didn't really know what they were after.

Anything, Cassie thought. *Anything that helps us figure out whether Jasmine's death was a mistake.*

Kiki said she wanted answers. Cassie could understand that. She still had so many questions about David, even if she fought to drive them from her mind during every waking minute. Because what would answers get them? Just more questions.

Why did David have to die? Why did Jasmine? Those questions didn't have a satisfying conclusion, and if anyone knew that it was Cassie. Why did people kill? Why did people have to die before they could grow old and lead a full life?

Jason's sharp knock drew Cassie out of her thoughts. She wished she could've shared them with him, but she knew better than to add to his burden. He was taking this investigation well enough, but she caught the sadness in his eyes when he didn't think she was looking.

After a second knock, they heard a muffled voice from the other side of the door. A few seconds later, a lock slid back, and the door cracked open. A chain kept the door from swinging wide.

The woman's voice was quiet. Confused. "Can I help you?"

She was the exact opposite of what Alan had described. She had short, straight, blond hair and bright blue eyes. Her skin looked like porcelain, and her makeup was light. Cassie saw the barest hint of pink eyeshadow without any eyeliner. There was a natural beauty to her that emanated softness and fragility. Her tank top made her look even tinier and revealed the fact that she didn't have any visible tattoos.

Cassie stepped into view so the woman knew she was safe. "Hi, my name is Cassie. This is Jason. I'm guessing you're not Charli?"

The woman blinked twice and then shook her head. "My name is Stephanie."

"Hi, Stephanie." Cassie put on her brightest smile. "Do you have a second? We have a couple questions about someone who might've lived here before you."

Cassie could see the woman calculating the odds. Were these people who they said they were? If she unlocked the door, would they try to come in? There must've been something in Cassie's smile that put Stephanie at ease because she nodded once, closed the door, unlatched the chain, and then swung it wide open.

Cassie didn't make a move to step forward, and the woman didn't invite them in. That was well enough because it didn't look like she had much furniture for entertaining guests. What little Cassie could see of the apartment looked spartan. There was a table and a single chair in the kitchen, and a single recliner in the living room. Beyond that was out of her view.

"Thank you." Cassie didn't allow her cheery façade to slip. "I'm guessing you haven't lived here for long?"

"About a month." Stephanie's voice was light and airy. Small. "I haven't really had time to make it mine yet."

"That's okay. I'm pretty sure I still have boxes I need to unpack that've been in my basement for years." Cassie gestured to Jason. "We're looking for a woman named Charli. We were told she lived here."

"I don't know anyone by that name, sorry."

Cassie twisted her mouth to the side. They hadn't come all this way for a dead end. "Do you know anything about the woman who used to live here? She had piercings and tattoos. She used to volunteer at the Tulane Medical Center?"

"I never met the person who lived here before me, but I think the landlord said it was a woman." Stephanie's voice remained small, but she seemed to relax. "I think she used to work at a bar, though."

"Oh?" Cassie couldn't decide if she felt elation or disappointment. Another lead was great, but she was tired of not finding anything of substance. "Do you know where it was?"

"Hang on." Stephanie retreated into her apartment, but kept the door open. She was back in less than thirty seconds, holding a glass in her hand. "There were a bunch of these left behind when she moved out. I didn't have anything with me, so I kept them."

Cassie took the glass from the woman's hands and peered down at the label. PETE'S BAR was emblazoned across the front in cherry red letters. She could see the silhouette of a pelican through the glass on the other side.

"I remember passing a Pete's Bar on the way over here," Jason said. "It's not far."

Cassie handed the glass back to the woman. "Thank you so much. This helps."

"I'm glad." She didn't smile. "I wish there was more I could do."

"It's okay. It was a long shot, anyway."

"Is she in some sort of trouble?" the woman asked. "Did she do something?"

Cassie and Jason exchanged looks. "No, she's not in trouble," Cassie said. "She might have some information about someone we know." She didn't want to give too much away, but she was hoping something might trigger Stephanie's memory. Maybe there was something else the woman had left behind in the apartment. "Since she worked at the hospital, I mean."

"Oh, okay." Stephanie hovered in the doorway, one hand on the jam and the other curled around the glass, which she clutched to her chest. "I'm sorry I couldn't be more help."

"That's okay. We appreciate your time." Cassie took a step back, and after a moment's hesitation, the woman smiled and closed the door with a soft *click*. They heard the latches slide back into place.

"Onto the next?" Jason asked her.

Cassie sighed. "Onto the next."

25

By the time they had arrived at Pete's Bar, Cassie was ready for a drink. Jason must've agreed because as soon as they sat down, he ordered himself a beer. Cassie wrinkled her nose and ordered a margarita.

Neither of them spoke until they had drained at least a quarter of their respective beverages. She could already feel the alcohol in her system. It relaxed her muscles and made the tips of her toes tingle. But it didn't lift the burden from her shoulders.

"What's our plan?" Jason asked.

Cassie looked around the establishment. It was rustic as far as bars went, but it had a certain charm. There were a few tables lined up along the back wall, but the extensive bar took up most of the room. About a dozen people were scattered down its length, either in pairs or solo. A single waiter ran the floor, and the bartender made sure everyone's drinks stayed topped up.

Cassie waited until there was a lull in orders before she caught the barkeep's attention. He sidled up to them and flung a rag over his shoulders, just like she'd seen in the movies. "I have a question for you, if you've got a second?"

"You're in luck." His smile was disarming. "I have several."

"This might take longer than several seconds."

"Doesn't it always?" He leaned against the bar and looked between the two of them. "What's on your mind?"

"We're looking for a woman who might work here," Jason supplied. "Her name was Charli?"

"Charli, yeah." He looked wistful. Cassie had seen that same look on Alan's face. "Couple of tattoos, a few piercings. She had a rough start here, but she got the hang of it, eventually."

"Rough start?"

"I don't think she'd ever been a waitress before." He chuckled. "I'm not sure she'd ever had a steady job, actually. But like I said, she got the hang of it. Turned out to be a pretty good worker in the end. We're gonna miss her."

"Did she quit?" Cassie asked.

The bartender frowned. It took him a second to respond. "She died."

"Died?" Cassie and Jason exchanged a look. "When?"

"About a month ago, I guess. Her sister came in, gave us the news."

Cassie resisted the urge to drain the rest of her margarita in one go. Another dead end. "What can you tell us about that?"

For the first time, the bartender looked dubious. "Why do you want to know?"

"Did you know Charli also volunteered at the Tulane Medical Center?"

"No, I didn't." He processed the information. "I'm kind of surprised, actually."

"Why?"

"If you saw her, you would know. I can't imagine many people being comforted by her."

"There had been some complaints," Cassie supplied. "The reason we're asking is because she got fired, and we're wondering if she knew something she shouldn't have."

"Hang on a second." The man walked the length of the bar and topped off someone's beer. He took a slip of paper from the waiter and made another margarita. On his way back, he poured two shots and grabbed a bottle of cider out of the mini fridge behind him. "Sorry about that. Where were we? Oh, yeah, Charli working at the hospital. That's news to me. Then again, I didn't know much about her. She only worked here for a couple of months. We talked a few times on breaks, but we didn't hang out. She wasn't very social."

Jason drained his beer. "Glass of water? Thanks, man." He waited until the bartender swapped his glasses. "How did you find out she died?"

"Her sister came in." He cocked his head to the side. "Well, I thought it was her sister. Maybe a cousin or something. I don't know, she didn't actually say. But they looked similar. I figured they had to be related."

"What did she tell you?"

"*Charli won't be coming in today.* I asked why. She said it was because she died. I said I was sorry. She picked up her check and left."

"You didn't ask how she died?"

"Didn't seem appropriate at the time."

"Fair enough." Jason sipped his water. "Did you get the sister's name?"

"Didn't ask. Sorry, man."

"That's okay. Thanks for your help."

The bartender pointed at Cassie's glass. "Another?"

"Just the check, please. Thanks."

Jason drained the rest of his water. They paid for their drinks, then swiveled around in their chairs and exited the bar. Outside, Cassie let the breeze play with her hair. Neither of them wanted to get back into the car. It's not like they knew where to go next.

"What are you thinking?" Jason asked. He leaned on the fender of his car. She joined him.

"I'm thinking we're at a dead end."

"No such thing."

She laughed. "I wish that were true."

"In my experience, a dead end just means we made a wrong turn. Or we're not seeing the secret passage. There's always an answer."

She smiled up at him. Bumped his shoulder with her own. "You're good at this."

"You are, too."

"I learned from the best." The words left her mouth before she knew what they meant. She was talking about David, of course. But she didn't want to. It was still too painful. "Do you think Charli is the right path?"

"I think it's interesting that she got fired and wound up dead a month later."

"I was thinking the same thing."

Jason ran a hand over his head. "Lots of people dead. We might have a coverup on our hands. Except—"

"Except that only makes sense if this had gone down in one hospital."

"And Don Chichetti upsets the balance. He connects UMC and Tulane."

"And leads us to a dead ex-volunteer."

"What the hell have we gotten ourselves into?" Jason chuckled, but she heard the nerves underneath. "What are we chasing?"

"I'm not sure. And there's a whole other dimension to this, too." Cassie waited for Jason to lift an eyebrow in question before she supplied the answer. "The Ghost Doctor."

He made a noncommittal noise.

"You don't believe me."

"Oh, I believe you." His eyes were wide, almost crazed. "But I'm not sure she has anything to do with this. Unless she can hop from one hospital to the other?"

"Not that I'm aware of." Cassie didn't finish her thought. *Then again, I'm not sure what she's capable of.*

After a moment of silence, Jason spoke again. "I keep going back to Charli. She's fired and then she dies. Something's off here."

"She could've found out something she shouldn't have." Cassie was guessing at this point. "Maybe both hospitals are dealing with an overload of malpractice lawsuits? Maybe they're working together to cover it up?"

"It's possible." Jason's tone indicated it wasn't likely. "If that's the case, then we need to find out what happened to her. But we don't have any more leads."

Cassie held up her phone. "We know a few details about her. Might be enough to find her social media profiles. If we can do that, we could track down her sister."

Jason slid off the fender. "It's worth a shot."

"Good. But I don't want to do this on my phone. We need a computer."

"You want to go back to Granny Mabel's?"

"I had somewhere else in mind."

26

THE NEW ORLEANS PUBLIC LIBRARY WAS RIGHT ACROSS THE STREET FROM THE Tulane Medical Center. It was a massive building full of books, newspapers, computers, and just about any resource they might need.

Cassie made a beeline for the bank of computers near the front entrance and snagged a station at the end. There weren't too many people milling about, but she didn't want to risk anyone seeing them cyber stalk a dead woman.

Jason pulled up a chair and watched as Cassie's fingers flew across the keyboard. "What are you looking for?"

"Anything." She tapped a few more buttons, then clicked around on the page. "First, we start with Facebook." She gestured to the computer in front of him. "You start with Twitter. Then we go from there. Instagram. YouTube. LinkedIn. Yahoo Answers."

Jason's fingers hovered over his keyboard. "Yahoo Answers?"

"Just kidding. Kind of." Cassie never took her eyes off the screen. "We need a last name and the names of her relatives. If she has the same username across all her social media accounts, like most people do, then we might find her in other places where she hasn't attached her name."

Jason took his instructions like a champ. But answers wouldn't come easily. Cassie couldn't find a single Charli on Facebook who lived in New Orleans and had worked at either Tulane or Pete's Bar. She'd even checked everyone's profile pictures, in case Charli hadn't put that information on her page. But she came back with nothing.

They kept digging. An hour passed. And then two. They couldn't find a single Charli that fit the description they'd gotten from either Alan or the bartender at Pete's. No social media presence. No work history. There wasn't even an obituary.

"It's like someone erased her," Jason said.

Cassie stretched her arms over her head. She saw Jason looking at her out of the corner of her eyes, but she found she didn't mind. "It's like she never existed."

"How is that possible?"

"It's not. Even if she had no online presence—which is pretty impossible these days—there's bound to be a relative who has one. You'd think she'd be in a picture somewhere. Some photo with all the cousins barely tolerating each other just so Grandma can hang it on her fridge."

"Which takes me back to her being erased."

"That would be difficult to do." Cassie thought for a moment. "But not impossible."

"The real question is why."

"The question is always why."

Jason continued to think out loud. "What did she know that was so big someone felt the need to erase her from the internet?"

"Something that could connect both hospitals and dozens of patients."

"Something doesn't add up." Jason had rolled up his sleeves at some point during his search, and Cassie liked the way his muscles flexed as he worked out the problem. "It's not just that we can't find her. It's that we can't find anyone even related to her. No one is talking about her being dead."

"No one we can find."

"Maybe she didn't have anyone. Maybe she was all alone."

Cassie bobbed her head. "That would make sense. She'd be an easier target to get rid of if that were true. But we know she had a sister or a cousin who picked up her check."

"Or someone who pretended to be her sister." He shook his head. "And if that's the case, then it puts us back at square one."

"Another wrong turn." Cassie echoed his words from earlier. "Maybe we went down the wrong fork in the road."

He looked at her out of the corner of his eye. "Meaning?"

"Meaning there was another reason why I wanted to come to the New Orleans Public Library."

"Oh?"

Cassie stood, knowing Jason would follow. She looked for the signs that would point her in the right direction, and once she found them, she headed for the section housing the city's local history. It was a robust area, and Cassie's heart quickened at the chance of finding answers.

Jason picked a book up off the shelf. "You think Charli is going to be in a yearbook from 1923?"

"No." Cassie laughed and took the book out of his hands, placing it back on the shelf with reverence. "I think we need to set Charli aside for a minute. *Just a minute,*" she said, when he raised an eyebrow. "I want to know more about our Ghost Doctor."

"I can't say I'm not intrigued. Where do we start?"

"She dressed like someone from the 1940s. And she looks like a doctor. I'm guessing there weren't too many female doctors back then. We're bound to find her."

"UMC isn't that old of a building." Jason frowned. Then his eyes widened. "But Tulane is old. It used to be a medical university."

"How do you know all this?"

Jason shrugged, but pride shone through his smile. "My dad likes history. Sometimes I remember what he says."

Cassie tapped a finger on her chin. "We never saw the Ghost Doctor at Tulane, but she obviously isn't from UMC if it's that new."

"Don't ghosts haunt where they die?"

"Not always." Cassie looked around and lowered her voice. No one was paying attention to them, but she didn't want to risk being overheard. "They go where they have particular ties, like where they died, where they're buried, even where their family is, even if they've moved across the country."

"And you said the Ghost Doctor is different from all the others, right? So, maybe she's stronger, which means—"

"—she's able to move around more freely." Goosebumps erupted over Cassie's skin. "If she started at Tulane, something could've pulled her away from there. Then she found UMC and stuck around."

"And just because you've only seen her at UMC doesn't mean she hasn't traveled back to Tulane."

A grin erupted over Cassie's face. "Are you starting to take my Ghost Doctor theory seriously now?"

"I'm not *not* taking it seriously," he said. "But we still haven't proven anything. And even if we figure out she's responsible for the uptick in murders, it doesn't mean we'll be able to do anything about it. Unless we can exorcise the whole hospital."

Cassie had never done an exorcism, and she told Jason as much. "Or we figure out what she wants and help her move on."

"But we can only do that if—"

"—we know who she is."

Cassie loved being on the same page as Jason. It reminded her of working with David, which could be as effortless as breathing. She and David had cultivated their relationship over an entire decade, and though David trusted her, he sometimes treated her like a kid. Jason, on the other hand, treated her as an equal.

"What's the goofy grin for?"

"Nothing." Cassie tried to stifle it, but she couldn't. And she didn't really want to. "I'm just glad you're here." Her eyes grew wide. "I mean, not because of the circumstances, obviously. I wish things were different. I wish we didn't have to be doing this. But since we are, I'm just glad it's you."

"I'm glad it's you, too."

Cassie held Jason's gaze for as long as she could before looking away, her face aflame. She kneeled and began perusing the bottom shelves. "I'll start down here. You start up there. Let's find anything we can on the history of the Tulane Medical Center."

Their second search proved more fruitful than the first. After about fifteen minutes, Jason ushered Cassie over to a table and splayed a thick volume in front of her. It smelled ancient and made her nose tingle, but there was something oddly satisfying about flipping through the yellowed pages.

"This one has pretty much everything you need to know about the medical center." Jason was bursting with pride. "There are a few books over there, but none of them had this." He flipped about two-thirds of the way through the book and pointed at a staff registry.

Cassie frowned. "But no pictures."

Jason held up a finger. He turned a few pages and swept his hands out in front of him as if to say *ask and you shall receive*. "This is Doctor Emma Thornton. She started off as a midwife, but she soon became a licensed physician.

She wasn't the first woman to become a doctor in New Orleans, but she was the first at Tulane."

Cassie leaned over the book. There was a crystal-clear, black-and-white photograph of the woman. She wore a black dress with a high collar. Her face fell in shadow, and she'd pinned her hair back into a high bun.

In other words, everything about her was wrong.

"This isn't the Ghost Doctor."

"I figured as much." Jason hadn't lost any of his enthusiasm. "She seemed a little too old. She received her license in 1876. So, I kept looking." He flipped the page. "Dr. Dorothea Bridge. She was Thornton's apprentice, eventually taking over her practice when Thornton retired."

The woman kept the same style as her mentor, only her dress was the customary white. "That's also not her."

Jason held up another finger, dramatically waiting a few seconds too long before turning the page again. "Bridge took on her own apprentice. Dr. Shelley Marie Cohen. She was licensed in 1932 and practiced until her untimely death in 1947."

Cassie sucked in a breath. She looked down at the page in front of her, and the Ghost Doctor stared back. She wore a gray dress with a jacket over the top. She'd pinned her dark hair back in curls. Even her hazel eyes were exactly as Cassie remembered them. And just as hypnotizing as in real life.

"That's her."

"Yeah?" Jason sat down next to Cassie. "You're sure?"

"Absolutely." She drew the book closer. "Does it say how she died?"

"She was administering to her patients when there was a gas leak. They couldn't evacuate the hospital in time. She refused to leave until everyone was out. She and twelve of her patients died."

"How?"

"They suffocated." Jason's voice was somber now. All the excitement from earlier was gone. "Painless, as far as deaths go, but no less terrifying."

"And no less tragic."

Jason seemed to sense Cassie needed a minute to absorb what he'd found. He left her to read through the woman's biography on her own while he perused the other books.

Dr. Shelley Marie Cohen had been a remarkable woman. She was twenty-eight when she became a licensed practitioner. She had known Dr. Thornton, but had never worked underneath her. That responsibility had fallen to Dr.

Bridge, who had treated Shelley Marie with a kind but firm hand. All three women knew their colleagues and the public would scrutinize them more than any of their male colleagues, so they worked twice as hard to prove themselves. Their track records were impeccable, and the community at large had come to respect them.

But that didn't mean Dr. Cohen walked an easy path. She never had as many patients as her male colleagues, and she wasn't allowed to work on the more interesting cases. She had a particular interest in the spread of viral infections, but she could never get close enough to study them on her own.

Her superior bedside manner meant she often had to break terrible news to patients and their family members. After a prominent New Orleanian socialite found herself on death's door, she begged Dr. Cohen to help her. Within days, the woman recovered and returned to her life as though nothing had ever happened.

Historians now believe Dr. Cohen merely examined the woman and found something another doctor did not, but at the time, rumors spread like wildfire. Whispers told tales of how Dr. Cohen had made a deal with Death. If she looked upon you favorably, she would spare you. But if she sat by your bed, took your hand in her own, and leaned close, then you knew your time was up.

Though there was no proof, some historians believed someone had set the gas leak. If there had been an explosion, as the arsonist had intended, it would've destroyed the tools used to open the gas valve, thus destroying the evidence. As it was, no one was convicted of causing the gas leak or killing thirteen innocent people. That day, New Orleans lost a pillar of their community and a brilliant doctor.

Cassie brushed a tear from her cheek. Dr. Cohen had been an exceptional doctor, but in a time when science bordered on the mystical, they had heralded her as some sort of angel of death. It made sense if she continued that role after her death.

Jason sat down next to her. "Find anything?"

"I'm not sure." Cassie stared at Dr. Cohen's picture. "She was amazing at what she did. People back then didn't understand that what she did was science, not magic. They thought she had superpowers, but she was just a normal person."

"You sound disappointed."

"I'm confused." Cassie looked up at him, not bothering to hide the tears. "I expected to find someone who had been cruel and inhumane. But she loved every single one of her patients."

Jason pointed to the book. "History doesn't always tell us the whole truth. Sometimes we have to find that out on our own."

"How?"

"Usually by talking to those that came before us." He grimaced. "Though there's no guarantee we'll be able to find anyone who knew Dr. Cohen well enough to give us answers."

"And if we can't get answers, then we can't figure out what she wants. Which means there's no way we can help her move on." Cassie blew a piece of hair off her face. "Another dead end."

"Another wrong turn." Jason laid a hand on her arm. It was warm and comforting. "But I thought of something else."

Cassie closed the book on Dr. Cohen, both literally and figuratively. "What?"

"Charli was a real person. She existed somewhere. Otherwise she wouldn't have been able to get a job."

It took Cassie a second to catch on. "The hospital. She'd need to give them some personal information to volunteer there."

"I texted Vanessa. She said most of the volunteer workers go through one or two major organizations." He looked at his watch. "It's too late now, but we could stop by tomorrow. See if they can help us figure out what happened to her."

"Sounds like a plan."

Cassie wished she felt something other than disappointment, but at every turn they made, an obstacle rose to force them into changing course. She was glad Charli wasn't a total dead end, but the Ghost Doctor remained an elusive mystery.

One she was tired of trying to solve.

27

JASON AND CASSIE STAYED IN THE CAR UNTIL SOMEONE UNLOCKED THE FRONT door of Dana's Friends, a non-profit volunteer organization in the heart of downtown New Orleans. The bank to its right and the grocery store on its left dwarfed the building, but the bright green sign in the window was enough to catch attention.

The temperature had dropped overnight, and even though it would hit the mid-sixties by that afternoon, the early morning was dim and wet. A steady drizzle made the city look hazy, and the ice-cold drops of water sent goose-bumps skittering across Cassie's skin when they finally exited the vehicle and rushed across the street.

Jason pushed through the open door with Cassie on his heels. It was a cramped room, with three large tables and a smattering of chairs. Posters and bulletin boards covered every inch of wall space. Several people huddled in the back over paper coffee cups. When the bell chimed, a woman with short curly hair and golden-brown skin set down her cup and greeted them. Up close, Cassie saw her coiled hair had streaks of magenta. She wore large, round glasses that made her look like she belonged back in the 1970s.

"Hey there." Her voice had a southern twang that made Cassie think of cowboy hats and Texas longhorns. "How are y'all today?"

Jason ran his hands up and down his arms. "Could do with a little more heat out there."

"I hear ya." The woman craned her neck to look through the front windows. "Supposed to stop raining at some point, but I'll believe it when I see it."

"My name is Jason." He held out his hand. "This is Cassie. We're hoping you can help us with something."

She shook both their hands. "My name's Poppy, and I'll do my damnedest."

"We're trying to contact one of your volunteers. Charli?"

The woman's mouth twisted into a sympathetic smile. "Unless you have a warrant of some sort, I can't give away anyone's personal information."

"We're not cops," Cassie said.

"And we're not looking for personal information," Jason supplied. "We just want to contact her."

"Unfortunately, that falls under personal information." When the woman shook her head, her curls bounced. "I'm sorry, but there's nothing I can do."

"Can you at least tell us if she worked here?" Cassie didn't hide the desperation in her voice. "Her name was Charli, without the *e*, and she had tattoos and piercings."

"I know who you're talking about." Poppy cast a glance around the room. "Maybe you want to look around for a bit? See if you're interested in helping us out sometime?"

Jason seemed to catch on before Cassie did. "Of course, thank you."

"Let me know if you need anything else."

Cassie waited until the woman walked away before turning to Jason. "Another bust?"

"Maybe not." He pointed to the walls. "Who knows what we might find."

Cassie took a step closer to one of the bulletin boards. There was no order to the chaos. People had pinned business cards to the middle of posters, which sat atop informational handouts. The topics ranged from insurance to proper care to women's rights and rampant racism in the health industry.

Then there were photos of the volunteers mixed in with everything else. Sometimes they were grouped in front of the hospital or standing over someone in a hospital bed, offering them food or reading them a book. It looked like Dana's Friends also organized fundraising opportunities throughout the city, from 5K runs to block parties to book sales.

Jason pressed a finger to a picture of a group of women standing outside a library pushing shopping carts full of books. Three of them were older, at least in their fifties. One of them was in her late twenties. Black hair. Tattoos and piercings. A forced smile on her face. She looked like she was trying to hide behind one of the other women.

"That's gotta be Charli, right?" Jason asked.

Cassie leaned closer. "Who does that look like to you?"

Jason placed his face next to hers. Their cheeks were almost touching. When he stood back, his eyes were wide. "Stephanie."

Cassie kept looking at the picture. It was hard to tell because they were night and day, but the two shared some similarities. The slope of their nose. The point of their chin. The angle of their cheekbones.

They kept looking and found two other pictures of Charli, though none of them were clear enough to make a hard call. It seemed she hated being photographed and usually turned her face to the side or hid in the back of a group. Still, there was no denying it. The two were hauntingly similar.

"This doesn't make sense." Jason pointed to a picture of Charli hoisting a bag of bottles during a can drive. "Stephanie said she had no idea who the woman was."

"People lie, you know."

"But why?" He shook his head. "I don't mean why do people lie in general. I mean, why would she want to lie? To us?"

"She only half lied. She said she didn't know Charli, but she sent us to Pete's Bar. Maybe she wanted to help but was afraid to."

"She might know more than she let on, then."

Cassie ran her fingers through her hair. "What if she's Charli's sister? Like the guy at the bar said? She could've been the one to tell them Charli died. The one to pick up her check."

"What if Charli's not dead?" Jason grabbed the back of his neck and squeezed. His entire forehead screwed up in thought. "What if she and Stephanie know something, and they were too afraid to tell us?"

"We need to go back."

He nodded. "But how are we going to get her to talk?"

"We'll worry about that when we get there."

Cassie twisted toward the door, but as she turned, the words HOSPITAL and JUSTICE jumped out at her from a poster near the front window. She stopped so abruptly that Jason nearly knocked her off her feet.

"Sorry—"

"Look." She pointed at the words that caught her attention. "Justice for Naomi. Hospital malpractice. Don't become the next victim."

"Call if you have any information," Jason continued, "or if a loved one has died under suspicious circumstances at UMC, Tulane, Curahealth, etc. Anonymous tips welcome."

Cassie looked at Jason and saw her own expression reflected on his face. What had started off as an investigation into Jasmine's death for the sake of the family's sanity had exploded into a case of multiple deaths across several hospitals, with no tangible evidence connecting them.

"I'm taking a picture of this." She held up her phone. "We can call the phone number after we talk to Stephanie again."

Jason nodded, but didn't speak. Cassie wondered if he was thinking the same thing she was.

What have we gotten ourselves into?

28

As they rounded the corner to Stephanie's apartment, Cassie and Jason pulled up short at the exact same time. She could feel his brain spinning with possibilities in tandem with hers, but it took her a full thirty seconds to understand what she was looking at.

The door to apartment 718 was wide open. A male voice emanated from somewhere inside. Pauses in conversation made Cassie think the man was on the phone. The silence between his sentences was deafening. Something was wrong.

Jason approached the door first. Cassie stood behind him and pushed up on her tippy-toes to see over his shoulder. Everything looked as it had yesterday—the kitchen table, a single chair, even the lone recliner. A pair of pint glasses sat on the counter. They had Pete's Bar emblazoned across the front.

A man emerged from the back room. He held a phone to his ear. Gray hair and a matching beard covered most of his face and head. His beady black eyes caught sight of them. His mouth turned down. He wore a t-shirt and a pair of sweatpants. Either he'd been lounging, or he didn't care about appearances.

The man hung up the phone and eyed the two newcomers. "Can I help you?"

"We're looking for the woman who lives here." Jason's voice was soft. "Stephanie?"

"She don't live here no more." The man's voice was gruff, but not unkind. Cassie got the impression he lacked people skills. "Moved out last night. Last minute."

"Do you know why?"

"Didn't ask." He looked them up and down. "You interested in renting?"

"No, sorry." Jason hesitated. "Did she mention where she was going?"

"Like I said, didn't ask." He never took his eyes off them. "What's it to you?"

Cassie took a step forward but made sure she didn't cross the threshold into the apartment. "We think she might be in trouble."

Her bet had paid off. The man softened. "What kind of trouble?"

"We're not sure." Cassie twisted her fingers together. "We talked to her last night because we're looking for her sister."

"Or someone we think is her sister," Jason corrected. "Apparently she lived in this apartment before Stephanie?"

"She's been living here for about ten months." The man gestured around him. "Didn't have any roommates that I knew of. If she did, I woulda charged more."

"Have you ever seen a girl with dark hair, tattoos, and piercings come out of here?" she asked.

He shrugged. "Mighta. Stephanie was strange. Got a few complaints about her screamin' and yellin', but I told 'em that's not my problem. Told 'em they could talk to her if they wanted her to be quiet. I'm not their parent. Kids these days don't know how to talk to each other. Always want everyone else to solve their problems for them."

Cassie gave him a sympathetic nod. "Why do you say she was strange?"

"Don't know." He scratched his beard. "Just was."

Jason gestured to the furniture and the glasses. "And she just packed up and left?"

"More like just left." He shrugged. "Told me I could sell anything she left behind. Don't bother me none."

"We're really trying to find her," Cassie implored. "Do you have any information that could help us?"

He eyed the pair of them. "Seems like she don't want to be found."

"It's important."

"I'm sure it is." He shrugged again. "But she always paid me in cash. I don't got no information about her." He shooed them across the hall. "Now if you'll excuse me, I got an apartment to rent."

Cassie and Jason retreated to the elevator, but neither pushed the button for the ground level. They both stared at it like it would give them the answers they sought.

"None of this makes sense." Jason looked up at her, concern lining his face. "None of it."

"Charli brought Alan back to this apartment to sleep with him. She got fired and then supposedly died." Cassie held out a finger for each statement she made. "Charli and Stephanie look too similar not to be related. She helps us by pointing us to Pete's Bar. Why?"

"She had to give us something," Jason said. "The bartender would confirm Charli was dead, plus it would give her time to vacate the apartment."

"Maybe she's afraid that whatever happened to Charli would happen to her."

"Now she's in the wind with no way of tracking her down."

"Maybe we don't need to find her." Cassie gestured to her phone, to the picture she'd taken of the poster at the volunteer center. "We just need to find what she was running from."

"On to the next," Jason said. He sounded tired.

"On to the next." She watched him press the down arrow, feeling like they'd never reach the bottom of this mystery.

29

HARRIS DIDN'T BOTHER BRUSHING THE FUR OFF HER JACKET BEFORE SHE knocked on Chief Clementine's door. There was no way this meeting would go in her favor, so why delay the inevitable? The detective rapped her knuckles on the door twice and heard a reply from within.

"Come in."

Harris pushed through the door and closed it behind her. Something else she was sure of: This wasn't a meeting she wanted anyone else to overhear. She had crossed the line yesterday, and she knew it.

"Sit."

Clementine didn't look up as she barked the order. Her voice was sharp as a knife, and it hit Harris dead center. Despite her crusty exterior, Harris hated disappointing people. She had a lot of respect for the Chief, and even though she didn't regret her actions, she regretted the trouble she'd caused.

"I trusted you, Adelaide." Clementine finally lifted her head. The familiarity of hearing her first name made Harris want to sink deeper into her chair. "I asked you not to be rash. You told me you wouldn't. You lied to me."

"I was doing my job, Chief." Harris tried not to sound like a petulant child and failed. "Gibson attacked me. I arrested him."

"Without backup." Clementine held up a hand before Harris could argue. "It was stupid and reckless. *You* were stupid and reckless."

"I'm sorry."

"Are you?" She shook her head. "Because I don't think you are. If you could go back in time and do it differently, would you?"

What was the point of lying? "No."

"Gibson told us you had a chat with Aguilar before you cuffed him. What did you talk about?"

"We talked about David." Harris could see the barrage of curses forming on Clementine's lips. "He brought it up first. I didn't say anything. I wasn't there to goad him."

"Weren't you?"

Harris sighed. Rubbed her temples with her fingers. She knew exactly why she'd charged into the steakhouse, and it wasn't just to arrest Gibson. If she was being honest with herself, it was because she wanted to look into Aguilar's eyes. She wanted to see for herself if he was the one who'd killed David. But she'd found out a lot more than she'd bargained for. "Was David undercover?"

Clementine's eyebrows pinched together. The question had clearly taken her off guard. Harris could see the calculations behind her eyes. "Why do you ask?"

"Something Aguilar said." Harris pressed the issue. "Was he?"

"No. Not to my knowledge."

"Wouldn't you know if he was? You're the Chief."

"As you're well aware, Detective Harris, sometimes cops like to go rogue."

"Do you think David went rogue?"

Clementine leaned back in her chair. She looked more than tired. Exhausted down to the bone. "If you asked me that a week ago, I would've said no."

"And now?"

"And now I don't have an honest answer."

"I didn't like the way Aguilar knew something that I didn't." Harris ran a hand down her face. "Something about David."

"He could've been messing with you." Clementine shrugged. "Someone like Aguilar gets off on manipulation. He enjoys pulling people's strings." Hardness crept into her voice. "And you fell right into his trap."

"What do you want me to say?" Harris asked. "That I'm sorry?"

"It'd be a start."

"Then I'm sorry." She leaned forward in her chair, shifted her weight to the balls of her feet. She could spring up at any second. Always at the ready. "I am, but you're right. I would do it all over again. Just to look him in the eyes. He knows something, Chief. I know he does."

"I'm not saying you're wrong, but we have to play this smart. He gave up Gibson too quickly." Clementine huffed. "The man gave one of the most detailed confessions I've ever seen in my life. And all we had to do was give him a pen and some paper."

"Then Aguilar wants Gibson in jail. Why?"

"Could be to deliver a message," Clementine said. "But he's got more convenient ways to do that."

"Unless it's the type of message that needs to be delivered by someone like Gibson." Harris teetered for a moment and then leaned back in her chair again. "Or Gibson is rallying the troops."

"Either way, we don't have any hard proof." Clementine glared at her. "And now Aguilar knows you're onto him."

Harris waved the comment away, trying to ignore the way the Chief's piercing gaze made her heart beat faster. "He already knew that."

"But now he's looking directly at you." Clementine pounded her fist on the desk. "Jesus, Adelaide. We could've used you to get close to him. Especially if what he said was true about David. You went in there hotheaded, ready to fight all of them single-handedly. You think he's going to believe you had a change of heart if you try to approach him down the line?"

For the first time since Harris left the restaurant, doubt creeped in. Clementine was telling the truth. Harris had wanted to go toe-to-toe with all of them, starting with Gibson and ending with Aguilar. She'd made sure he knew what kind of cop she was. No fear. No remorse. No bullshit.

Harris hung her head. "So, what now?"

"You're suspended."

Harris' head snapped up. "What?"

"You heard me." Clementine pointed at her desk. "Hand over your badge and your gun. Two weeks."

"You're joking."

"Do I look like I'm joking?" Clementine raised a single eyebrow, as if daring Harris to question her again. "Badge and gun. Now."

Harris stood. She unclipped her badge. Set it on the desk. Pulled out her gun. Set it on the desk. She stood there, arms hanging at her side, feeling small and stupid and helpless. What was she if she wasn't a cop? What was she if she couldn't solve David's murder?

"What am I supposed to do now?"

Clementine's mouth was still a hard line, but her eyes softened. "Take a break. Go on vacation. Read a book. Find some inner peace, Adelaide. This is temporary. I need you back at peak performance. When we're ready to take down Aguilar—*if* we can pin this on him—then I want you there to cuff him yourself."

Harris' phone buzzed. She pulled it out. Unknown number. She stuck it back in her pocket. Looked up at Clementine. She didn't know what to say.

"Deal?" Clementine asked.

Harris knew she was right. She'd let her anger get the best of her. Now Aguilar knew she'd stop at nothing to pin him. She was safer if she was out of the limelight. She was safer if she wasn't on duty. Otherwise, she might end up like Officer Steve Warren. Or Detective David Klein.

"Deal."

"Good." Clementine pulled Harris' badge and gun toward her and dropped them in a desk drawer. She didn't look up again. "Dismissed."

Harris walked out of the room feeling more lost than when she'd entered. As she pulled the door shut, her phone buzzed again. It was the same unknown number. She thought about declining it again. Probably just spam.

She hit *answer* instead.

"Harris."

"Detective Harris?" The man's voice was high and panicked. "It's Randall."

Harris paused. It took her a moment to place the name. Randall Sherman. The witness they'd been planning to meet with the night David died. He was potentially the last one to see David alive. "Randall?" She was still processing. "I thought you might be dead."

"They tried." His voice quivered. "I'm faster than I look."

"Lucky you." She didn't bother to keep the bitterness out of her voice.

"I heard about Detective Klein." A pause. "I'm sorry."

"Are you safe?"

He laughed. "For now."

"Why are you calling me?"

Another pause. Confused silence. "I'll tell you what I told David. I have information on Aguilar. Information that could put him away." He let his words hang in the air. "Forever."

"That's good to hear." Harris bypassed her desk and walked straight to her car. "Tell me where to meet you."

30

By the time Jason and Cassie pulled up to the curb outside a lavish green-and-cream Queen Anne-style house, someone was already there to meet them. Thankfully, the earlier rain had subsided and the sun peeked out from the clouds.

After leaving the volunteer center, Cassie had called the number on the poster. The woman on the other end of the line introduced herself as Marsha, Naomi's mother. It hadn't taken Cassie more than two minutes of explanation before Marsha had agreed to meet with them. She'd given them her address, but Cassie would've known which house it was from a mile away.

Marsha had filled the yard with posters screaming #JUSTICEFORNAOMI in bold purple letters. Purple and white streamers hung from the trees, and if the wind caught them just right, it looked like they were dancing.

Marsha waved from the end of the driveway. She wore a white t-shirt with a picture of Naomi in the center. Her skin was a dull beige, mottled with age spots borne from too much sun-exposure. She was fit for her age, which Cassie guessed to be around fifty, and wore a diamond bracelet and matching necklace. From the house alone, Cassie could tell the family was several tax brackets above her league. She felt cheap just pulling up to the curb.

"Cassie?" Marsha leaned down to investigate the car. "And Jason?"

"That's us, ma'am." Cassie got out of the car and waited for Jason to join her. "Thank you for taking the time to talk to us."

"Thank you for calling." Marsha put her hand on Cassie's arm and squeezed. "Naomi sent you to us, I just know it."

Cassie kept a smile plastered on her face. Naomi had definitely not sent her, but she wouldn't say that out loud. "I hope so."

Marsha didn't move to invite them inside or even onto the porch. She shifted her weight to one hip and placed her hand on her waist. "You said you had a family member who died, too?"

"My cousin," Jason said, forcing Marsha to shift her focus to him. "Jasmine. We don't know if something happened, but the whole situation feels off."

"And we've encountered a few other families who recently lost their loved ones under strange circumstances." Cassie gestured to the woman's shirt. "Can I ask what happened to Naomi?"

"She had a tumor in her stomach. It was benign. She went through surgery. The doctor took care of it. There was a chance another tumor would grow back, but they didn't seem worried about her chances. She was only twenty-six."

"Were there complications from her surgery?" Jason asked.

"That's what the doctors said, but I don't believe it." Marsha brushed a piece of hair out of her face, but Cassie saw it for what it was—a nervous habit fueled by rage and frustration. "She was fine after the surgery. They were going to keep her for a couple nights because she was in a lot of pain. But she was recovering. Then one day, she got worse."

"Do you know why?"

"No." Marsha looked at Cassie and shrugged. "I was with her that night. She was in so much pain. She started crying and talking to someone who wasn't there. In the middle of it all, she had a heart attack and died."

"Talking to someone who wasn't there?" Cassie looked at Jason. Her previous theory reignited against her better judgement. "Did she say who? Did she describe them?"

Marsha frowned and looked at Cassie like she had a screw loose. "She was out of her mind. I think it was all the drugs in her system. She didn't actually see anyone."

"Of course." Cassie smiled to reassure her that no, of course she didn't think her daughter had been talking to someone who wasn't there. "How did the hospital respond?"

"We requested an autopsy, and we'll be suing them for malpractice, of course." Marsha flipped her hair again. "The money doesn't matter to us.

Justice for Naomi does." She gestured to the signs in her yard. "They thought they could settle out of court. Buy us off. They made the wrong move."

"Have you heard of any other families being offered compensation like this?"

"I know of several." She shrugged. "A few have reached out to me anonymously. Others are easy to spot. They have cars or houses or boats they never would've been able to afford before. And none of them will talk to me. Cowards."

"Some people can't afford to say no to that kind of money," Jason said. Cassie heard the hard truth of his voice past the polite exterior.

"Justice is more important than wealth." Marsha stared him down. "Lives are more important than money."

It's easy when you're the one who already has the money, Cassie thought. "Did you know someone by the name of Charli? She was a volunteer at the Tulane Medical Center."

"A girl named Charli?" Marsha scrunched up her face. "No, I would've remembered that. Besides, Naomi was at UMC."

Cassie forced a smile. "It was worth a try. Thank you so much for your time."

"Oh, before you go." Marsha handed Cassie a pamphlet she'd been carrying in her back pocket. "This is for you. We're having another rally this weekend for Naomi. Trying to spread the word. We're going to march at the hospital. You should come. We're printing sashes with the names of the people we've lost. You can write Jessie's name on it."

"Jasmine." Jason's voice didn't hold any of the kindness she'd heard earlier. He took the pamphlet. "She was my cousin."

"Of course." The woman's smile was as artificial as the whitener she used on her teeth. "Jasmine."

"Thank you for talking with us." Cassie put her hand on the doorhandle just as Jason walked around to the driver's side. "I can tell you really care about everyone you're fighting for."

And with that, Cassie punctuated her sentence with the slamming of her door.

31

Jason had a death grip on the steering wheel as he drove away from Marsha. He hit the gas and the brakes too hard, and Cassie could tell their interaction with Naomi's mom had frustrated him.

"Maybe that would've been worth it if we'd learned something new," Jason snarled.

"Maybe we didn't learn anything new." Cassie closed her eyes against the morning sun as he turned a corner. "But one part of her story stood out to me."

"The part where Naomi was talking to someone who wasn't there?"

A cloud passed overhead. Cassie opened her eyes again. "It sounds like the Ghost Doctor, if you ask me."

Jason had calmed considerably, but he hadn't relinquished his grip on the steering wheel. He cast a glance at her, and she saw something close to sympathy in his eyes. But for what? "I'm having a hard time believing a ghost is behind all this."

"I'm right there with you." As much as it pained her to say it, she didn't want to lie. "The entire thing is unbelievable, and I'll be the first to admit I've never seen anything like this. But something is going on, and with Stephanie and Charli nowhere to be found, what other choice do we have?"

"Fair point." Jason took a left and then another left, pointing them in the direction they'd just come from. "Back to UMC?"

"It's the only lead we've got right now."

"What's the plan, then?" He shrugged and shook his head. "Go up to the ghost and ask her why she's killing people?"

"I wouldn't have put it exactly like that, but yeah, I guess." Cassie tipped her head back against the seat. The car was stuffy and hot and her qualms about coming face to face with the Ghost Doctor didn't make her feel any better. "Most spirits try to reach out to me when they know I can see and talk to them. Even if they can't communicate directly, I can feel their desire to move beyond this plane of existence."

"But Dr. Cohen's different?"

"Very different. She doesn't try to reach out. It's like she's single-minded about doing whatever she's doing."

"Killing people."

Cassie studied a spot on the roof of the car above her head. "Whatever it is, she doesn't care that I can communicate with her. But if what Marsha said is true, and Naomi was talking to her, that means she can talk back. If I can catch up with her, I'll know a lot more."

"And if we find out a ghost has been killing all these people?"

"Then we stop her."

This didn't offer Jason any peace of mind. "And what about the families of all those people? They'll never know what really happened to their loved ones. We may never really know if that's what happened to Jasmine."

Cassie stopped short of telling him sometimes that's just how it went. On the rare occasions Cassie had revealed the true extent of her abilities to people, she inevitably got dozens of questions about how it all worked and if she'd be able to communicate with someone's grandmother or dead wife or lost child.

But life is messy. There are rarely any clear-cut answers, and even when Cassie could shed light on the mystery of what happens after a person dies, it inevitably led to more questions. People prefer to live in absolutes but wanting something didn't require the universe to provide it.

Jason interrupted her thoughts. "I'm sorry. That's a lot of pressure to put on you. I'm grateful for your help. I hope you know that."

She laid a hand on his arm. "I do know that. And it is a lot of pressure, but I kind of signed up for that. I'll do the best I can. I may not be able to give you all the answers, but I want to see this through to the end, too. Dr. Cohen is a mystery I'd like to solve, and with any luck, that'll bring us some answers about Jasmine, too."

Jason smiled. They remained lost in thought for the remainder of the ride. When they arrived at the hospital, he reached for her hand. She held onto his with a smile on her face. They still had plenty to talk about, but for now she could find comfort in the fact that he was by her side. And if the way he held onto her was any indication, he felt the same way.

As soon as they walked through the sliding doors to the waiting room, they both stopped and turned to each other.

"What now?" he asked.

"She either comes to us, or we try to find her."

"Why would she come to us?"

Cassie led him over to a chair and sat down. "I don't know for sure that she's been seeking me out, but she's waited for me to notice her both times I've seen her here. She's not afraid of me. And maybe she doesn't want me to stop whatever she's doing, but she is trying to tell me something."

"So, we wait." He looked around the room like that was the last thing he wanted to do. "Or you figure out a way to locate her?"

That hadn't occurred to Cassie. "I've never done that before."

"Sabine Delacroix seems to think you're capable of a lot more than you think you are."

Cassie couldn't deny that. The way she had opened Cassie's world hadn't rocked her to her core, but it had shifted the way she viewed her abilities and the spirit realm. She had seen through the veil. She could walk into a hospital without being overwhelmed. She had come face to face with a ghost more present and powerful than any she had seen before.

Who knew what else she could do?

Cassie closed her eyes, reaching out invisible tendrils of her own. It was easy to feel the spirits surrounding her in the waiting room. No matter where she went, she always felt watched. She had grown accustomed to it years ago.

But now she pushed her reach beyond the limit of her current position. She searched for that invisible line she'd felt the last time she saw the Ghost Doctor. But there was so much noise. The hospital was full of pain and death and sadness. The spirits were restless. They wanted answers. They wanted someone to see them for who they were now. One by one, they awakened to Cassie's presence. She could help them. If only she would listen to what they had to say.

Cassie felt the pressure building. She had opened a two-way communication with an entire hospital worth of spirits. They grew louder, a cacophony of voices in her head. She couldn't make out the words, but she knew what they wanted from her. And she couldn't give it to them.

The line grew taut. It pulled against her, trying to wrench free of her grasp. The spirit on the other end didn't need Cassie to interfere. It didn't need her help. It was strong enough to do what needed to be done. Nothing would stop it.

Cassie's eyes snapped open. "Fourth floor." She turned to Jason. She couldn't stop tears from forming in her eyes. "I don't know for how long, but she's there now."

They moved to the elevators. Jason ran a finger down the directory until he hit the fourth floor. "Long-term care."

"Someone else is going to die." Cassie wiped the tears from her eyes. "I can't explain—"

"You don't need to." Jason punched the button for the elevator. "I believe you."

Those three simple words were all Cassie needed to hear. She had spent so long pushing people away because she thought they'd think she was crazy. Her parents, her sister, even Harris and David. She was always trying to explain her world to them in a way they could comprehend. In a way they could accept.

And here was Jason, following her on this bizarre journey, without question. She knew it wouldn't be easy, but something slid into place during that elevator ride to the fourth floor. She felt relaxed and powerful and whole for the first time since she could remember.

And she'd fight with everything she had to never lose that feeling.

When the door slid open, Cassie was ready to face Dr. Cohen. She could feel the eyes of hundreds of spirits following her every movement, but she had closed the door against them, no longer allowing them to reach her. They had to stay at a distance. Most went about their business, not strong enough to push past her defenses. One tracked her as she moved closer.

When Cassie turned the corner and stopped an arm's length away from Dr. Cohen, it was like seeing the woman for the first time. She looked the same—gray dress, pin curls, hypnotic eyes—but there was a humanity to her that hadn't been there before. Even if she didn't have all the answers, Cassie understood her better now.

Dr. Cohen turned away from Cassie, her skirts fluttering at the movement. She walked down the hallway with such grace and determination, appearing as though she were floating. Cassie chased after her.

"She's here," Cassie said. "I see her."

Jason was on her heels. "What's she doing?"

"Walking."

"Where?"

Cassie waited, never close enough to reach the ghost. Not that she'd know what do to if she did. How could you stop something you couldn't touch? She had no control over a spirit's body. All she had was her words.

And she had no idea if that would be enough.

Dr. Cohen halted in the middle of the hallway. Cassie pulled up short and Jason slid to a stop, watching her face in attempt to figure out what was going on. She wanted to tell him every detail of the woman in front of her, but breaking the silence of the hall felt like committing a crime.

A few nurses passed by, but no one paid them any mind. They had their own work to do, their own lives to live. Little did they know what was happening under their noses. Cassie wondered how many went home and cried themselves to sleep after losing a patient, never knowing that it had all been out of their control.

Dr. Cohen turned to a closed door and stepped through the wall. Cassie didn't hesitate. She couldn't. She told Jason to stay where he was and entered the room herself. His protests fell on deaf ears, and she shut the door behind her before he could convince her she'd made a mistake.

The room was dark, the air inside stale. No one had opened a window in some time, though with the current weather, Cassie supposed that wouldn't have been a good idea. Still, she felt her lungs protest. They screamed for fresh oxygen.

The Ghost Doctor hovered over an elderly woman with paper white skin. She had bruises along her arms, hidden in the folds of accumulated wrinkles. If Cassie had to guess, the woman was at least a hundred years old. It would be her time sooner or later, but Cassie would fight to make sure she'd last as long as possible.

When Dr. Cohen reached a hand to the woman, Cassie didn't think. She acted. She sprang forward to stop her, reaching for the doctor's arm even though she knew her hands wouldn't latch on. But maybe the movement would startle the ghost. Maybe she'd think twice about taking this one.

Dr. Cohen turned toward her, hazel eyes boring into Cassie's soul. As soon as Cassie's hand passed through the woman's translucent skin, a vision erupted in her mind, splitting her skull and making her knees buckle.

Cassie watched from the eyes of the Ghost Doctor as she saw a blonde woman in a short pink dress and yellow cardigan walk down the hall, wallet in hand. She stopped at a vending machine, debating her afternoon snack. She looked at her reflection in the glass and adjusted her hair. It was a wig.

A man rounded the corner. He stared at his phone, not seeing the woman standing in front of him. He knocked into her, causing her to drop her wallet. Cards and money hit the floor with a *splat*, sliding in all directions. The woman cursed and bent down to pick up her things.

Cassie, still seeing through the doctor's eyes, moved closer. The man apologized and bent down to help her. She thanked him, tight-lipped, and shoved everything into her purse. But she didn't see the credit card that had slid under the machine. Would she ever notice it was missing?

The woman brushed past the man, her afternoon snack forgotten. She kept her head down, as though she didn't want to draw too much attention to her face. But it was too late. Cassie had already seen who it was.

There was no mistaking the blond hair or the face that looked so identical to Charli's.

Stephanie walked right through Cassie without ever knowing she was there.

32

Cassie blinked away the vision, now staring into the hazel eyes of Dr. Cohen. There was a sad look on the woman's face, something between remorse and weariness. But before Cassie could think of what to say, a line of light cut across the room as the door opened behind her.

"Excuse me, ma'am?" A nurse stood silhouetted against the frame. "You're not supposed to be in here."

Cassie turned her back on Dr. Cohen. Jason was right behind the nurse. "I told her you were looking for your aunt." The words rushed out of him. "Is this not the right room?"

"Oh my gosh, I'm so sorry." Cassie turned back to the woman in the bed. The Ghost Doctor had disappeared. "I think they gave me the wrong room number." She was already making a retreat. "I'm so sorry. This is so embarrassing."

"Ma'am, I can't stress enough—"

"I know, I know." Cassie held up her hands as she slipped past the nurse and out of the room. "I understand. I'm going to call my mom right now. I'm so sorry."

Jason and Cassie all but ran down the hall. At the corner, Cassie cast a glance over her shoulder. The nurse was still watching them like a hawk. She ducked her head and made a beeline for the elevators. She didn't hesitate as she punched the arrow back down to the first floor.

"I'm sorry, I stalled her as long as I could." Jason wrapped a hand around the back of his neck. "She was kind of intimidating."

"It's fine." Cassie's heart was racing. "I got what I needed."

"You did?" The panic washed from his face. "What happened in there?"

"I saw Dr. Cohen." Cassie was still sorting through the vision, one frame at a time. "I touched her, and I saw *Stephanie*."

"What?" Jason looked like he had no idea how to compute that. "Why?"

"She wears a wig."

He shrugged. "Lots of people wear wigs."

"No, I know." She shook her head to clear her mind. "But things aren't adding up. She dropped her credit card under a vending machine. I think Dr. Cohen was trying to give me a clue."

"She's helping?" The elevator arrived, and the two of them stepped inside. An overweight gentleman with a thick head of hair stood in the corner. Jason lowered his voice. "Why would she do that?"

"Just add it to the mystery." Cassie eyed the other man in the elevator, but he was busy scrolling through his phone. Still, she wouldn't take any chances. "For now, my *aunt* seems to be fine."

"Good." Jason's shoulders relaxed. "So, what next?"

The elevator doors opened with a *ding*, and Cassie stepped out. "I'm hungry. What about you?"

She didn't know which vending machine Stephanie had been standing in front of, or whether a custodian had collected her credit card, but she was certain the woman had been on the first floor.

"There was a sign for the cafeteria," she explained. "So, it's gotta be around here somewhere."

Jason let Cassie lead him around the entire floor. At the end of every hall, she stopped and stared, trying to determine if it was the same one from her vision. They didn't find the right vending machine until they had made a complete circuit of the first level. But when she stood near the front entrance and looked back over her shoulder, everything aligned.

A woman and her three-year-old son took their time picking out a bag of chips from the machine. Cassie was already on her hands and knees, sliding her fingers under the machine. It came back covered in dust, but she found what she was looking for.

The two of them moved off to the side and put their heads together. It was a plain Visa credit card with an unfamiliar name stamped on the front.

"Heather Stephens." Jason looked up at her. "Who's that?"

"And why would Stephanie have someone else's credit card?"

Jason pulled out his phone. "Heather Stephens," he mumbled. "Charli. Stephanie. Nothing associated with those names is coming up."

"Stephanie was wearing a wig. She looked so similar to Charli, who supposedly died. The second we asked her about Charli, Stephanie abandoned her entire apartment." Cassie knew there was just one more piece of the puzzle to put together before the whole thing took shape. "If Heather Stephens is on her credit card, maybe that's her real name."

Jason deleted a few of his search terms. He hit enter. "She had a Facebook page. And an Instagram."

"Go to her Instagram." Cassie waited until he complied. "Scroll through. See if Charli or Stephanie pop up."

Heather Stephens looked exactly like Stephanie, only she had strawberry blonde hair. She had one tattoo on her stomach, but it was nothing like what Alan had said to describe Charli, and she didn't have any piercings. Most of her outfits were bohemian, long skirts and flowing tops.

"Heather hasn't posted in almost a year. Everything before that is normal, except her most recent picture." He turned the phone to Cassie so she could see it better. "Rest in peace, Daisy. Bloom eternal."

"Look up *Daisy Stephens obituary*."

Jason swiped his thumbs across the keyboard. "Died a year ago. Look, there's an entire article on her. She was having surgery on her back and the doctor made a mistake. They paralyzed her from the neck down and she fell into a coma from some bacterial infection. She died shortly after."

"She could be patient zero," Cassie offered. "The first one in a long line of deaths due to malpractice. It would fit the pattern."

"Maybe Heather was the first person to notice something off." Jason stared at the picture of Daisy. "Maybe she's doing her own investigation. And that's why she keeps changing her identity."

"It's been a year." Cassie tried to fight off dejection. "And she hasn't found enough to come forward?"

"Maybe she has, and that's why she's hiding." Jason clicked on a few more articles, opening and closing them to see if they offered any additional information. "What I don't understand is how this is happening across multiple hospitals."

"Maybe the doctor has moved from one to the other?" Cassie shrugged.

"Then again, I'm not sure that would fit the timeline. We still don't know which patients died under unusual circumstances."

"Heather's parents own a small bakery just outside the city." He tilted his phone again so she could see the spot on the map. "They might have more information."

"So, what, we show up and ask them about their dead daughter?" She plastered a smile on her face and mimed paying in cash. "Hello, I'd like half a dozen red velvet cupcakes. Can you tell us exactly how Daisy died? Hang on, I have the thirty-six cents."

Jason rolled his eyes. "Maybe with a little more tact than that. Although, I approve of the red velvet." He slipped his phone into his pocket. "Maybe Heather's parents are worried about her. If she's living on her own, moving apartments, changing her identity, it's possible they haven't seen her in a while. Or have no idea what she's been up to. Maybe they'll be grateful we've seen her recently."

Cassie enjoyed the way Jason's brain worked. He was clearly good at thinking through these situations. And she still relished the fact that she didn't need to do this on her own. "You're right." He beamed, and she couldn't stop herself from smiling. "It's worth a shot."

33

THE BAKERY WAS A TINY BUILDING THAT COULD'VE BEEN A HOLDOVER FROM THE 1950s. The striped awning looked new, and the brick appeared as though they'd restored it sometime in the last decade. Everything else about the building retained its original character. The sign that read *Flora's Bakery* in delicate script looked original.

There was no bell as Cassie pulled the door open, but the woman behind the counter noticed when they entered. She looked up with a smile, setting aside her book. "Hi, there! Welcome to Flora's."

"Hi, how are you today?"

"Can't complain." As Cassie approached, she saw similarities between Heather and the woman. They had the same nose. "How about you?"

"The weather could be better." Cassie was stalling. "Are you Flora?"

"Flora was my mother." She pointed to a black-and-white portrait of a woman draped in fur and a diamond necklace. She looked like a movie star. "This was her pet project while my father was busy designing the city's infrastructure."

Cassie didn't miss the way she'd said *designing* rather than *building*. Though she'd never heard of them, she'd bet the Stephens were from the wealthier part of the city. Especially if Flora Stephens had taken on an entire bakery as a pet project.

"And now you run the shop?"

"My husband and I, yes." She gestured around the store, and Cassie noticed how they had positioned antique lamps and signs next to modern conveniences. Everything about the store screamed *money.* "Our attempt to keep a little slice of history alive."

"That's wonderful."

"Do you know what you might like to try today?" She pointed to a sample tray next to the cash register. "These are peanut butter and jelly cupcake bites. They're one of our best sellers."

Cassie hesitated. They had gone over the plan on the car ride over, but now that she was face to face with the woman, she hated darkening her day. But then Cassie thought of all the people who had died, including Jasmine, and she allowed their spirits to spur her forward. "I'm sorry, I didn't catch your name."

The woman looked delighted Cassie had inquired. "Lily."

"Lily, my name is Cassie. This is Jason." She took a moment to breathe. "We're looking for your daughter, Heather."

Lily frowned. "I'm not sure I'll be able to help you."

"It's important we find her."

"Is she in trouble?" Lily looked from one of them to the other. "Who are you? Police?"

"No, we're not the police."

"Reporters?"

"No, it's nothing like that." Cassie felt the conversation getting away from her. "Jason's cousin died recently, and we think Heather might know something. We just want to talk to her."

Something in Lily broke. Her lip quivered and she looked down at her hands. "Were they friends?" When she looked up again, there were tears in her eyes. "Heather and your cousin?"

"No, ma'am." Jason's voice was slow and gentle. "At least, not that I'm aware."

"Good." She tried to steel herself, but there was so much pain in her eyes. "We don't talk much anymore. At all, actually. Heather hasn't been the same. Not since her sister died."

"We read about her. Daisy." Cassie tiptoed through the conversation. "We know she had back surgery and something went wrong. She got a bacterial infection?"

The woman nodded. "She was paralyzed. Put into a coma."

"My cousin had heart surgery. Something went wrong, too." Jason didn't hold back the emotion in his voice. "She died and she shouldn't have."

"I'm sorry to hear that." Lily said it like someone who knew how painful that could be. What a far cry from how Marsha had handled their situation. The two of them looked like they could've been friends at their daughter's PTA meetings, but their personalities were worlds apart. "They weren't sure Daisy would recover. We were willing to wait. We're lucky money wasn't an issue. Heather hated seeing her like that, dead and alive at the same time. It wasn't easy on any of us."

Every question had to be asked with the utmost delicacy. Cassie laid a gentle hand on the counter between her and the other woman. "What happened?"

"I don't know." Lily dabbed at the corner of her eye with the tip of her finger. "She was on life support. The doctors couldn't explain how her ventilator turned off without the machines alerting us. They said it was a glitch. Our lawyer recommended we sue the company for a faulty device." She hung her head. "But I'm just so tired. I don't want their money. I want my daughter back."

"Were Heather and Daisy close?"

"They were very similar." Lily's smile was sad. "They fought a lot, but they loved each other fiercely. Heather was the one who found her. I don't think she'll ever forget that."

"No one should ever have to go through that."

"She was inconsolable," Lily continued. "For days. She became a recluse. She stopped going to school. It devastated her."

"Did something else happen? Something to make you two stop talking?"

"We wanted answers. We kept asking her if she saw anything, remembered anything. Our lawyer wanted to talk to her about it, to get her account of what happened. But she shut us out. She packed up and moved out the next day. Told me in no uncertain terms that she never wanted to see either of us again. I haven't talked to her since. I lost both my daughters within weeks of each other. And somehow the worst part is that Heather is still out there. She's just choosing not to return my phone calls."

Cassie saw a glimmer of hope and reached for it. "She still has the same number?"

"Not anymore."

Cassie deflated. "Do you have any way of getting in touch with her? Any idea where she might be?"

Lily looked back down at her hands. "I'm not proud of it, but I hired a private investigator to find her." She looked up again, desperation in her eyes. "I just wanted to know she was okay. My husband thought I was crazy. I didn't want to bother her, and I wasn't going to reach out if she didn't want me to. As a mother, I just wanted to make sure she was still out there somewhere."

Cassie leaned forward. "Do you have her address?"

Lily once again looked between the two of them. "What's this about?"

"We're not sure yet." At least that was partially true. "We met Heather when she was pretending to be someone named Stephanie. And we think she was also using another identity, Charli."

Lily furrowed her brow. "I don't understand. Why?"

"That's what we're trying to find out." Cassie looked to Jason, but it didn't appear as though he had the right words to explain this either. "We know she's been volunteering at multiple hospitals under these different disguises. There has been a string of deaths due to so-called complications from surgery or other procedures."

"And you think Heather is looking into these deaths because of what happened to Daisy?"

"That's what we're hoping to find out."

Lily held Cassie's gaze for what felt like an eternity. When the woman finally looked away, she grabbed a piece of paper and a pen from under the counter. She scribbled something down and handed it to Cassie. It was an address.

"I only hired the private investigator for about a month, right after our fight. This was the address he gave me. Sometimes I still drive by there, but I've never seen her. She might've moved."

Cassie took the paper and clutched it to her chest. "Thank you so much."

"I hope you find what you're looking for." Lily's shoulders drooped. "And I hope she's—" She broke off. "I don't know. I hope she's okay."

Cassie didn't know what to say. Lily got up and grabbed a tissue to blow her nose. They took that as their cue to leave. When Cassie and Jason filed through the door into the fresh air, Cassie finally felt like they were one step closer to figuring out what Heather Stephens knew that they didn't.

34

HEATHER STEPHENS LIVED ON THE FIRST FLOOR OF AN UPSCALE APARTMENT complex that had its own courtyard, swimming pool, and enclosed basketball court. Every other car in the parking lot was a BMW, and Cassie couldn't help but feel they stuck out like a sore thumb, even if Jason's sedan was brand new just a few years ago.

Jason slid the car into one of the guest spots. "How does she afford to live here?"

"How does she afford to have multiple apartments?" Cassie peered through the windshield to get a better look at the building. "The other place wasn't as nice as this, but we know she worked part time at a bar and volunteered at the hospital. She wasn't making a ton of money on her own."

"It must've been for appearances then. Or just extra pocket change."

Cassie's eyes lit up. "That was probably the money she used to pay rent and anything else she wanted to use cash for. I bet she still has access to her parents' bank accounts to afford a place like this. Either that or she's using a college fund."

"You think her parents would let her do that?"

"Her mom definitely would. She wouldn't want Heather to be on her own with nothing."

"True." Jason turned to her. "So what's the plan?"

"We knock on her door."

"That much I figured."

"We ask her what she knows."

"What if we spook her?" Jason gestured toward the building. "She's already met us once. She'll know we figured out her multiple identities."

"We'll tell her the truth, then." Cassie unbuckled her seatbelt but didn't move to open the door. "We tell her about Jasmine and say we think something is going on. Maybe we can put our heads together and figure out how much these different hospitals are covering up. If she's volunteering at two or more of them, she's probably putting together proof about what she's seen."

Jason's voice was quiet. "How big do you think this is?"

Cassie shook her head. "Honestly, I don't know. I still can't wrap my head around it. Is it one doctor or nurse moving from hospital to hospital?" Cassie thought back to Langford and how long he'd gotten away with ripping hearts out of people. Then again, he hadn't done it while he was at work. It had been an after-hours activity. "Or have the bigwigs at these hospitals started working together to avoid malpractice lawsuits?"

"That's the thing, though," Jason said. "They're not avoiding it. They're settling out of court, which means they're paying more."

"So, it's not about the money." Cassie tucked a piece of hair behind her ear. "It's about reputation. They don't want to lose public support or government funding. Maybe they don't know what's going on either and instead of looking into it themselves, they're willing to hush it up to protect their own asses."

"I think that'd make me even angrier than if one specific person was behind all this." Jason hooked a couple of fingers around his doorhandle but didn't push it open. "I can understand murder. Evil. Impulse. But I can't understand laziness if you're dealing in people's lives."

Cassie got out of the car and met him around front. She wasn't sure what to say. She'd seen evil up close. Locked eyes with it. Survived it twice. But she'd never understand it. And she didn't want to. How could she ever want to understand why one person chose to kill another?

Silence hung between them as they each were lost in their own thoughts. They approached the building. Each apartment was like a miniature home. It had its own front gate, driveway, and garage. They slipped through the gate and approached Heather's door. Cassie wasn't sure how Jason was feeling, but her heart was pounding in her chest. They were so close to the answers they'd been looking for all this time. All she had to do was knock.

Jason beat her to it.

They both waited, holding their breaths. Time crept along. They exchanged a look. There was no sound from within. Jason knocked again. More silence. More looks.

"Maybe she's not home?"

The twisting of a doorknob and the sound of keys jangling caught their attention. A woman emerged from the apartment next door. She had dyed black hair, pale freckled skin, and wore yoga pants, a sports bra, and a loose zip-up hoodie. The front of her apartment looked exactly like Heather's, except the woman had a summer wreath hanging from her front door. She caught them staring at her.

"Are you looking for Heather?"

"Yeah." Cassie put on her most innocent and cheerful voice. "We're in town on a whim and wanted to surprise her. I guess she's not home."

"She usually leaves for work about this time." The woman locked up her house and walked around to the driver's side door of her car. But she didn't get in. "You probably just missed her."

"Darn." Cassie smiled. "Does she still work at the hospital? I forget which one. Tulane?"

"UMC."

"Right! That's the name of it. Thank you so much."

"No problem." She opened her door. "Have a good day."

"You too!"

"So, Stephanie wasn't the persona who worked at UMC," Jason said. "It's been the real Heather all along."

"I'd hate to corner her at the hospital and bring more attention to whatever she's doing there."

"I'd also hate to wait all day until she comes back home. She might run away again if she sees us sitting outside her apartment. At least at the hospital she can't go far."

Cassie couldn't argue with that logic, so she and Jason got back in his car, returning to where all of this had started.

UMC was busier than usual when they stepped into the waiting room for the second time that day. Cassie felt like they were running in circles. The activity around her only added to the chaos. Families were arguing and patients were crying and nurses were trying to calm everyone down. Cassie stepped up to the registration desk, but a single finger held her at bay. The nurse was on the phone, listening intently. She moved the receiver away from her mouth and hissed something into the ear of the nurse sitting next to her. Cassie only caught the end.

"—Dr. Amos. Find him."

"Now?"

"Yes, now. It's a Code Blue." She listened to the other line for a moment. "Send him to 619."

Cassie didn't wait. She knew her way around the hospital now. She punched the elevator button and waited for what felt like eons until it arrived. Four people got off. Two more ahead of her and Jason got on. They stopped at floors three and four and five until finally—*finally*—they arrived on six.

Cassie was out the door and halfway down the hall before she heard Jason call out for her to slow down. Hearing Code Blue was enough for her to take a chance that it was happening again, despite how close they'd come for answers.

She took the corner too sharply, and her feet almost slid from underneath her. Jason had caught up just in time. He steadied her. At the other end of the hall, outside room 619, a group of nurses were shaking their heads. Some were crying. Some were angry. Some stood staring at the ceiling as if asking why God had taken another person in their prime. Cassie's heart sank as she took in the scene.

They were too late.

35

Cassie hadn't seen Heather Stephens at the other end of the hall, but Jason pointed her out with a single finger. Cassie followed the length of it and met the eyes of a brunette who wore her hair in a messy bun. She wore slacks and a cardigan and looked much older than Charli or Stephanie. Though she looked nothing like the bohemian beauty they'd seen on Instagram, there was no mistaking who this was.

As soon as she saw Jason pointing in her direction, Heather took off around the corner. "Cut her off." Cassie shoved Jason in the opposite direction while she slipped through the crowd and followed Heather. There were only two ways off this floor: Down the elevators, or down the stairwell. They had to cut off her egress points before she could get away for a second time.

Cassie saw the forest green of Heather's cardigan disappear around the corner. If Cassie chased her, she'd draw too much attention. But the stairwell was on this side of the building, and she couldn't risk Heather getting off on another floor. There were a million rooms she could hide in.

Jason appeared at the other end of the hallway, and Heather skidded to a stop. It was clear she'd been heading toward the elevators. It was the quickest way down, after all. Now she looked to her left and sprinted toward the door that led to the stairs. A few more seconds and she'd disappear forever.

Cassie made it to the door ahead of Jason and before it had time to swing shut behind Heather. She all but jumped from one landing to the next. One second they were feet apart, and the next they were face-to-face.

"Heather." Cassie was gasping for air. "Please don't run. We're not here to hurt you."

"What do you want?" Her eyes were wide. This close, Cassie could see she was wearing colored contacts to make them look brown. "Who are you?" Dawning spread across her face. "I've seen you before."

"We came to your apartment. You introduced yourself as Stephanie."

If Heather felt ashamed for being caught in a lie, she didn't show it. "What do you want?"

"We don't want to hurt you."

"Then why are you chasing me?"

Cassie's breath was under control now. "To be fair, you're the one who ran."

"I don't have to explain myself to you." She went to move down the stairs, and Cassie threw out her hand to stop her. "I'll scream."

"Something tells me you don't want to draw that kind of attention to yourself." Cassie held up her hands in surrender, though she stayed at the ready to move in either direction if Heather attempted to run again. "Look, I think we might be after the same thing."

Heather barked out a laugh. "I doubt it."

"We know about the deaths here at UMC. And Tulane. And the other hospitals."

She grew still. "And?"

"And we want answers." Cassie lowered her hands slowly. "We spoke with your mother. We know what happened with your sister."

Silence hung in the air.

"Did you know some coma patients feel pain just like the rest of us?" Heather's eyes were wild. "She was suffering. And my parents would've kept her alive for years if they could. Until all the money ran out. No one deserves to live that way."

Cassie's mind split in two, exploring each possibility simultaneously. On the one hand, she could see Heather as she always had. Devastated by the loss of her sister. Frustrated that she had no one to blame but a faulty machine. A mere glitch that took her sister away. Angry and upset, she knew Daisy wasn't the only one to have suffered like that. She began volunteering to get closer to the patients. She figured out this was happening at more than one hospital, so she created different personas to gather more data. All she had to do was put it together, and she'd be able to prove liability. It would shock the nation to hear what had gone on in New Orleans, right under everyone's noses.

But there was a second path, one that hadn't previously occurred to Cassie. The loss of her sister had devastated Heather, but the idea of her sister suffering for years, unable to express her discomfort, was even more traumatizing. Frustrated, she broke the machine, feeling as though she had done her sister a favor. She left home, knowing her parents would never understand. Heather didn't want anyone else to suffer like that, so she began volunteering to get closer to the patients. She created different personas so she wouldn't bring attention to herself. Thanks to her parents' money, she even got a separate apartment, so if anyone came looking for her, they'd never know her true identity. She could do anything she wanted, right under everyone's noses.

The true irony here was the Ghost Doctor had been an unwitting accomplice. Cassie had yet to solve that mystery, but Dr. Cohen had pointed her toward the true culprit. She had shown Cassie who Heather really was. They had spent so much time looking into the doctor that it had allowed Heather to claim another victim.

They had wondered if Dr. Cohen was an angel of death when they should've asked the same of Heather. All the pieces slid into place and Cassie remembered stories of people like Donald Harvey, who had spent years killing patients, claiming he was euthanizing them for their own good. Did Heather know anything about him? Had she studied his methods?

"It was you." Cassie didn't bother asking it as a question. She couldn't deny the truth now. "You killed all those people. Why?"

"*No one deserves to live that way,*" Heather repeated. She didn't bother trying to get away. She stood tall. She believed in her cause. "They were in pain. I was helping them."

Whether Jason had come to the same conclusion as Cassie or if he understood what she was implying, Cassie didn't know. But he was standing right beside her, his voice deadly quiet. "Do you even know who they were? Did you know anything about them?"

"I remember all of them." She was defiant. "I knew everything about them."

"Jasmine Broussard. Did you kill her?"

Heather looked away. But not before they saw the recognition in her eyes. And the fear.

Jason stepped closer. "She was my baby cousin." His voice broke. He recovered. It hardened into steel, and Cassie's heart shattered. "She would've survived that surgery if it weren't for you. She would've had years left to live."

"Years full of suffering." Heather didn't meet his eyes. "She didn't deserve that."

"You don't get to make that call." Jason's voice was steady, and that scared Cassie even more. She wanted him to yell, to be angry, to explode the way she wanted to explode. Somehow, this was worse. It was like he was turning in on himself, shutting everything down. And something deep inside her feared he'd never open up again. "You took her choice away. How could you ever think that was right?"

Cassie had been in this position before, wanting to understand the mind of a killer. Jason had said he understood evil, but this was something else. In her own twisted mind, Heather thought she was doing the right thing. Her sister's comatose state broke something inside of her, and when she put herself back together, she did it all wrong.

"You know what it feels like to lose someone," Jason continued. "You know how a piece of you dies with them. You know that, and yet you've done that to dozens of families. How could you?"

For the first time since they'd confronted her, Heather didn't have an answer. She opened her mouth to respond, but before they could hear whatever excuse came next, the door at the top of the stairs opened.

"—heard voices down here."

Two figures stopped at the top and looked down at them. One was a nurse, her face pallid and weary. The other was a security guard, his face rich brown and startled.

"That's her." The woman extended a finger to point at Heather. "That's the volunteer I kept seeing outside the room. And I've seen her other times, too. Last month, they asked her about another patient who died. She'd been the last one to see him alive, too."

Heather didn't hesitate. She threw an elbow at Cassie's face with the intention of either breaking her nose or, at the very least, knocking her off her feet. What she didn't expect was Cassie's quick reaction time. Years of finding herself in these kinds of situations and a few self-defense classes had paid off.

Instead of enduring a bloody nose, Cassie blocked the elbow with her palm. She pushed back at the same time she put a leg behind the other woman. The momentum threw Heather off-balance, sending her sprawling back into the wall instead of down the stairs. Jason was there in an instant, making sure Heather couldn't escape. The security guard already had his cuffs out by the time he hit the bottom step.

Cassie looked down at the woman huddled in the corner. She pitied her for everything she had been through with her sister, even understood the way her own mind had twisted her drive to make sure no one had suffered the way her sister had. But none of that made it okay.

Jason, Cassie, and the nurse followed them back up the stairs to the sixth floor. The security guard led Heather to the elevator. He would call the authorities as soon as they hit the first floor. Cassie and Jason would have to stick around to tell them what she had confessed, but now that they caught her, it wouldn't take too much digging to find the paper trail. She had thrived on living just under the radar, but now that the spotlight was on her, she had nowhere to go.

"I feel bad for her parents," Jason said.

"I can't imagine how Lily will feel once she learns what Heather did."

The pair of them walked along the hall, giving the security guard and Heather time to make their exit. There were still a few nurses going in and out of the room where the last patient had died. Cassie peeked into the room as she passed it and came to a halt.

The man in the bed couldn't have been much older than Cassie. Someone had pulled the blankets back, and even from the doorway, Cassie could see he was missing an arm and a leg. Was that why Heather had chosen him? Fury swirled through Cassie's veins. Heather saw people as a combination of their illnesses and disabilities. She'd played God with people who had full lives ahead of them. And even if their time on earth had to be cut short, they had the right to live it however they wanted.

For the first time, Cassie realized that ten years ago she might've been on Heather's list. Lying broken and bruised in a hospital while a team of doctors tried to put her back together. She still carried those scars with her wherever she went, but she was no lesser for it.

It was simply a part of her story.

But none of this was why she pulled up short. Next to the bed, Dr. Cohen stood over the deceased. She placed a gentle hand on the man's arm. When she pulled back, his spirit sat up and slid off the bed. If he felt confusion or anger or sadness at what Heather had done to him, he didn't show it. He held Dr. Cohen's hand and didn't look back.

Cassie watched with wide eyes as Dr. Cohen walked across the room with the man in tow. She held Cassie's gaze, her hazel eyes as bright and entrancing as ever. They rooted Cassie to the spot. The truth dawned on her. Dr. Cohen had spent her entire life trying to save lives and now she spent her death saving souls. The Ghost Doctor had never once stolen a person from their body. She'd simply been there when it was their time to go. She helped them let go of their physical form. She knew, in the way only another spirit could, how to transport them from this world to the next.

Dr. Cohen smiled. It was a beautiful, mysterious thing. It held all the secrets of life beyond this one. Cassie had so many questions for her, but she held her tongue. It wasn't her place, and it wasn't her role. She stepped to the side and allowed the doctor to pass.

The man kept his eyes on the doctor, trusting her to carry him to the next life. And together, they walked down the hall, tall and sure, until they faded from view.

Jason placed a hand on Cassie's shoulder and brought her back to the land of the living.

"Everything okay?"

"Yeah." She smiled. "Everything's okay."

36

DETECTIVE ADELAIDE HARRIS WASN'T PRONE TO MAKING MISTAKES, BUT EVEN she could recognize throwing caution to the wind. It was strange—she was as calm, cool, and collected as ever, and yet here she was, meeting the same witness who had contacted David right before his murder.

Harris wasn't naïve enough to brush away the idea that it could be a trap. She'd confronted Aguilar the day before. The man had to know she was onto him or, at the very least, would risk everything by going after him.

She pulled over to the side of the road and shifted her car into park. When she cracked the window, a cool, night breeze and the smell of her car's exhaust filtered in. She was a good mile from where she'd told the witness to meet her along River Street. David had met the man in private and still found himself at the wrong end of the barrel. She wanted somewhere open. Somewhere she could see others coming and going. She could use the crowds to her advantage.

It was closing in on nine o'clock. The sun had gone below the horizon hours ago. Few people would still be along the river in December, but there were always a few. She hoped that if anyone wanted to get a jump on her, multiple witnesses would dissuade them.

She'd worry about tomorrow when it came.

Harris shut the car door with a *click* and hit the button on her fob. A small beep emanated from the vehicle, and she listened for any movement in the shadows. Having heard none, she pulled her cap lower, stuck her hands in her jacket pockets, and headed toward the riverbank.

She didn't have the same affinity for being on the edge of the water as most other people. Growing up in Montana meant she preferred the mountains over the ocean, no matter how many times someone tried to change her mind.

That said, she had to admit the river walk was nice, especially at this time of night. A few people milled about—couples walking hand in hand, families returning to their cars after a full day, lone travelers who stopped to stare out across the water like it held the answers to all their problems.

It was serene, to be sure, but the wind made her pull her collar up around her face. It was probably for the best. She needed to keep her face hidden long enough to scope out the area ahead of her meeting time. She memorized the faces of every person who passed her. Did she recognize them? Could they work for Aguilar? Had she seen them pass by once already?

The thought that she was overreacting pushed its way to the forefront of her mind, but she brushed it off. Maybe Aguilar had no intention of going after her. Maybe he'd already forgotten her name and face. Then again, he hadn't gotten to where he was today by being lazy. No, he probably had someone keeping tabs.

She kept thinking of what he'd said at the restaurant about David, but she pushed that away, too. She wouldn't second guess David's actions until she had more proof. For now, she had to rely on what she knew. Otherwise, she'd drive herself insane trying to pull answers from thin air.

Unfortunately, she knew little about the witness. His name was Randall Sherman. He was an accountant by trade, which meant it wasn't a stretch to think he ran Aguilar's books. If they couldn't get the kingpin on murder, then perhaps they'd be able to get him on fraud. The tactic had worked before.

She had seen a picture of Randall. It wouldn't be difficult to pick him out of a crowd. He didn't look like much—a small, mousy man who wore glasses and had a slight hunch in his back. He didn't look like the type of person to get in bed with a criminal like Aguilar, but who knew why people made the choices they did? She wouldn't let her guard down, regardless.

Harris stopped and leaned against the railing to look across the river. She was about three hundred feet from where she needed to be, and at least a half hour early. The chilly air drove the crowd away, but there were still dozens of partiers with drinks in hand.

Harris put her back to the water and scanned the surrounding faces. A man sitting on a bench in a baseball cap glanced her way, but as soon as his buddies joined him, he forgot all about her. He was no one. She moved on, lingering on every person, committing each set of features to memory.

When she felt safe, she pushed off the railing and kept walking. She had her backup piece tucked away in a holster on her hip, and the weight was a comfort as she closed the distance between her and Fool's Errand, the bar she'd told Randall about. They were to meet on the bench directly across from the establishment, the one that faced the water.

She tried not to let the irony of the restaurant name distract her.

Harris walked by the bench twice, peering at people's faces and scouting the areas where someone could hide. When she passed by a third time, Randall occupied the space, staring at his phone. He had no sense of self-preservation. If he had, he would've kept his head on a swivel.

Still, she ducked away and circled behind him. Peered over his shoulder. He was staring at her phone number, his thumb hovering over the call button.

"No need," she said, and he jumped. "I'm here."

"Detective Harris." His voice was breathier than it was on the phone. He was terrified. His skin was pale and sweaty, but his cheeks were a rosy red. If she didn't know better, she would've thought he had the flu. "You scared me."

"Let's go."

"Go?" He turned his head in one direction and then the other. "Go where?"

She nodded the way she'd come. "There's a bench down there with better cover."

"Better cover?" He stared in the direction she'd indicated, but didn't move. "Why?"

"Less chance of someone seeing us. Less chance of someone shooting me."

"Shooting you?"

She was tired of him repeating everything she said, so she didn't bother answering. She turned and began walking to the other bench. There was no way he wouldn't follow her, so she didn't bother looking back over her shoulder.

The second bench was more secluded. Tree branches hung lower. Enough cover for a brief conversation. She brushed crumbs off the seat and sat down. Randall stood in front of her.

"Sit," she ordered. He complied. There was a foot between them. "Closer."

He scooted to the side a few inches. "Closer. People will avert their eyes if they think we're together."

Randall swallowed audibly but complied. His leg pressed up against hers. She could feel heat radiating off him. "Is this okay?"

"That works." She let the man breathe for a moment. In and out. In and out. A dozen times. There was no point in delaying the inevitable any longer than that. "Do you know what happened to David?"

"Someone shot him."

"I'd gathered as much." She tried to keep the venom from her voice but failed. "Why aren't you dead, too?"

"I ran."

Harris bit down on her tongue. She couldn't blame someone for their survival instinct. Something told Harris he wouldn't have been much use to David anyway. Not that it made it any easier to hear he'd abandoned her friend as he bled out on a warehouse loading dock floor.

"Do you know who shot him?" She asked.

"Not exactly." He was shaking now. "But I have a guess."

"Guesses don't do me much good. I need proof."

He produced a flash drive. "This is all the proof I have. It's not much, but I hope it'll be enough."

She eyed the flash drive but didn't take it. "Why are you giving me this?"

Randall searched for the words, and when he found them, he deflated. "I can't do it anymore."

"Do what?"

"Help him." He swallowed. "Help Aguilar."

"How are you helping him?"

"It's all on here, okay?" For the first time, Randall took in his surroundings, as though it had finally occurred to him he wasn't safe out in the open like this. "This is what I wanted to give to David. But they killed him before I could."

"Why now?" Harris asked. "What's changed?"

Randall looked up, staring into her eyes. There was a type of clarity there she hadn't seen before. His voice was quiet, but steady. "Everything."

She needed specifics. She had to know she could trust him. "Like what?"

"My wife's having a kid." The smile that blossomed over his face was like the sun after a rainstorm. "It's gonna be a—"

Harris saw the red blossom across his forehead at the same time she heard the gunshot. She felt the spray of blood hit her cheeks and lips. Her eyes closed involuntarily, but Randall's face burned its way into her memory. The shock on his face. The vacancy of his eyes. The slackness of his smile.

He was dead before his body hit the ground.

Harris knew she had to make a decision. She could either launch herself after the flash drive, which had bounced off the bench and skittered across the walkway, or she could vault over the bench and use it as a shield against whoever had fired at them.

The few people left along the walkway screamed and ran away. All except for one man. The shadow cast by his hoodie hid his face, but the streetlights glinted off the pistol in his hand. He raised it and pointed it at her.

Harris made her choice. She launched forward into a somersault, grabbing the flash drive just as she began her roll. When she came up, she had already cleared half the distance between her and shooter. She could either throw herself to the side or run straight at him, taking him by surprise. All it took was the passing idea that this might've been the person who killed David. As soon as the thought entered her mind, it locked in, and she made her choice.

The shooter adjusted his aim, but Harris was already on the move. A bullet whizzed by her ear, close enough to make her flinch. But she didn't stop moving. She dropped and rolled to the side, forcing the man to recenter himself to get off another shot.

As Harris came up, she was close enough to take two more steps to reach out and wrap her hands around his neck. She could see the whites of his eyes now, the green of his irises. She could hear his ragged breaths mingling with her own.

His arm adjusted. He had her in his sights.

She was close now. Close enough to take him down.

Who had the faster reaction time? If she ducked to the side, would he compensate quick enough?

The last thing Harris heard was the crack of a gunshot.

And the last thing she felt was the heat of a white-hot bullet piercing her flesh.

37

THE LAST TWENTY-FOUR HOURS HAD BEEN A WHIRLWIND OF ACTIVITY. NEW Orleans' finest had arrived on scene shortly after the hospital's security team collected Heather. They'd taken her downtown in handcuffs. A hush settled over the hospital as they escorted her through the doors, and even those who didn't know why they'd arrested her sensed something momentous had happened.

Two officers stayed behind to get Jason and Cassie's side of the story. It was clear they hadn't expected them to have conducted a thorough investigation. There was still plenty of evidence to collect, but at least the authorities knew where to start. They had information about the second apartment and knew about Heather's sister. It wouldn't be hard to put together a timeline, even with Heather's multiple personas.

Heather knew they had caught her red-handed. They had seen her coming out of the room seconds before the man with the amputated limbs had died. They'd given her a warning a month prior for improper conduct, though Cassie didn't know the specifics. Tulane had fired Charli over similar circumstances, so it seemed like Heather's UMC persona, Brooke, had already been one step away from a similar fate.

The hospital staff had reacted in one of two ways. They either blamed themselves, or they blamed the hospital. The ones who blamed themselves cried in the hallways or the breakroom as they learned the truth of what had happened across the city in the last year. Cassie heard dozens of names whispered from one medical staff member to the next. There would be no way to tell for sure if this patient or that had been one of Heather's victims, but the police had promised to investigate every death that fit the profile.

The ones who blamed the hospital were not as easy to console. Talk began to circulate about medical malpractice and how the hospital had swept it under the rug. Settling out of court. Doctors not being written up when they should have been. Mistakes not being reported. People not being held responsible. Those who had been flying under the radar got defensive. Those who had turned the other way confessed their sins. It wouldn't be easy to sort through all the stories to find the truth, but it would happen in time.

By that evening, the UMC's CEO had released a statement condemning Heather's actions and promising to investigate all allegations of misconduct. Other hospitals echoed his sentiments, though they felt empty. Those who knew the people in power had done their best to cover up the misconduct refused to sympathize with the position they were in now.

Word spread quickly and the story was on every major news channel, locally and nationally. They didn't name names, but it was only a matter of time. The public outcry was enormous, and as friends and family learned what had truly happened to their loved ones, the despair would only grow. Cassie couldn't imagine what they were going through, not even Jason and his family.

Kiki channeled her anger into action. She became the unofficial point person, working to keep families organized and informed as they showed up at the hospital, demanding answers. The police set up barriers on the surrounding streets to keep everyone at bay. It took half the department to ensure ambulances could get in and out without delay.

It was dark by the time Cassie, Jason, and Kiki left for the night. Cassie had a late-morning flight the next day, and even though Jason wasn't leaving until the day after, he wanted to spend as much time with his family as possible. Kiki had already agreed to return the next morning, and there was talk about demanding a meeting with the hospital's CEO and his board members. The families of the victims wanted answers, and they would make enough noise to get them.

The night air hit Cassie as soon as the sliding glass doors opened, brushing her hair off the back of her neck and providing cool relief for the first time in hours. Police barricades lined the sidewalk on one side of the entrance. The officers had instructed all protestors to stay out of the road and allow a single thruway for foot traffic.

Kiki led them in the opposite direction and around the corner to where they had parked in the general lot behind the hospital. There were at least twice as many vehicles now, and Cassie was sure half of them belonged to those protesting out front.

As they crossed the street, a man emerged from between a pair of vehicles, shifting a pair of eyeglasses to the top of his head and hoisting a briefcase higher on his shoulder. He looked about Kiki's age, a little younger than Cassie, with bronze skin, shining white teeth, and perfectly gelled hair.

He stopped when he saw Kiki and a smile spread across his face. "Ms. Broussard, what a pleasant surprise."

Kiki faced him, flanked by Cassie and Jason. "Pleasant is not the word I would use today."

"You're right." He molded his smile into something a bit more appropriate for the situation. "I apologize." He held out a hand to Jason and then Cassie. "My name is Jonah Washburn."

"He's a member of UMC's legal defense." Kiki didn't hide the derision in her voice. "We've run into each other before."

"Kiki is one of the best." Jonah's jealousy was well-concealed, but Cassie still picked up on it. "You always know you're in for a fight when she's sitting at the table opposite yours."

"At least you know what's about to happen." Kiki didn't look nervous. "Your boss is about to have several very bad days."

Jonah's face grew serious, but Cassie saw a spark behind his eyes. He enjoyed a challenge, and he especially liked it when Kiki played the challenger. "UMC will fully cooperate with all the families who suffered a loss at the hands of Heather Stephens. We'll do anything we can to make this right."

"Anything?" Kiki took a step forward. Next to her, Jason's hand twitched, as though he thought he might need to hold her back but changed his mind. "Do you mean that?"

"Of course." His smile widened. "Why wouldn't I?"

"Because UMC has a lot to answer for. So do the other hospitals that allowed Heather Stephens to roam free in their halls."

"Hang on." Jonah looked confused. "Allowed her to roam free?"

Kiki took another step forward. Jonah took a step back. Jason's hand didn't twitch this time. "We have dozens of hospital staff coming forward about their experiences being told to keep their mouths shut."

"The hospital itself is not liable for individual people's mistakes. Nor is the CEO."

"I disagree." A grin spread across Kiki's face, but it was a predator's smile. "I've heard enough to draw some conclusions. A hospital's success rate is important to its CEO, isn't it? To the board? Wouldn't you say that's motive?"

"This has nothing to do with the Heather Stephens case."

"This *is* the Heather Stephens case." Kiki gestured to the hospital over her shoulder. "The only reason Heather Stephens exists is because UMC allowed her to. The only reason she could do everything she did was because UMC allowed her to. Because they care more about their numbers than their people."

"These are big accusations." Jonah wasn't smiling anymore. "You'd have to have some pretty big balls to not only go up against UMC but Tulane and Curahealth, too."

"I don't need balls to do that." Kiki turned her back on him. "Consider this warning a professional courtesy. I look forward to seeing you in court."

Cassie had the pleasure of seeing Jonah Washburn's face go slack before he pulled out his phone and rushed toward the hospital. Something told her he wouldn't sleep much that night.

38

WHEN THEY ARRIVED AT GRANNY MABEL'S HOUSE, CASSIE TUGGED ON JASON'S hand to make him hang back while Kiki walked through the door ahead of them. She looked down at her shoes and noticed a new scuff. "I think I should go. I don't want to interrupt. You need time with your family."

"They want to see you." He smiled and stepped closer. Lifted her chin with a finger. "And I want you to be here. We couldn't have done this without you."

"Hey, lovebirds." Kiki smiled back at them. "You coming?"

Cassie nodded and watched as a smile blossomed across Jason's face. He stepped back, and she realized she'd been holding her breath. She blew out her lungful of air. She could already smell Granny Mabel's cookies, and her mouth watered in anticipation.

A group of people had crowded the kitchen before the newcomers arrived. Granny Mabel stood at the counter, placing a batch of cookies on a plate, fresh from the oven. Mama T stood at her side, mixing another batch with a wooden spoon. Auntie Kay sat at the table with what Cassie recognized as her customary cup of tea. Janelle sat next to her, phone face down on the table and fresh tears cascading down her cheeks.

The room hushed when Cassie entered, and everyone turned to her. The heat of the oven wasn't the only thing that made her cheeks flush, and she had an urge to inspect that new scuff on her shoe again.

Janelle was the first to make a move. She stood and walked up to Cassie, wrapping her in a hug so tight that it squeezed all the air out of her lungs. But Cassie never wanted to escape it. Everything the young woman wanted to say was in there, and Cassie was so grateful, it brought tears to her eyes. When Janelle finally let go, there was a clarity behind the sadness. As difficult as all of this had been, at least she had answers about her sister.

"You did this family a service we can never repay." Granny Mabel's voice was watery, and she saw Mama T and Auntie Kay wipe tears from their eyes. Cassie got the impression it was a rare occurrence to see the Broussard family matriarch cry. "We are forever in your debt."

Cassie wiped her own tears away, but new ones took their place. "Please, you don't have to thank me."

Granny Mabel wiped her hands on a towel and walked up to Cassie. She laid a palm on both of her cheeks. They were still warm from the cookies. "We will never be able to express how much this means to us. You are a gift from God, Cassie Quinn. I hope you know how special you are. To all of us. You have given us peace. Our hearts will mend in time now that we know the truth."

"Suing the pants off all those corporate jackasses will help too." Kiki raised a cookie as a toast.

Auntie Kay clicked her tongue. She said, "Kailani, language." Mama T held up her own cookie and said, "Here, here." The room laughed.

"That means more to me than you could ever imagine." Cassie had spent years struggling to make peace with her abilities. She had helped countless people, but they didn't know what she had done to give them that peace of mind. The Broussards understood what she had endured. "Y'all have made me feel more accepted in the last couple days than I've felt in my entire life. You've done as much for me, trust me."

"Accept nothing less," Kiki shouted.

Cassie's heart swelled with love for this family. She didn't know what the future had in store for her, but she was sure she wanted it to include Jason and Granny Mabel and Kiki and all the rest of them. If she could spend an evening crying and laughing and eating cookies and never once feel self-conscious for what she could see or do, she figured this was something she'd fight to hang onto.

Hours later, after all the cookies disappeared and eyes were drooping,

Jason drove Cassie back to her hotel. He held her hand as he walked her to her room. When they reached the door, neither one of them rushed to say goodbye.

Jason broke the silence first. "I think this is the most time we've ever spent with each other."

"We can't admit that to Magdalena." Cassie smiled up at him. "She'll never let us forget it."

He chuckled. It was a low rumble that shifted something in Cassie's stomach. "I wish this had been under different circumstances, but I don't regret spending a single minute with you, Cassie."

"I feel the same way."

"I'm glad to hear that." Jason smiled. "Don't make any sudden movements."

Cassie froze. "Why?"

"Because I'm going to kiss you now."

Cassie's brain had just enough time to register the words before Jason stepped closer and pressed his lips against hers. She felt every point of his body that touched hers, from his lips to his fingers curled around her waist. The happiness that filled her heart threatened to explode right out of her chest.

When they broke apart, they were breathless. Cassie smiled up at him. "I'd say that went better than the first time."

He looked as dazed as she felt. "Much better."

"When we get back to Savannah, maybe we could do it again?"

"The kissing or the whirlwind adventures?"

"Well, you're bound to get one if you want the other."

"I'm okay with that."

Jason took her face in his hands and kissed her again. Something uncoiled in her stomach. He pulled her closer, and everything inside her screamed to invite him in. But something told her there would be plenty of time for that later.

When they broke apart for a second time, Jason took a step back and shoved his hands deep inside his jacket pockets. "If I don't leave now, I never will."

"I know." It made her heart flutter to hear him say that. "Text me?"

"Of course." He leaned in and kissed her once on the lips, then placed a tender kiss on her forehead. "And text me when you land tomorrow."

"I will." She was dizzy with excitement as she watched him walk down the hall. He looked back once when he reached the corner, smiled, and then disappeared. Cassie wasn't even sad. The prospect of seeing him again once they were home was enough to keep her spirits high.

Once inside her room, Cassie began the arduous task of throwing all her clothes back into her suitcase. She was grateful she had packed some extra outfits in case of emergency, but for now, all she wanted to do was get a full night's rest. It wasn't until she'd attempted to stuff the paperwork from the museum into a side pocket in her suitcase that she realized something was already there. Once she pulled the envelope out, she remembered slipping David's letter inside in case she could gather the courage to open it.

This entire trip had been a distraction from what had happened in Savannah. What had happened to David. She'd used it as an excuse to leave her problems behind, only to realize it had delayed the inevitable. Seeing Jason confront the death of his cousin and his family grateful for any scrap of truth had been enough to make her realize she needed to know what happened to David. Otherwise, his death would forever be an unanswered question bouncing around inside her brain. And if that had been David in the graveyard, encased in shadow, she owed it to him to figure out whether he was in a better place or if something sinister took over to his soul.

Celeste Delacroix's words made their way back to her. *This trip will be good for you, Cassie Quinn.* And as difficult and heart-wrenching as it had been, Cassie couldn't argue with that.

With another second's hesitation, she slipped a finger under the flap of the envelope and flipped it open. A single piece of white paper, folded in thirds, rested inside. Lisa had said David wrote it about a month ago. It still smelled faintly of his aftershave. Her eyes welled as she breathed it in. A flood of memories came back at once, but she pushed them aside. There would be time to explore each of those in turn. Preferably alongside Harris or Lisa or even her sister. And an enormous glass of wine.

Cassie unfolded the letter as though it were a delicate flower blossoming for the first time. If she had expected a lengthy letter from David, reality would have disappointed her. She blinked away her tears to bring the page into focus.

· · ·

CASSIE,

I've spent a lifetime trying to do the right thing, only to trip and fall at the finish line. Tell Harris none of this was her fault. I knew what I was getting into. She won't believe it, but I want her to hear it from you, anyway.

After everything we've been through, you would think I'd have taken some comfort in knowing there's a life beyond this one. Only, I'm not sure I'll be heading upstairs. I've made my peace with that. I hope you'll be able to, as well.

I only have one request. Let my secrets stay buried with me. Tell Harris to let it go. Tell Lisa I'm in a better place. It won't be easy to lie to them, but it'll be better than the truth. Consider it one last favor from a foolish old man who always tried to do right by you.

With love,

David

CASSIE'S CONFUSION over the meaning of David's letter kept the tears from falling once more. She had expected a final goodbye—maybe even a joke about how he hoped he didn't see her on the other side. But this letter was nothing like she had expected.

And it terrified her.

Before Cassie had a chance to read it a second time, her phone rang from across the room. Jason had promised to text, not call, and it was well past midnight by this point. The only person who might reach out at a time like this would be her sister, but Laura had no reason to think Cassie was still awake.

When she picked up the phone, it surprised her to see Harris' name. The last time the detective had called her was to inform her someone had attacked her. Panic filled Cassie as she hit the button to answer.

"Hello?"

"Cassie." Harris breathed a sigh of relief tinged with static from a poor connection. "Did I wake you?"

"No." She looked back down at the letter. "No, I'm still awake." She cleared her throat. How would she ever be able to tell Harris what David had left for her? "I was just packing for the trip home tomorrow." There were muffled voices in the background. "Where are you?"

"Internet cafe." She laughed. "Did you know these still exist? Someone at the emergency room recommended this one. They're only open for another half hour, so I've got to be quick."

"Emergency room? Are you okay?" Cassie was on high alert now. "What happened?"

"I was shot." She rushed on as soon as she heard Cassie's gasp. "I'm fine. It was in the arm. Honestly, it's a flesh wound. I wouldn't have gone to the hospital if Clementine hadn't made me. So don't get all worked up."

"Who shot you?"

"Some guy who works for Aguilar." There was a pause while she waited for a pair of voices to fade into the distance. "Well, he didn't admit that, obviously. But it wouldn't have been the first time this week, would it?"

"Should it concern me you sound so"—she searched for the word —"chipper?"

"Normally, yes, but I've got good news."

"Better than the fact that someone shot you?"

"I know who killed David."

Cassie froze. She looked down at the letter, but she couldn't stop herself from asking. "Who?"

"At first, I thought it was the guy who attacked me and the witness. But the gun was different, and so was the whole method. The other guy used a police-issued sniper rifle. This guy had a pistol. So, I looked through the flash drive. There's a lot here. I started with bank transactions. Follow the money, you know?" She was breathless. "I don't have his name. But I have information on a bank transfer from the night David died."

Cassie tried to draw out the explanation to give her time to think. "What does Clementine think about this?"

"She doesn't know. She suspended me."

"What?" Cassie stood now, almost dropping the letter. "What did you do?"

"I walked straight up to Aguilar and told him I wasn't afraid of him. It may have come off more like *hey, I'm onto you, and I won't stop until I take you down.*" Harris sighed. "Not my finest hour."

"I'll say."

"I met the witness who was with David the night he died. He handed over a flash drive before that guy killed him. Clementine doesn't know and I'd like to keep it that way."

"You don't trust her?"

"I need to do this." For the first time, Harris sounded dead serious. "She'll pull me off the case, and I'll be learning everything secondhand. I couldn't live with that, Cassie. I can barely sleep at night as it is." She took a deep breath. "David was hiding something from me. I need to know what it is. Are you in?"

Cassie looked down at the letter in her hands. It had raised more questions than it had answered. Part of her wanted to fulfill David's request, no matter how much it hurt to walk away from the mystery mounting in the wake of his death. But another part didn't care. David was dead, and he'd left her and Harris behind to deal with the aftermath. How could he ask her to forget about him? To let the person who'd killed him walk away?

He should've known better when he wrote the letter.

"I'm in." She felt a thrill saying it out loud. "Where to?"

"Pack your winter coat." Cassie could practically hear Harris smiling through the phone. "We're going to Chicago."

Cassie Quinn returns in *Concealed in Shadow*! Order your copy now, or read on for a sneak peek:
https://www.amazon.com/dp/B09CDWZNHT/

Join the LT Ryan reader family & receive a free copy of the Cassie Quinn story, *Through the Veil*. Click the link below to get started:
https://ltryan.com/cassie-quinn-newsletter-signup-1

LOVE CASSIE? **Hatch? Noble? Maddie?** Get your very own L.T. Ryan merchandise today! Click the link below to find coffee mugs, t-shirts, and even signed copies of your favorite thrillers! https://ltryan.ink/EvG_

THE CASSIE QUINN SERIES

Path of Bones

Whisper of Bones

Symphony of Bones

Etched in Shadow

Concealed in Shadow

Betrayed in Shadow

Born from Ashes (Coming Soon)

Love Cassie? Hatch? Noble? Maddie? Get your very own Cassie Quinn merchandise today! Click the link below to find coffee mugs, t-shirts, and even signed copies of your favorite L.T. Ryan thrillers! https://ltryan.ink/EvG_

CONCEALED IN SHADOW
A CASSIE QUINN MYSTERY (BOOK FIVE)

by L.T. Ryan & K.M. Rought

CONCEALED IN SHADOW: CHAPTER 1

Joseph Arthur Zbirak did not consider himself a picky eater. He did, however, take his steak seriously. It needed to be well-seasoned and medium rare. Warm and pink in the middle. Delectably juicy. Anything less than a perfect cut would not enter his mouth under any circumstances.

So, it was with an apologetic smile and a soft voice that he sent his steak back to the kitchen. Medium *rare*, he had said, emphasizing the last word, hoping the young woman serving them would relay the message to the cook. She was a bubbly girl, with her dark hair in a ponytail and a smattering of enamel pins attached to her waist apron. Zbirak would give her a hearty tip, regardless of the mistake. It wasn't her fault, after all.

"Hope you don't think I'm going to wait for you," said the man sitting across from Zbirak. He was a rotund, ruddy-faced individual with a bad comb-over. His mustache was untrimmed, and years of sweat stained the armpits of his shirt. Shoving a third of his burger into his mouth, the man talked around his food, spraying as much as he swallowed. "I never knew you had such delicate sensibilities."

Zbirak wanted to glower, but he refrained from taking the bait. Despite sharing the same first name, he and Pisano had nothing in common. Where the other man was fat, rude, and incapable of thinking for himself, Zbirak was lean, quiet, and clever. Genetics had blessed him with an average face and enough brains to know when to take action and when to sit back and bide his time.

Pisano, however, was all bluff. It had carried him through forty-two years on the police force, but not unscathed. In his youth, his fists sealed the deal when his words failed to do their job. Now it was merely arrogance. For someone who couldn't throw or take a punch without wheezing, he sure was a cocky son of a bitch.

"I like what I like." Zbirak shrugged, a playful smile tugging at the corners of his mouth. He wouldn't let this man get under his skin. "And when I make a request, I expect it to be fulfilled."

For the first time, Pisano revealed the disquiet Zbirak instilled in him. "Look, it wasn't my fault." He shoved the rest of his burger into his mouth and licked a bit of mustard from his pinky finger. After draining his beer, he dove into his fries, shoving them into his mouth three at a time. He didn't even make fleeting eye contact. "But I'm taking care of it."

"Oh?" Zbirak raised an eyebrow. The return of the server held his inquiry at bay. She set his new plate in front of him. "Thank you."

"Please let me know if that's to your liking, sir."

Zbirak took his fork in one hand and his knife in the other, cutting the steak against the grain to reveal a pink center. Juice poured from the opening and pooled beneath the meat, threatening to mix with the heap of mashed potatoes sitting to one side. He looked up at the server and smiled with all his teeth. "It's perfect. Please thank the chef for me."

"Of course." The woman flicked her ponytail over her shoulder to get it out of the way. "Is there anything else I can do for you, gentleman?"

"That'll be all, for now." Zbirak kept his smile steady and noticed the way it mesmerized her. "My friend and I have some business to attend to. Would it be all right if you gave us some privacy until we're ready for the check?"

"Absolutely." The woman backed away. "Flag me down if you need anything else."

Zbirak watched as she retreated before returning to his steak and cutting a healthy portion from one end. It was exactly what he had been craving all day. His mouth watered as he sunk his teeth into that glorious first bite. The restaurant was three stars at best—rustic in an upscale sort of way—but they had a solid menu. Most people would've been happy with the cut they'd received, but Zbirak was nothing if not a perfectionist.

"You got an unhealthy relationship with your meat, pal." Pisano's rough voice cut through Zbirak's moment like a knife through flesh. "Let me know if you need a minute alone."

Zbirak scoffed. Of the two of them, he wasn't the unhealthy one. But Pisano's barbs were blunt and not worth Zbirak's time. "Tell me exactly how the problem is being taken care of."

"All right, all right. Keeps your pants on." Pisano wiped his hands on a napkin and threw it back onto the table. He looked Zbirak in the eye for the first time in several minutes. Ah, there was some of his renowned bluster. A man who had failed one too many times took more offense to being called out for his shortcomings than a man with the confidence he would not disappoint a second time. "Would I lie to you?" He laughed, and it was a great guffaw that turned several heads. "I'm stupid, but I'm not that stupid."

"Yes, you would." Zbirak took another bite, but he found he couldn't enjoy his meal under these conditions. He placed his knife and fork on the table. "And yes, you are."

"I don't like your tone."

This time, it was Zbirak's turn to laugh. It was a quiet chuckle that no one heard but Pisano. He often found humor in the men who knew better than to test hi, but did so because their pride meant more to them than their life. Zbirak leaned forward, though he didn't relish in being any closer to Pisano than absolutely necessary. "I gave you a job. You failed."

"A momentary setback is not a failure." Even Pisano seemed surprised by his rather insightful retort. "She slipped away for now. We'll get her back. Just you wait and see."

"And how, exactly, did she slip away?"

Pisano must've gotten a sense that Zbirak already had the answer because he didn't bother lying. "I sent my nephew to grab her, and she got away. Simple as that."

"I was very specific in my instructions that you were the one to pick her up. No one else."

"I had a prior engagement. Look." Pisano shifted in his seat. He placed a hand on his side and winced. When he spoke again, there was a strain in his voice. "I didn't think some random woman would be that hard to nab. She didn't know we were after her."

"Gender has nothing to do with survival instincts." Zbirak leaned back in his chair, no longer able to maintain his proximity to Pisano's form. "Society has trained women not to trust anyone, let alone a dim-witted thug such as your nephew. Your police uniform, however, would have lured her into a false sense of security."

Pisano burped, but it didn't appear to relieve any of the pain in his side. Sweat had accumulated along his brow. "I said I'll take care of it." He peered over his shoulder. "They got a bathroom in this place?"

"There's no need. I did it myself."

Pisano turned back to him. "The woman? You found her?"

"No, your nephew." Zbirak pushed his plate away. The smell emanating from the sweaty man across the table had ruined his appetite. What a shame. "I took care of him."

Pisano groaned, but Zbirak couldn't decide if it was agony over losing his nephew or the agony in his gut. "My sister is going to kill me."

"I assure you, she is not." Zbirak wiped his mouth with a cloth napkin and tossed it on the table next to his plate. He stood and wrapped one of his large hands around Pisano's fleshy arm, trying not to recoil at the dampness of the man's shirt. "Come on, I'll help you to the bathroom."

"How do you know?" Pisano was sweating profusely now. Every word sounded like a struggle.

Zbirak didn't answer right away. First, he led Pisano into the men's bathroom and directed him to the last stall. It was wheelchair accessible, which allowed both men to fit comfortably in there at once. Pisano collapsed to the floor and crawled on his hands and knees until he slumped over the toilet, his nose practically touching the water in the bowl. Zbirak closed the door behind them.

"I know your sister will not kill you because I already have."

Pisano lifted his head enough to look at Zbirak, but the light in his eyes was fading. "Wh-what? Wh-why?"

"As I said previously," Zbirak responded, taking a step closer to the man. He didn't want any of his words to be misinterpreted, even with death looming overhead. "When I make a request, I expect it to be fulfilled."

"I'll find her," Pisano blustered. "I-I'll do it. Please." He coughed, and blood-laced spittle ran down his chin. "Help me."

"You're far beyond help now." Zbirak tried not to revel in this man's undoing, but it was difficult. It was not the first time he had considered killing him. "I had a simple request, Joseph. Kill Mrs. Sherman. I sent you because you are a cop. Instead, you employed your nephew, who has as much tact and brains as you do, but without the badge to back it up. He spooked her, and now she's in the wind. I will find her eventually, but I will waste valuable time and resources to do so."

"I-I'm s-sorry." Pisano's breaths were wet and gasping. Red blooms filled the toilet water, having dripped from his mouth and nose. "P-please—"

"Don't beg." Zbirak didn't hide his disdain now. "You should've known better, Joseph. The only thing I hate more than having my time wasted is a loose end. Mrs. Sherman is a loose end that my employer expects me to trim. I entrusted that job to you, and you failed. I killed your nephew because you gave him information that was not yours to share. I killed you because you have been a pain in my ass for two decades, and my patience has finally run thin."

Pisano was purple in the face. His mouth opened and closed like a fish gasping for oxygen, but the sound of air moving through his lungs was ostensibly absent. The man only had a few moments left, and he would spend them in excruciating pain. It was a blessing, all things considered. If Zbirak had more time, he would've dragged Pisano's death out for days.

"You're a disgusting, arrogant bastard who only made it this far in life because of the handouts you received along the way." Zbirak wanted to spit on him but resisted. "If you had a modicum of self-awareness, you would've come here begging for your life instead of maintaining your mask of false bravado. I may have even considered sparing your life, though the chances would've been slim."

Pisano's body had gone still, and the smell emanating from his pants indicated he could no longer hear Zbirak's words. It would take a few hours before anyone realized there was a dead body in the stall, and that would be more than enough time for Zbirak to put distance between himself and the restaurant.

As he exited the restroom and returned to his seat, Zbirak motioned for the server. "My friend is ill," he said, rearranging his face into a frown, "so I'm going to take this time to pay for the bill while he is otherwise occupied."

"Oh no." She glanced down at Pisano's empty plate. "Do you think—"

"Doubtful." Zbirak transformed his frown into another brilliant smile. "He's got a sensitive stomach. I keep telling him he'll eat himself into an early grave."

She followed his cue and laughed at the joke, then pointed to his plate. "Would you like a box for your steak?"

Zbirak couldn't stomach the idea of trying to reheat his meal without overcooking it. He'd rather see it go to waste. "Just the check please."

The woman took their plates, but when she reached for Pisano's beer bottle, Zbirak's hand shot out to stop her. He wrapped his fingers around the neck and smiled up at her. "This can stay." If the woman thought his actions were strange, her face didn't betray her. Instead, she bounded away, returning a few moments later with the check. He waited for her to retreat once more before dropping a wad of cash on the table, sliding the beer bottle into the pocket of his jacket, and striding out the front door.

Once the staff realized Pisano was still in the bathroom, they would send a busboy in to check on him. When the kid discovered the dead body, they would call the police, who would question Zbirak's server. She'd describe the man at the table as white, with brown hair and a kind smile. He had an average build and was likely in his forties, with no distinguishing features. By then, the kitchen staff would have washed away any evidence of fingerprints from their leftover food. He'd wiped off the lock on the stall and the handle on the door before exiting the bathroom. Not to mention he'd tossed the beer bottle in a dumpster three miles across town. Any traces of the poison he'd slipped into its open mouth while Pisano was distracted would be gone in a matter of days.

And just like that, Zbirak would slip back into the shadows like he had for the past twenty-five years. His spirits were high as he merged onto the highway half an hour later, certain no one had followed him. His only regret was that he'd let Pisano ruin his dinner.

No matter. Once Mrs. Sherman was out of the picture, he'd sit down for another steak dinner. And this time, he wouldn't make the mistake of inviting anyone else to the table.

CONCEALED IN SHADOW: CHAPTER 2

The Chicago Historical Society was founded in 1856 to study and interpret the city's storied past. After pieces of their collection succumbed to fire on two separate occasions, the CHS moved their museum and library to Lincoln Park, where it still stands to this day, boasting over twenty-two million items exploring the city's influence on American history and vice versa. With the city providing a backdrop to the West and Lake Michigan to the East, the Chicago History Museum collects snapshots of time and preserves them for all to witness.

One of the great ironies of her life was that Cassie Quinn loved museums. The smell, the atmosphere, the people, the history, the influence—all of it. You could walk into a museum and transport yourself to Ancient Egypt, where a toilet was merely a hole in a stool, and then fast forward to a time in which a man named Marcel Duchamp could place a urinal upside down in a gallery and call it a fountain. Nowhere else in the world can you find such a strange amalgamation of historically and intellectually significant objects. The breadth of human achievement placed under the same roof was astronomical.

But Cassie could not celebrate museums without also acknowledging the elephant in the room. Lord Elgin famously stole pieces of the Parthenon and transported them to Britain, where they continue to reside in the British Museum. Vandalism and theft were not solitary events, and many European museums have refused to return the legacies of other countries to their rightful places. If Greece cannot retrieve their beloved history, imagine the likelihood that an African nation could convince England to give up their cultural property, nearly all of which dwells outside of the continent.

Even the Chicago History Museum has an uncomfortable past to atone for. Lincoln Park was once a municipal burial ground for over thirty-five thousand people, many of which had died of cholera. But the earth at the edge of the lake was loose and sandy, and they had buried the bodies below the water table, which meant they were at risk for contaminating the city's water supply.

In the mid- to late-1800s, the bodies were transferred from the park to rural cemeteries outside the city limits. But with so many people buried there, it was impossible to locate and move them all. The Great Chicago Fire of 1871 destroyed many of the markers, further complicating the situation. Estimates indicate ten thousand bodies could still be buried beneath the soil of the park, and every time someone brings in a backhoe—like during each of the Chicago History Museum's several expansions—more bones surface.

And there was the irony—Cassie loved museums with every fiber of her being, but they tested her mental fortitude like no other place on the planet could. When she crossed the threshold into a cemetery, she knew what she was getting into. There was bound to be a ghost who approached her, begging for help. But in a museum, there were no rules. Ghosts and visions assaulted her senses. Millions of objects harbored information from the past, waiting for the right person to walk by. Pair that with tens of thousands of spirits who had passed through the grounds, and it was hard to say whether Cassie could truly have a good time within the confines of such a place.

But something had shifted in New Orleans. Sabine Delacroix had turned a key and unlocked Cassie's powers. Her abilities were nowhere near stable or perfect, but for the first time in her life, she was confident. She had patience. She trusted the answers would come in due time. That trip to New Orleans had opened her eyes to an infinite number of possibilities. She didn't want to run and hide anymore; she wanted to help those forgotten by the annals of time. With a newfound purpose in hand, Cassie walked a little taller.

Nevertheless, exploring the Chicago History Museum was no easy feat. She could feel the artifacts tugging on her consciousness, begging to be heard. Spirits drifted by, untethered and yet imprisoned within a world where they had been relegated to myth and legend. The older the ghost, the further gone. But the younger ones were still hungry for answers, and they often went to great lengths to seek her out.

Unfortunately, Cassie already had a mission, and the museum was merely a pit stop along the way. She wandered aimlessly, allowing the current of the universe to determine her destination, until she stopped in front of one of the most prominent oil-on-canvas paintings in the building. *Memories of the Chicago Fire in 1871*, painted from memory forty-one years later by Julia Lemos, who had witnessed the historical event firsthand.

Billowing clouds of smoke stretched across the sky as tendrils of flame consumed buildings from the inside out, like a parasite, with no concern for the longevity of its host. Its fuel was too willing to accept its embrace, and so the fire feasted like a king.

Dozens of people fled the scene, their dark clothes in contrast to the pollution overhead. Cassie could hear the calamitous event like she had a crackling speaker up to her ear. People shouting, horses neighing, and wood crackling as the blaze consumed the city without pause or prejudice.

Cassie had been to Chicago once in her youth and vowed never to return. As a teenager, she had buried her abilities so deeply within herself that they were nearly non-existent. *Nearly*. The city had always given her a headache and caused her stomach to twist in response to an unseen force. While the migraines were a distant memory, the knot in her abdomen curled in on itself until Cassie winced. She consciously had to loosen the muscles and tell her body to relax. But it was difficult to convince herself she wasn't in any immediate danger when she could feel the inferno's heat caressing the back of her neck.

A vibration in her pocket broke Cassie from her daze, and when she saw Jason's name light up her phone, a smile broke across her face. Her skin cooled, the knot loosened, and the sound of screaming men, women, and children faded away to a dull roar that she tucked into the deepest recesses of her mind.

"Hey." Cassie's voice was breathless with surprise, and she winced. Even from a thousand miles away, he had that effect on her. "Miss me already?"

"Can you blame me?" There was a chuckle in Jason's voice that made her heart skip a beat. Even if he was playing into her joke, it was nice to hear. "How was your flight? Did you make some more friends?"

Cassie's laugh echoed around the hall. A few heads turned, and she winced in response. Stepping back from the painting, she nestled into a corner where she wouldn't disturb anyone else. "Yeah, I met a wizard who could travel through time. Nice guy. Poor fashion sense."

Jason laughed, but the humor didn't linger.

"What's wrong?" she asked.

"Jane Livingston asked Magdalena if you're still interested in your job."

Cassie froze. "What? Why?"

"You've been missing a lot of work."

"They've approved all my time off."

"I know." Jason sighed, and the air from his mouth made the phone crackle in her ear. "That's probably why Jane hasn't said anything to you. But if she's asking Mags whether you're still interested, then they're probably wondering if all this time off is becoming a pattern." There was a deadening silence on the phone before Jason blew out another breath of air. "I'm sorry, I feel like I'm being the bad guy here."

"You're not. I know you're not." She tapped her foot on the ground until someone looked at her pointedly and she stopped. Putting her back to them, she lowered her voice. "Has Jane said anything to you yet?"

"No, but I'm not sure if she's aware of our... relationship."

Cassie's heart fluttered at the word. The last time she'd seen Jason, they'd shared a kiss outside her hotel room. They hadn't talked about labels or exclusivity, and Cassie was afraid if she broached the topic, she'd jinx the whole thing. "I'm choosing not to worry about it for now," she declared. "They approved my time off, so there's nothing they can say about it. When I get home, I'll work overtime to make sure I wrap up all my projects. And then some."

"Do you know when you're coming back yet?"

"No idea. I'm supposed to meet Adelaide in a few minutes. Once I talk with her, I'll have a better idea of what's going on." She wasn't used to sharing her fears with people, so she had to force out the next words. "I'm worried about her."

"How come?"

"She's not acting like herself." Cassie sagged into the wall. All she wanted to do was crawl back into bed. "She won't leave Chicago without answers."

"I know she's important to you," Jason started, "and not just because she was also important to David." He hesitated, like he was measuring each word to make sure it held exactly the right weight. "But don't let her drag you into something you're not ready for, okay? It's hard enough losing someone, but it's a whole different ballgame when you have to investigate their death, too. Trust me, I know."

Jason hadn't shared his story with Cassie yet, but this wasn't the first time he'd mentioned he knew how she was feeling. Even without all the details, the idea comforted her—momentarily, at least. Then she'd remember how David had written her a letter specifically telling her not to look into his murder, and she'd feel guilt swell up inside her again. "Thank you." A comforting silence filled the phone. It was nice just to exist together. "You probably have to go soon."

"Keep me updated, okay?" There was a strain to his voice. "And be careful."

"I will," she said, though it wasn't really a promise she could make. "I'll text you once we know anything new."

After Cassie hung up, she took a moment to breathe. Somewhere over the course of the conversation, her anxiety had ratcheted up, threatening to constrict her throat and lungs against her will. The heat of the museum didn't help matters, so with great abandon, she wound her way back toward the entrance and into Chicago's winter air, relishing in how it pierced her skin and shocked her body into forgetting about the burden she carried.

Turning left, Cassie strolled down the street toward a tiered fountain at the end of the road. Hooking left again, she meandered along a path lined with bare trees. The city had seen its first snow a month ago, and the frozen ground made sure it couldn't melt away. The end of December was approaching, and unlike Savannah, Chicago rarely went without a white Christmas.

As Cassie neared a crossroads, a figure rounded the corner and stopped in the middle of the path. Even from a distance, Cassie recognized Harris' telltale silhouette, complete with a slicked-back ponytail and a pair of aviators. A long wool coat covered most of her outfit, but Cassie could tell Harris had given up her pantsuit for a pair of jeans. The Timberlands on her feet were in stark contrast to the glossy sheen of the pavement.

Cassie looked past Harris and out across the expanse of Lincoln Park. She felt the spirits more than she saw them, and she wondered how she could navigate a city so full of tragedy without being pulled under the waves. At one time, she would've been happy to lean on Harris for support, but these days,

Cassie couldn't trust that the detective wouldn't risk her drowning just to get a few answers.

But it was too late to turn back now, and when Harris raised her hand in greeting, Cassie returned the gesture, plastering a smile on her face and praying to God that the Windy City wouldn't blow them off course.

CONCEALED IN SHADOW: CHAPTER 3

Cassie waited until she was within earshot of Harris. "Hey, how are you doing?"

Harris pursed her mouth. "Don't say it like that."

"Like what?"

"Like you're *worried* about me."

"What's wrong with being worried about you?"

"How would you feel if I asked you that?" Harris placed a hand on Cassie's shoulder and stared directly into her eyes. *"How are you doing?"*

"I would be grateful."

"You'd be offended."

"Fine." Cassie rolled her eyes. "I'll pretend like I don't care."

"You're not supposed to worry about me," Harris amended. "I'm supposed to worry about you."

"Okay, now I *am* offended."

A smile broke across her face. "Good."

"Seriously, though." Cassie didn't want to press the subject, but they couldn't avoid it forever. "You dragged me to Chicago on a whim. I'm allowed to check in."

"It wasn't a whim, and I didn't drag you here. From what I remember, there was little to no hesitation before you agreed to meet me," Harris said. "And yes, I'm fine. All things considered."

All things considered. Cassie let the phrase roll around in her mouth. It tasted bitter. The *thing* they were considering was David's death. She supposed she was also fine if she didn't incorporate her feelings about her best friend's murder into the equation. But how could she not? It took up every inch of her brain space. She couldn't get away from it if she tried. And she'd definitely tried.

"Whim or no whim," Cassie said, "I can't stay here long. People are already asking questions at work. I can't miss too many more days."

Harris' playful air vanished. "We're talking about figuring out what happened to David. *David*," she said, like Cassie had forgotten who this was all about. "Let them ask questions."

"I can't lose my job, Adelaide."

Harris took a big breath and held it for a few seconds before exhaling through her mouth. "I know. I'm sorry." She looked like she meant it, but frustration still coated her words. "And I appreciate you coming out here with me. The dead of winter isn't exactly the best time to be in Chicago."

As if on cue, an icy breeze tore through the park. Cassie pulled her jacket up around her neck. "I miss Savannah."

Harris spread her arms wide. "Don't get me wrong, I love Chicago. It reminds me of Montana." She cut a glance sideways. "But I can't deny that you're less likely to lose a couple appendages to frostbite in Georgia."

"Let's walk." Cassie gestured to the path ahead. "I can already feel the hypothermia setting in."

"Don't be such a baby," Harris replied, but she cut to the left and led Cassie down another path.

Cassie pushed her hands deep into her pockets. "Tell me more about this flash drive."

"I haven't looked through the whole thing yet—"

Cassie stopped dead in her tracks. "So, you see one piece of information that points to Chicago, and you decide to hop on a plane? You haven't even gone through the entire drive yet?"

Harris rolled her eyes and grabbed the crook of Cassie's elbow, dragging her forward. "Relax. There are a lot of files on the thing, and they're not all labeled. I've gone through a good portion of it, but there's still a lot to figure out. Some of it's coded. Some of it's a bunch of numbers without context. It's going to take time."

The chill in the air made Cassie snippy. "And remind me again why we're here?"

With all the patience of a parent explaining to her child why the sky is blue, Harris said, "Randall Sherman was an accountant. He came forward a few weeks ago wanting to turn on Aguilar. We figured he was running Aguilar's books." She patted the pocket of her wool coat. "And considering what's on here, it looks like we were right."

"What made him want to turn?"

"His wife is pregnant. He thought he was in too deep, and he got cold feet."

Cassie felt like a broken record. "And Chicago?"

"There's a folder full of bank transactions. They went back a couple of years. There were only about four or five variations in the numbers." Harris paused to see if Cassie followed her train of thought, but when only silence met her, she continued. "It reads like services rendered. A flat fee for a project completed. The night of David's murder is on that list."

"Services rendered?" Cassie didn't like the way her mind was putting two and two together. "You're talking about an assassin."

Harris shrugged. She looked far too casual for the topic at hand. "Someone murdered David with a police-issue sniper rifle. It was a professional job. It makes sense."

"Let me get this straight." Cassie's teeth rattled, and she wasn't sure it was just from the cold. "We're in Chicago, following a lead on the *assassin* that killed David?" No matter how many times she said *assassin*, it didn't make the word any easier to swallow. "Does that not sound insane to you?"

"We're following the money trail. If this person is doing jobs for Aguilar, they could be anywhere—Savannah, Chicago, Tallahassee, Rome."

"You think Aguilar needs to take care of business in Rome?"

"Probably not, but the point still stands. I doubt we're going to run into David's killer unless we sound the alarms, and we're going to do everything we can to avoid that." Frustration flashed across Harris' face. "We have a bunch of numbers in a bunch of files, but nothing tied to physical evidence. That's why we're here. We need to figure out where that money went and prove it was a payoff for David's murder."

"You mentioned an address?"

Harris bobbed her head. They were approaching the end of the path, and yet another fountain rose in the distance. "I imagine Sherman put together the information on the flash drive quickly, hoping to offload it to David and get out of Dodge as soon as he could. Some folders make more sense than others. This one didn't have much context, but he had included an address. So, that's where we start."

Cassie stopped at the foot of the fountain and looked up into the metallic face of the sixteenth president of the United States. *Abraham Lincoln: The Man* was cast in 1887 and stood twelve feet tall. It depicted the former leader rising from a chair, preparing to give a speech. He holds his lapel and looks down in contemplation. As with most representations of the historical figure, the statue exudes a regal air of quiet intelligence.

Looking into his face reminded Cassie of Lincoln's complex history. Though many consider him the Great Emancipator, historical evidence suggests that while the president didn't agree with the institution of slavery on the whole, he also didn't view Black Americans as equal. As beloved as Lincoln is, and as wonderful as his accomplishments were, he was still only human—full of flaws, contradictions, and secrets.

Cassie turned to Harris. "David left me a letter."

The detective's eyes widened. "When?"

"I'm not sure when he wrote it. Lisa gave it to me that day of the funeral."

There was a beat of silence. "You never told me."

"I didn't open it right away." Cassie found it hard to swallow past the lump in her throat. "I wasn't sure what to expect. But that last day in New Orleans, I decided to see what it said."

Harris' voice was soft. "You don't have to tell me."

"He wanted me to." A pressure settled into Cassie's chest, and she had to fight to get enough air to speak. "He wanted me to tell you that this wasn't your fault. That he knew what he was getting into."

Harris blinked rapidly. When she spoke, there was emotion in her voice. "I don't understand."

"I don't either." Cassie fought her own tears. "I don't know what he was talking about. But he said he wanted his secrets to stay buried with him. He wanted me to tell you to let it go."

"Let it go?" Harris' voice was no longer soft. "Why?"

"He said it would be better than the truth." Cassie took a deep breath and blew it out, but it did nothing for the mounting force threatening to steal the air in her lungs. "I've never heard him talk this way before." Her voice shook. "I'm scared."

Harris looked down at her shoes. Cassie could see the gears turning in her head. "You're here, which means you won't try to talk me out of following this lead."

"No," Cassie said. "I won't."

"We're in this together." Harris looked up. A tear had slid down her cheek. "Right?"

Cassie didn't answer right away. Harris' question wasn't a small one. David's final request meant something to her, and the last thing she wanted was to be disloyal to her friends, in life or in death. But he had clearly gotten himself mixed up in something big. And he hadn't told Cassie. The sting of that betrayal battled against her fear of learning the truth.

There was no other person on the planet she had revered and respected as much as David, but he was still only human—full of flaws, contradictions, and secrets. The prospect of digging up his skeletons terrified her, but now that she knew they existed, she couldn't imagine a life where she wouldn't spend every waking moment wondering where they came from.

Cassie gazed up into Lincoln's face and then over at Harris'. Their eyes met, and Cassie knew her answer.

"There's no turning back now."

ORDER *CONCEALED IN SHADOW* NOW!
https://www.amazon.com/dp/B09CDWZNHT/

Join the LT Ryan reader family & receive a free copy of the Cassie Quinn story, *Through the Veil*. Click the link below to get started:
https://ltryan.com/cassie-quinn-newsletter-signup-1

ALSO BY L.T. RYAN

Find All of L.T. Ryan's Books on Amazon Today!

The Jack Noble Series

The Recruit (free)

The First Deception (Prequel 1)

Noble Beginnings

A Deadly Distance

Ripple Effect (Bear Logan)

Thin Line

Noble Intentions

When Dead in Greece

Noble Retribution

Noble Betrayal

Never Go Home

Beyond Betrayal (Clarissa Abbot)

Noble Judgment

Never Cry Mercy

Deadline

End Game

Noble Ultimatum

Noble Legend

Noble Revenge

Never Look Back (Coming Soon)

Bear Logan Series

Ripple Effect

Blowback

Take Down

Deep State

Bear & Mandy Logan Series

Close to Home

Under the Surface

The Last Stop

Over the Edge

Between the Lies (Coming Soon)

Rachel Hatch Series

Drift

Downburst

Fever Burn

Smoke Signal

Firewalk

Whitewater

Aftershock

Whirlwind

Tsunami

Fastrope

Sidewinder (Coming Soon)

Mitch Tanner Series

The Depth of Darkness

Into The Darkness

Deliver Us From Darkness

Cassie Quinn Series

Path of Bones

Whisper of Bones

Symphony of Bones

Etched in Shadow

Concealed in Shadow

Betrayed in Shadow

Born from Ashes

Blake Brier Series

Unmasked

Unleashed

Uncharted

Drawpoint

Contrail

Detachment

Clear

Quarry (Coming Soon)

Dalton Savage Series

Savage Grounds

Scorched Earth

Cold Sky

The Frost Killer (Coming Soon)

Maddie Castle Series

The Handler

Tracking Justice

Hunting Grounds

Vanished Trails (Coming Soon)

Affliction Z Series

Affliction Z: Patient Zero

Affliction Z: Abandoned Hope

Affliction Z: Descended in Blood

Affliction Z : Fractured Part 1

Affliction Z: Fractured Part 2 (Fall 2021)

Love Cassie? Hatch? Noble? Maddie? Get your very own L.T. Ryan merchandise today! Click the link below to find coffee mugs, t-shirts, and even signed copies of your favorite thrillers! https://ltryan.ink/EvG_

Receive a free copy of The Recruit. Visit:

https://ltryan.com/jack-noble-newsletter-signup-1

ABOUT THE AUTHOR

L.T. Ryan is a *USA Today* and international bestselling author. The new age of publishing offered L.T. the opportunity to blend his passions for creating, marketing, and technology to reach audiences with his popular Jack Noble series.

Living in central Virginia with his wife, the youngest of his three daughters, and their three dogs, L.T. enjoys staring out his window at the trees and mountains while he should be writing, as well as reading, hiking, running, and playing with gadgets. See what he's up to at http://ltryan.com.

Social Medial Links:

- Facebook (L.T. Ryan): https://www.facebook.com/LTRyanAuthor

- Facebook (Jack Noble Page): https://www.facebook.com/JackNobleBooks/

- Twitter: https://twitter.com/LTRyanWrites

- Goodreads: http://www.goodreads.com/author/show/6151659.L_T_Ryan